ALSO BY CHRIS HARDING THORNTON

Pickard County Atlas

LITTLE
UNDERWORLD

LITTLE
UNDERWORLD

CHRIS HARDING
THORNTON

MCD

FARRAR, STRAUS AND GIROUX

NEW YORK

MCD
Farrar, Straus and Giroux
120 Broadway, New York 10271

Title-page art by drante / Getty Images.

Library of Congress Cataloging-in-Publication Data
Names: Harding Thornton, Christina, author.
Title: Little underworld / Chris Harding Thornton.
Description: First edition. | New York : MCD / Farrar, Straus and
    Giroux, 2024.
Identifiers: LCCN 2023038954 | ISBN 9780374298333 (hardback)
Subjects: LCGFT: Detective and mystery fiction. | Thrillers (Fiction). |
    Novels.
Classification: LCC PS3608.A725386 L58 2024 | DDC 813/.6—
    dc23/eng/20230928
LC record available at https://lccn.loc.gov/2023038954

Our books may be purchased in bulk for promotional, educational,
or business use. Please contact your local bookseller or the Macmillan
Corporate and Premium Sales Department at 1-800-221-7945, extension
5442, or by email at MacmillanSpecialMarkets@macmillan.com.

www.mcdbooks.com • www.fsgbooks.com
Follow us on social media at @mcdbooks and @fsgbooks

1   3   5   7   9   10   8   6   4   2

For my grandparents, great-grandparents,
and great-great-grandma, who've left this world
a little ahead of me:

Iva Cates 1883–1978

Frances Warkentien 1906–1989

Fred Buel 1908–1990

Herb Cohrs 1899–1991

Eula Harding 1906–1996

Bernice Buel 1909–1999

Alma Cohrs 1906–2002

Norma Cohrs 1931–2004

Priscilla Wilber 1931–2016

Marlin Cohrs 1928–2020

Dale Harding 1932–2021

"Se non e vero, e ben trovato."
(Even if it's not true, it's believable.)

—ORVILLE D. MENARD,
RIVER CITY EMPIRE: TOM DENNISON'S OMAHA

LITTLE
UNDERWORLD

1

One night, late March 1930, Jim Beely and his brother Ward squatted on a sandbar, a sliver of bank jutting from the Omaha side of the Missouri. They took turns plunging another man's face in the cold current. The river was black and slicked with stars.

Jim could hardly make out Vern beneath his brother. For as much wreckage as the son of a bitch wrought, Vern Meyer was puny. Maybe being small was how the sneak blended in, got away with the wreckage. Jim and Ward couldn't blend in. They were too big. Too tall and wide. Even if they'd been reasonable-sized, people eyed their black hair and olive-tinged skin like a puzzle to figure out. At least being big meant they could hold their own. Ward spent days slinging four-hundred-pound ice cakes with cast-iron tongs. He must've had a pint of whiskey in him, and Vern was still light work. Ward just sat on him. Clamped the puny shit's upper arms and elbows to his sides. About all Vern could do was kick his feet and claw the muddy sand.

When his fingers dug with a frenzy, Jim said, "Air."

Ward pulled Vern's head up so he could gasp and hack,

get a good lungful. Then Ward plunged him back under. Vern gurgled.

Right then, mid-gurgle, Jim knew this was no good. There should've been a crumb of relief in roughing up Vern, in knowing he'd leave town and never come back. But Jim felt worse. He felt like a goddamned rube for chasing a crumb— for thinking the constant squeeze behind his ribs would let up a minute. The squeeze was like a laundry mangle wringing his lungs and stomach.

Jim needed to finish what he'd started. Get through it. He'd try taking stock of what he'd be glad about if he were some ninny who walked around being glad all day. Aside from the gurgling, Jim guessed it was quiet down here. He was up-wind of the downtown sounds that ricocheted through his office every night: screams and laughter. The thuds of drunk heads hitting pavement or cobblestones and the scramble of pockets and purses being picked. Shoes getting ripped off a sap's feet. Every Sunday paper, some variation of the same classified ad ran: PLEASE RETURN SHOES TAKEN OUTSIDE PAT DOYLE'S. At least down here on the river, there were no Victrolas and radios, no bawdy stage shows or movie theaters letting out, belching chatter into the air. Hell, the air itself was decent for late March. Warm enough Jim was in his shirtsleeves.

That didn't do it—taking stock of what to be glad about. Jim still had the squeeze in his chest. His knees ached from squatting, and the tongues of his cheap oxfords gouged his bent ankles. A corn on his left foot stabbed like a hot poker.

And somehow, the worst of it all was he could see too far—clear to Iowa. The night-dark cliffs of the bluffs made the horizon too high, like he was at the bottom of a pit. Any colder a night, the city's soot would've at least walled off the distance. Walled off now from whatever came next.

Vern's fingers stretched straight and bent back high like he was being electrocuted.

"Air."

Ward pulled up Vern's head to let him gasp, then plunged it again. Under the visor of his flat wool cap, Ward peered toward the river, too. Jim wondered if Ward saw they were in a pit. Jim doubted it. They had the same eyes, their dad's, dark umber like buckeyes. But they didn't see alike. People only saw half of what was in front of them. The other half was fogged up by everything else they'd ever glimpsed. Memory was a goddamned cataract.

Ward's voice was deep and rough like sawteeth gnawing through bark. "Still say we drive him out to Washington County. Grab what cash he's got, send it to Molly and Addie. Tell Shumway he was at the Burlington, hopping a train." Shumway was sheriff up in Washington County. "They'll lock him up till trial. Then let the pen have him."

"Molly don't want money. She did, she would've wired the address. Stenos get paid same in Spokane as here. Probably got Addie working at a laundry. Two more weeks, they'll be worth three of me." Another man would've been bothered by that. Jim was used to it. Molly never let him forget his worth.

"She's too hard on that kid."

"Molly's too hard on the whole goddamned world. And kids—Christ, look what having kids's got us down here doing."

Jim shouldn't have said it. When it came to kids, Ward

got moody. Jim wasn't up for one of Ward's moods. He tried to head it off. "Look. Maybe it would've been different with you and Loretta. Or you and Cel." Ward's first two wives and kids were dead. Loretta bled to death, pushing out a stillborn. Then Celestina overdosed on morphine two months after theirs died of fever. "All I know's me and Molly never figured it out—the kid thing. We never figured out much."

"Ma would've said me and Cel cursed it, naming that baby after Loretta."

"Old wives' tales are good at that—explaining what already happened. Be a hell of a lot handier if they said what's coming."

"I don't know what I ever did." To deserve it all, Ward meant, though there was never self-pity in how he said it. He sounded stumped.

"Christ. Not like there's a tally anywhere. Besides, you got Edith now. We'll drop this prick at the depot, get you back to Pop's." Pop was Edith's dad. He ran a saloon in South Omaha billed as a soft drink parlor. "This way the son of a bitch skips town. I'm fine with him skipping town. So long as it's permanent."

"Don't fix what's wrong with him. Half drowning and throwing him on a train don't."

"Can't be fixed," Jim snapped. "A kid-diddler's a mad dog. You want him fixed, cut off his head. Airmail it to Chicago." He'd done that with a dog once, when Addie was too young for school yet. He'd had to. If he hadn't, the health department would've. A mad dog bit Champ, then Champ bit Addie. Jim shot him, used a hacksaw, and put his head in a crate. Tests came back negative. Waste of postage and a good goddamned dog—the best goddamned dog there was—and all for what? So his fifteen-year-old daughter could get knocked up by a pervert. At least she'd lost it—the kid. Hell of a bright side, but Jim took what he could get. "Air."

Ward yanked up Vern's head to sputter and wheeze, then dunked it. "Heard any more? From Molly?"

"No. The once. Knowing her, that'll be it." Her sister lived in Spokane. Molly wired a week and a half ago, said she and Addie made it there. No address, no telephone number.

Jim wondered when he'd get served the papers. Or if he'd get served any. He wouldn't put it past her to never file. If she didn't file for divorce, she could keep looming over him like some disembodied harpy who sent telegrams. Wire an occasional reminder that he was the lousiest eighteen-year-long mistake she'd made. If he knew where the hell she was, if he had money to burn on lawyers, he'd have sent Molly some goddamned papers.

"Here," Jim said. "Switch."

Ward held Vern down and Jim maneuvered himself over, lifted Vern's head. As soon as Vern coughed out, "Fellas," Jim dunked him.

"You hear that?" Ward said.

"What?"

"Owl."

"Stop talking like an old woman. It ain't no omen. Owl hoot's an owl hoot. It's a goddamned bird."

Ward was fishing in his shirt pocket, eyes on the far riverbank. He pulled out a smoke and lit it. The match head hissed when it hit water. "Think he'll stay away from Spokane?"

"She's fixed it so I can't even find them up there. That sister of hers remarries twice a year. I'd find Atlantis sooner than her latest last name. Molly's way of making a point. Saying I'm a shitty PI, too. Shitty husband, shitty father, shitty PI. No. He'll just find another Addie." He shoved Vern's head till he felt resistance, Vern's nose and chin meeting the sandy mud. Jim made himself lighten the push but felt the knobs at the base of Vern's skull, the void between, where the spine met. "Hell, he already found the one."

That'd been what did it, what made Molly pack up and leave two weeks ago. What finally did it, nearly a year after Vern Meyer swooped in and out of their house and left everything that'd been rotten to begin with a goddamned wreck, Molly saw an article in the morning *Tribune* about Vern and a twelve-year-old up in Kennard. Molly had the trunks packed, her and Addie boarded on a westbound train before the evening edition's ink dried.

"How much time's he looking at?"

"Three, five years. Tops."

"You'd know where he was, at least."

"Sure, I'd know. For three, five years I'd know. Then he's dumb enough to show his face again, and I'm right back here doing this shit. He skips town now—hell, even Vern's bright enough to stay gone-gone. I want the son of a bitch invisible." Beneath him, Vern wanted air. He kicked and wriggled, tried to buck Jim off. Vern should've known there was no use. Jim had over a hundred pounds and a foot of height on him. If Jim wanted to snuff him out right now, the only chance Vern had was Ward's intervention. Jim eyed his brother. Ward still smoked and stared at the river, half drunk.

Jim pulled Vern's head up by the hair. Vern didn't try to

talk. He was too busy gasping. He huffed. A clod of sand plopped from his nose. Jim dunked him.

Three to five years. Then this shit again.

An image of Molly hovered in Jim's head. Her standing on the porch after she'd caught Vern messing with Addie. She was waiting for the cops, but Vern had hightailed it. Molly stared hard from the doorstep and told Jim to stay the hell away, said he'd caused enough problems. For a flicker, then and now, he thought of what Vern must've done. Under Jim's own goddamned roof.

His face flooded with heat. He felt those knobs of Vern's skull. The back of Vern's head cupped against his palm.

Jim pushed. He pushed, felt the resistance of sand and muck, then pushed harder. He pushed that head deep as it could go. Then he held it. Air bubbled up around Jim's elbow and burst.

Vern squirmed and kicked, but Jim was braced. He held his shins steady and used the whole of his weight to press Vern's body into the grit. Vern Meyer would disappear. If Jim did nothing else worth doing in fifty-one years on this earth, he'd erase Vern Meyer from it.

After the last few twitches, the river lapped and glimmered. A frog chirped in the brush at Jim's back—it was too peaceful. Too scenic. It scraped against the images he tried to shake from his head: Molly at the doorstep. What Vern must've done.

The air had stopped moving and gone thick. Jim's collar was already unbuttoned. He used his free hand to loosen his necktie another nudge, get a decent breath.

"Shit," Ward said like he'd been daydreaming. "Air."

"He wouldn't know what to do with it."

"Jim," he said. "Jim—you didn't—"

"If I wanted to kill him, I got a .38." It was a dodge, not an answer, but he couldn't lie to Ward any sooner than he could say the truth. And he did carry a pistol, in a shoulder holster. He only used it for leverage and knocking down cans, but carrying it was habit from years as an on-again, off-again cop. "Heart attack, maybe."

"Jesus." Ward heaved himself upward to stand. "Jesus Christ."

"Don't panic."

" 'Don't panic,' he says. Jesus. Jesus goddamn Christ, Jim."

Jim sat back from where he'd knelt. He sat back on Vern's skinny ass-bone like it was a piece of driftwood.

Ward double-, triple-puffed his cigarette. "So what the hell now?"

"We say he went for a swim, owl hoot killed him."

"Should I go call Duffy? He'll vouch it was a heart attack—aneurysm—whatever it was—leave us off the report." Duffy had been police surgeon for years. When Cel died, he'd been good to Ward. He'd put "pulmonary hemorrhage" on the certificate. Said she died of TB.

"Retired. Couple months ago. Who's deputy?"

Hat off, Ward scratched his hair so it stood like brush bristles. "Hell, I don't know. Favano? Favana? Favara?" Then he seemed to focus. He looked like he was doing math in his head, measuring dimensions of river and sand. "Floater? Grab whatever's on him—license, letters, anything with a name—roll him out, let him drift?"

It was an option. Floaters were common enough. The

river was good for nothing but fishing, dumping garbage, and drowning. The bottom was fickle. Shallow stretches dropped to deep ruts. The bank was fickle, too. Water flooded and receded, redistributed shore. Made one state bigger, the other smaller. After the last big flood, dry silt piled up north of the dump. Squatters built a shack town on it. Between the sand and mud and water strewn with dead trees, the Missouri was made for floaters.

Jim was tempted. They could roll Vern in, let him bob alongside some bloated pig carcass. But anything that easy would go wrong. "He'd screw that up, too. Get caught on a tree trunk downstream. Some kid fishing at dawn spots him, they find him while he's still got a face—it's no good. Somebody might've seen us leave Pop's with him."

Jim could think of only one option. "Let's take him to Gilson."

2

Jim had never killed anyone. He'd roughed up plenty, and like any PI, he'd been arrested for false imprisonment more than once. But when he and Ward hauled Vern back to the car, Jim wondered if he'd planned to kill Vern to begin with. It'd felt spontaneous enough, but earlier that night, after Ward called, said Vern had shown up at Pop's, Jim pulled the canvas tarp from the trunk and spread it over the backseat and floor of his '24 Ford Touring. He told Vern he'd been hauling paint. He told himself the tarp was in case Vern got scared enough to shit himself.

Whatever Jim's intention, now that Vern had indeed shit himself, Jim was glad for the tarp. Ward helped slide Vern in the backseat and tuck up his legs. Jim draped the extra canvas over him. As they drove, the tarp hid all but the stench. The Ford's top was up, so they ducked their heads from the windows and held their hats. Jim's was felt with a crease. It looked more formal than Ward's driving cap, but it was cheaper than Jim's shoes.

Pete Gilson's undertaking rooms weren't far, up F Street on Twenty-Fourth, but the distance was multiplied by all the zigging and zagging around Riverview and Syndicate Parks and through Clontarf. Clontarf had been a backwoods no-man's-land so set against being annexed and taxed, they'd slashed their streets diagonal to the Omaha and South Omaha grids. They'd been annexed anyway, just like South Omaha and Dundee and Benson. They'd all had assets for Omaha to seize, taxes to be levied. The Empire of Omaha annexed everything. Built over everything. Then the city knocked it all down and built over it again. Pain-in-the-ass streets were the only evidence Clontarf had ever been.

The mortuary was almost a mile from the south side police station, at the end of what passed for a quieter block in South O. Being that close to the station wasn't ideal with a body in the backseat, but longtime south side cops were fine. Or at least Jim knew what to expect. He'd been one for a while, before South O got gulped up. The cops you had to worry about were downtown station, the county sheriff's department, the feds, and the morals squad. Granted, somebody from any of those could've been reassigned to south side this week, because that was the goddamned racket.

City commissioners shifted themselves between departments: Finance, Streets, Parks, Public Improvements, Fire, and Police. They made everybody dizzy over who oversaw what so nobody said boo when they handed in-laws and nephews bids to sod the courthouse lawn or install City Hall's light fixtures. Whichever commissioner drew the short stick got the pointy end—Police. In a city where half the businesses dealt in liquor, gambling, or prostitution, cops were not popular. Their incompetence, their unwillingness to solve murders and thefts, didn't help. That meant police commissioners rarely got reelected, but they all tried like hell to be the exception. They'd dole out demotions and promotions, shuffle patrolmen and desk clerks between downtown and south side, or temporarily disband morals. Or the volunteer force. There was also the goddamned volunteer force. After Jim and Ward's last living sister died, a volunteer shot and killed her youngest son. Said the kid was stealing gas. Shot him in the back while he ran across the country club golf course northwest of town. Fell dead on the sixteenth green.

When the Ford puttered to a stop across the intersection from Pete Gilson's, Ward said, "Tvrdik."

Just then a pair of passing coupes blocked Jim's view across the street—he couldn't see who Ward meant. There were three Tvrdik brothers. The oldest, Eddie, worked at Burlington station. Sold tickets, Jim thought. Another, Tony, ran a saloon registered as a pool hall.

When the coupes passed, Jim saw it was Frank, the one Tvrdik who was a cop. He was in his street clothes, hatless, slicked-back brown hair falling forward in a long curve. His short, wiry frame bobbed down the sidewalk. He was nearing the bricks of Gilson's chapel-fronted mortuary, squinting at a newspaper under the streetlights.

"I'll take you to Pop's," Jim said. "Come by when I'm done."

"You'll need a hand carrying him in."

"He's a shrimp. I got it. Less time between leaving Pop's and getting back, less to account for."

Jim hung a left on Twenty-Fourth, drove south to N, and made a right. He stopped outside the storefront.

"What if he's there? Tvrdik," Ward said.

"At Gilson's? Don't see why he would be. Kava and Kucera

deal with dead Czechs. He was probably walking by. If he wasn't, I worked with Frank. I'll deal with Frank."

Ward gave a snort. "Sure thing. He's reasonable. Real even keel."

"Yeah, well," Jim conceded. "He was in his street clothes, at least."

Ward nodded at Pop's storefront windows. "What do I say?" To Pop and Edith, he meant.

"Say I'm at Maymie's." Maymie's was a brothel.

"Christ, Jim. I'm not up for getting bawled out."

"They start bawling you out, they forget Vern a minute. They ask, say he took off for the depot. Said he was skipping town."

They sat in the stink and silence. Putting their heads out the windows wouldn't have helped. They were downwind of the stockyards and packing plants that'd built South O.

Ward eyed him. "You all right?"

"Sure, I'm all right. Don't I seem all right?"

Ward stopped studying him and looked to the storefront again. "Seeming all right ain't being all right."

"Does the same job."

Ward didn't answer or get out.

"I'm all right." Jim tried to sound definitive. He shouldn't have needed to try, but that kind of question was a trap. Nothing made somebody doubt he was all right like being asked if he was. Jim punctuated his all-rightness with a good-natured punch to Ward's knee. That was either reassurance enough or Ward figured Jim's well-being was a lost cause. He said he'd see Jim in a bit and got out.

Jim drove back north toward F. When he saw no sign of

Frank Tvrdik, he hung a left off Twenty-Fourth, then swung into the alley behind the mortuary. He parked between Pete Gilson's two hearses. The newer looked like a paddy wagon with curtained windows. The older was a carriage, horses retired to a stable for the night. From the driver's seat of the Ford, Jim checked the side mirror for onlookers. The buildings across the alley behind him were strung with laundry and telephone lines. Light and voices came from a pair of upstairs tenement apartments. He couldn't tell which language. The city had to hire translators for thirteen languages in the ward back when he was an election inspector. All he made out now was singing, laughing, a barking shout. A sheet and a kid's dressing gown hung from the splintered banister of a fire escape. Nobody looked out. Maybe it didn't matter if anyone did. He was dropping off a body where people dropped off bodies.

Jim got out, crossed the short distance, and rapped a knuckle on the steel door to the basement. A steep embankment made the back entrance a floor lower than the front. When Pete didn't answer, Jim pulled the doorbell. He didn't hear it ring, but the bell was probably upstairs, wherever Pete slept. Jim waited around until the peep window shifted a touch, then slid over. Pete Gilson was bug-eyed. Not at seeing Jim. Pete was naturally bug-eyed.

"Jim!" His voice was too damn loud.

"Yeah, yeah," Jim whispered back, trying to get Pete to tamp it down.

The window slid shut and what sounded like a bar and lock shifted on the other side of the steel. Pete swung the door open, wide awake and still dressed, smiling like Jim was company come to dinner. Near the stairwell at the other end of the room, a bare light bulb hung above a pair of steel gurneys. Pete ushered Jim in with a "Come in, come in," and asked how he'd been.

Jim said he'd been fine. "How's business?" he asked, then decided he didn't want to know. "Hear they almost caught that Burke fella? Bet you wish you'd set up shop in Chicago."

Pete looked at him, blank.

"Burke. The one they say did the warehouse deal. Saint Valentine's thing last year. Seven guys gunned down."

Pete was still blank.

"Forget it. I got a favor to ask."

"What can I do you for?" Pete was pale white and slim, permanently bent a little at the waist. He grinned, toothy mouth slackened, the way old men who were hard of hearing gaped. Like their mouths could catch words.

"There's a fella." Jim tilted his head toward the back door, hoping Pete could fill in the rest.

If Pete thought anything strange about Jim bringing him a dead fella in the middle of the night, he didn't show it. "Ah!" he said, waving his arm majestically at the narrow red-brick space. "Plenty of room. I'll throw him in the cooler." An oak cooler lined the far wall, opposite the staircase from the gurneys. It was a bunk-bed setup. One compartment sat atop another, each with a lever handle like you'd see on an icebox. Without the handles the cooler could've been an absurdly long filing cabinet straight out of a Harold Lloyd feature.

"Thing is, Pete—I'm a little light on cash right now." Right now. As if Jim had ever been flush in his life. He made a show of kneading the sweat at the back of his collar and looking at the cement floor. It sank toward a perforated metal drain. Jim wasn't certain what the drain was for but could guess. He avoided looking at it.

Pete screwed up his mouth and tapped a finger to his chin, like he was doing figures in his head. "You know I want to help, but the bank account's run low since they put the kibosh on inquests."

"I know it. Hell of a thing." Jim shook his head in sympathy, though he had none. Pete was the reason the state axed the county coroner's office a decade before. He'd served three terms and declared nearly every death suspicious. Suspicious deaths meant inquests, so Pete billed the county to investigate and charged the families for undertaking. He'd made enough money to never work another day in his life—which said something, that Pete would weigh retirement against a job prepping dead people for burial and pick dead people.

"You tell me," Pete said. "How's a county attorney qualified to say a manner of death?"

"Got me there." Above, the floorboards creaked. Jim looked up and traced the footsteps. "Little late for company."

Pete's mouth gave a quick, embarrassed twitch. "Like I said, Jim, no inquests—I still have bills to pay." A door creaked and a slim needle of light widened down the stairwell. "Be right up," Pete called back over his shoulder.

Then he flicked the crown of his head toward a corner of the room behind Jim. Jim hadn't noticed it before, a door of weathered barn wood. He hadn't smelled the tang of mash, either, but embalming fluid was sharp.

"You running a still?"

"Vent it through the crematory." On the wall to Jim's left was a heavy cast-iron plate on hinges.

"That a customer upstairs, or somebody got you on the hook?"

Before Pete could answer, Frank Tvrdik came bobbing down and ducked the ceiling where the stairs ended, although he could've cleared it by half a foot standing straight. He must've been up there the whole time.

Frank Tvrdik was usually deemed a police sergeant, sometimes demoted to patrolman, and once in a while relegated to vice, which Omaha called morals squad because it sounded pious. Frank was a few years younger, but he and Jim were appointed special officers together twenty-five years before, during a meat-packers' strike. Even back then, more than a decade before Nebraska made liquor illegal, reformers found a way to blame booze for the strike. Jim and Frank were assigned to saloons, making sure everybody closed at eight and stayed shuttered on Sundays. The two of them did their jobs, then made sure strikers knew which back doors and sheds to go to instead. Frank stayed with the police, while Jim was fired, rehired as a truant officer, fired again, hired for morals, and fired again with an explicit order to never come back. So he'd started the private agency. Since cops didn't bother solving cases, he'd have plenty of business. RESULTS GUARANTEED, the ad read, and they were. Jim guaranteed somebody'd get pinched. Nobody innocent if he could help it, but there wasn't much risk of finding anyone innocent in Omaha.

Grin half-cocked, face round and impish like a Kewpie

doll, Frank bounce-strode over and shook Jim's hand. Then the environs seemed to dawn on him, and the grin straightened. "Hope you're here on business. Or a social call."

"Sure," Jim said, like he'd ever be in a room with Pete Gilson on purpose. "I was telling Pete it's too bad he didn't set up shop in Chicago. Hear they almost caught that Burke fella?"

"The Valentine's thing?"

"Who's your money on?"

Frank shrugged. "My bet's what it looks like. Two uniforms, couple plainclothes drive up in a squad car, go in, mow down everybody but the dog. But they'll pin it on somebody. Burke, Purple Gang, Capone."

If Chicago's municipal racket was anything like Omaha's, the theory was solid.

Frank's gaze sank to his shoes with gravity. He wasn't one for gravity, and the shift gave Jim heartburn. In the space of a minute, that mischievous doll face could joke, turn hotheaded, get misty-eyed about his grandmother, then go menacingly quiet. Terror-inducing. But even the way Frank bobbed when he walked—gravity didn't have much hold on him. "Hate to break it to you—" He kept his head bowed but his eyes rose to meet Jim's. "You got a dead guy in your backseat."

Jim didn't breathe for a beat. Two beats.

Then Frank reared his head back in a laugh.

"Christ, Frank."

"Need a hand?"

"I got it."

"Nah, come on, Big Jim Beely. I only look like a squirt."

They used the tarp to carry Vern in and dropped him on

a gurney Gilson wheeled to the door. Frank flipped the canvas off to see who it was. "Shit. Ain't that Vern What's-it?"

"Meyer."

"Get his head stuck in a toilet?"

"Cistern," Jim said. "Freak accident."

"Got the freak part right. No offense," he told Pete.

Pete said none taken.

"Seen he got more statutory charges—Washington County? Twelve-year-old?"

Jim let a short, disgusted breath through his nose. He nodded and waited for questions—about the cistern, about why Jim was here with the body.

"How'd Molly take it? News about the charges."

"Yeah, real well. She left two weeks ago. Took Addie. Didn't want her in any more headlines." Some prick at the *Tribune* got word when Molly called the cops on Vern. The editor had a grudge against Jim and ran the story on the front page. Bottom corner, but a headline was enough for Molly to pull Addie out of school.

"Papers in this town are garbage." Frank turned to Pete. "I smoke right now, will the whole place blow?"

Pete handed him a box of matches.

Vern's eyes were open. So was his mouth. Jim had brushed and scooped and shaken the muck from both, plus his nose, but his face still had a thin crust of pale dried mud.

Frank lit a cigarette, waved out the match, and dropped it in Vern's mouth. "Couldn't've happened to a better fella." The burnt match head stuck where Vern's tongue had bunched up at the back of his throat. The wood jutted past his front teeth.

Jim's clenched shoulders loosened a bit. Frank had kids.

He knew what Vern was. Maybe murder and taking protection weren't level ground, amorally speaking, but Jim sensed that if Frank suspected anything, he wouldn't ask questions. Not if Jim didn't. "I got a few bucks. He don't need the cooler, just light him up. How much?"

"Ah, hell," Frank said. "Pete can do this one on the house, can't you, Pete?"

Pete stared at the matchstick, his face a wince. Jim wondered if he took offense—at desecration of bodies and whatnot. Jim doubted it. More likely, Frank had Pete in a bind over the still. Word around town said Frank's protection was reasonable; he mainly charged wholesalers who manufactured or ran import operations, not saloonkeepers who advertised their joints as soft drink parlors, pool halls, or cigar stores. Wholesalers could generally afford it, and in Jim's experience, people who could afford it generally deserved it. Besides, if they didn't pay, the only backlash was a raid and watching their still get hauled off or their stock hacked open and drained in the street. They'd skip court and forfeit bond, which cost more than Frank did. At least with Frank, they wouldn't take a hit on the booze and lose any business licenses they had. But Pete's liquor sales couldn't have been good to begin with. Not with newspapers across the country running stories anytime somebody dropped dead from guzzling embalming fluid.

"I like his tie," Pete said, eyes fixed on it. Christ, Pete could give Jim the creeps.

Vern's tie was hand-painted with a trio of horseshoes, which always struck Jim as odd. Vern was an auto mechanic. Or he said he'd been. He was out of work when they'd met. He'd helped Jim get the Ford running when it'd stranded him west of the city limit. Vern had looked harmless, down on his luck, and he'd helped Jim out. Not a lot of people did. So Jim let him stay in his house like a goddamned chump, in exchange for odd jobs. "It's all yours," Jim said of the tie. "And I'll pay—I'm good for it. Give me a week. Three bucks, the tie—how much more you want?"

"Nah, see—I got a thought." Frank smiled and tapped his temple. Pete looked at Frank. Jim couldn't tell if the look was hope or his natural expression of bug-eyed awe. "Pete here's behind on some bills." Frank ashed in Vern's mouth and took a drag. "And I got a problem money don't fix anyhow. It's my brother, Antonín—you met him—goes by 'Tony' so he don't sound so bohunk. Better for business with the dagos." Frank's brother ran a pool hall that sold liquor near Tenth and Hickory. People called the area Little Italy, but like most neighborhoods that weren't rich, it was as mixed as the League of Nations. "Some teetotaler running for city commission's gunning for pool rooms, soft drink parlors, any joint's got booze." An election was coming in May. "Commission's renewing business permits, next meeting. This guy wants anybody selling booze denied."

Anybody caught selling booze in the last year was already denied. The teetotaler must've been gunning for anybody not caught. "Campaign stunt?"

"What else?" Frank shrugged. "The guy wants private investigators. To suss out which joints sell liquor." He held an open hand to the side of his mouth and whispered as loud as his speaking voice, "Say, some operatives. From a detective agency." He dropped the whisper and the hand. "Except it'd be good if operating ain't their strong suit."

"Who is he? The dry."

"Hell, I don't know. Some smug nitwit, Independent Federation slate. You know anybody on the ticket? Personally?"

The Independent Federation was the latest name of some longtime local politicians who rarely got elected. Cross-burning nativists. They used to campaign as the "reform" ticket. Their idea of reform was to rid Omaha of booze, prostitution, gambling, and, while they were at it, immigrants, non-whites, non-Protestants, and anybody poor who didn't make them rich. "Not if I can help it."

"That's good." Frank mulled something over. His eyes skated across the concrete floor like he was reading fine print. "If you don't know the guy, all he knows about you's what he seen in the papers, yeah?"

"That's not always good."

"Not so bad, neither." Frank searched for a word. He had an unexpectedly large assortment of them tucked in that big doll head. "Inscrutable," he landed on. "Big Jim Beely: truant officer, booze hound, election judge—"

"Inspector."

"Sure. Plus loiterer, larcenist, judge puncher—you got a real detective pedigree. Nobody ever knows your angle."

Jim didn't like being called a detective. "Investigator," he said. "Let Pinkertons bust strikers' heads."

Frank wasn't listening. He was hatching a scheme and getting fired up—Frank could get real wound up—like he was on the edge of solving a riddle. "Nah, it's perfect. Anytime you fall down on the stand or get pinched looks like retaliation. Like you got too close to something somebody don't want out. I put it like that, you're in."

"Put it to who? And into what? What're you cramming me into?"

Frank smiled big, like there was a good punch line coming. "Whoever this Federation dolt is hired Harry Donnegan to get the investigators, give some anti-liquor, clean-up-Omaha speech at the meeting."

"Donnegan," Jim repeated, to make sure he'd heard right. Harry Donnegan's formal title was defense lawyer. Less formally, he was a goddamned clown and a sloppy drunk. He had two courtroom strategies. One was endless delay. The other was getting clients immunity from prosecution, then making them memorize testimony.

"I know it. Ventriloquist Donnegan. He'd get immunity for a guy who killed Missus Donnegan if it made a buck."

"But he's a defense lawyer. It'll look like he's trying to put half his clients out of business."

"Correct. Not his purview. But the teetotaler's after publicity, and Donnegan gets headlines—every closing argument, same sob story about his mother on her deathbed, begging him, 'Sonny. Sonny-boy, promise me you'll get off the sauce.' Ain't you heard? Donnegan's bona fide reformed now."

"He's bona fide full of shit." He'd ordered a barrel of whiskey from Pop's last week, when Ward was tending bar.

"Yeah, well." Frank shrugged. "Donnegan's gotta be short for O'Donnegan, right? Point is: Besides the *Tribune*, a reform guy couldn't get a front page to cover him if he was a wet, naked baby on a snowbank. And the best part? Donnegan wants the Federation idiot's plan to go haywire. How else does he stay soused? His clients know the fix—hell, my brother was the one told me about it."

"And some Independent Federation guy trusts Donnegan." Jim was skeptical.

Frank took a drag off his smoke and dropped his gaze in thought. "Yeah, I don't know. Whatever it is, it's politics—always politics. Hell, you know that con. Try and untangle whose hand's in whose pocket, you get a date with the Insanity Board." Frank was being literal. Two of the three-man Insanity Board were political appointees. You got in their way, you got railroaded into the booby hatch.

Frank said he'd tell Donnegan to put Jim on the job. Donnegan could tell the Federation candidate Jim had been a liquor agent for a while. Got fired for not looking the other way on joints that were protected.

That was true in spirit, Jim guessed. And Ward knew plenty of drunks from helping at Pop's. There must've been one or two who'd gladly get paid to go around and find booze. "I could get a couple rounders."

"You charge half up front?"

Jim said he did. Plus, Donnegan would be on the hook for expenses, which Jim could pad if Frank wanted a cut.

"Nah. Keep it. Tony stays in business, Jennie and me don't gotta put him and his whole brood up at the house. Between that and watching the commissioners' meeting turn into a circus? That's payoff enough." He stubbed his cigarette out on the gurney. "So? How's that for a deal? You get paid, pervert gets burnt, Tony stays in business. All that, plus me and Pete here are square."

"Hell of a deal," Jim said, even if he wasn't so sure. They shook on it.

3

Jim waited at Pete's until the crematory was heated and Vern was incinerating behind that cast-iron door. Pete was already wearing Vern's tie, the one with three hand-painted horseshoes. Jim thought to say not to wear it a few months, but mentioning the tie could only raise suspicions about how Vern wound up dead. And all that mattered, for Jim and the rest of the world's sake, was that Vern Meyer was no more.

Jim drove back to Pop's. When he walked in, Ward and Edith were at the far end of the bar. They were drying glasses, leaving them bottoms up on a thin towel. Edith talked too low to hear but looked worried. Ward was flushed, either from more whiskey or henpecking.

No, Edith was all right. She was good for Ward and she wasn't bad-looking—skinny redhead with a frizzy bob, gestures twitchy like a bird's. Tonight she wore an oriole-orange dress to match. It was one of those shapeless flapper types that'd once been the rage. Jim thought they looked like dolled-up flour sacks with arm and head holes.

Between the low-hanging fringe and the stockings, you wouldn't know she was missing half her left leg unless you studied her walk. She had a real slight lope, wood foot landing a little louder than the other. Jim hadn't noticed until he'd seen the leg without Edith attached once. The worn leather harness had leaned against the entryway hall of her and Ward's row house. There were newer legs, he thought, lighter, ones that moved easier, but they were probably expensive or reserved for vets. Or maybe the leg was like marriage or anything else a person lived with so long they barely thought about it. She was over forty; she'd lost the leg when she was a kid. She'd been around longer without it than with it and got by fine. She had a day job as a labeler at the packing plant.

Pop squatted behind the front end of the bar, which was old-fashioned but regal—carved mahogany, ornate, with a big back mirror and an arch lined in bronze lion heads. The cats spit tubes of gaslight into milk-colored balls. Maybe the bar was locally made, but the whole setup looked special-ordered, shipped in about the time Pop Nelson stepped off a nearby boat. He'd come from Denmark, a decade or three after Germany invaded and started drafting Danes into their army. Jim didn't remember the details.

The old man was rearranging a display of cigar boxes. Colonitas and Caballeros. They smelled rich and just sweet enough to tug the roots of Jim's teeth. Pop glanced up and gave Jim a *hmf*, but the old man wasn't so much a grouch as he was formal. He held his chest rigid like a bust. Even the way his hair receded was dignified. His thick, long mustache was combed to a tight trim, his eyes ringed in wire spectacles. He looked ready-made for a lecture tour ad in the newspaper. One with some overly complicated nonsense title: THE

DESPOTIC TENDENCIES OF THE PSYCHIC MECHANISM.
He didn't look a damn thing like a saloonkeeper, much less somebody who'd run a so-called soft drink parlor, but Pop was a man of principles—a self-proclaimed conscientious objector to liquor prohibition.

The room's four tables were rounded by empty chairs. In a few weeks, they'd be full until the last games' box scores were chalked on the slate at the bar's far end. Outside baseball season, most customers phoned in orders, then swung by or asked for delivery. When people did stop in, they didn't stick around upstairs. Since Ward and Edith were up here, the basement bar must've been empty.

Jim asked Pop how business was.

"Fine," the old man said, curt. "Not so fine as Maymie's, I'll bet."

Jim knew he was in for it, but he was glad Ward stuck to the story. "I don't get it, Pop. You're a forward-thinker. What's wrong with a few hardworking men and women meeting demand with supply? Seems like any other job."

Pop never had much retort on the topic, at least not from an ideological standpoint, and Pop consisted primarily of ideals. On prostitution, he was a quibbler. He slid the display case closed and stood. "It's no place for a married man."

"I'm deserted."

"It's no wonder," Pop said. " 'Men and women.' You talk about men and women in those places. Half are barely older than children."

A short splintering crack came from the end of the bar. Edith had flung the glass she'd been drying to the floor. She gripped her towel in a fist and glared at Jim. Judging by the cockeyed aim of her eyes, she was tipsy. She could be trouble tipsy.

"Well? I didn't throw it," Jim told her. "The hell you looking at me for?"

"You're a goddamned piece of work."

Ward said he had to take a leak. Pop told Jim to lock up and turned to busy himself at the register. As soon as the old man was occupied counting IOUs and change, Edith waved Jim over with the towel. Jim took as much time as he could locking the door and closing the shades before he went to her.

"You let him leave town," she hissed, hot-breathed from the booze. "That's it?"

Jim stared back with a practiced, hardened blankness, though he was grateful Ward stuck to the story with her, too.

"I swear to God, Jim, if letting that son of a bitch go means you dragged Ward—"

"You're the only person ever dragged Ward into anything. Thought he was heartbroke, latched on like grim goddamned death."

He knew she wanted to smack him. He'd been smacked enough he could smell it coming like rain. But she didn't. She said, "You're useless. Good for absolutely nothing, you know it?"

Jim did know it. He knew it a good deal better than Edith ever could.

She turned away and crunched through the shards of glass to grab a broom and dustpan.

The bathroom door opened, and Ward came out. His hairline was wet, like he'd splashed water on his face. He grabbed his coat and hat and lit a cigarette. They all told Pop good night, Edith gave the old man a peck, and they left.

In the car, Edith sat where Vern had when they'd driven to the river. Jim rolled down his window.

"You plan on telling what happened?" she said.

"He's gone, honey," Ward said. "I told you. That's it."

"Humor me. Walk me through the genius reasoning that lets that son of a bitch off the hook."

"I told her," Ward said, loud over the engine and whipping air. "We were gonna shake him down. Figured he goes to the pen, no use letting money sit in a drawer however many years. Might as well let Molly and Addie—"

"How long would he get? You know, anything would be something. Anything would be better than nothing." She lit a cigarette and threw the match from the window.

"His lawyer's a snake," Jim said. "Plans to argue the girl looks older. He'll tell the jury what happened between her and Vern's happened between her and plenty others. He'd get a wrist slap. She'd be in a reformatory longer than he'd be in the pen." That'd been what Vern said, anyway, and he wasn't bright enough to make it up. Jim's pulse beat an angry thump in his head hearing Vern's voice tell it again. Jim looked at Edith in the rearview. Her eyes were fiery green and set on his, waiting for the rest. "So I made him swear he'd leave town." He looked back down at the road. "Roughed him up." That much was true. Vern swore he'd leave town, Jim roughed him up.

"That's it, then," she said. "That's your goddamned answer."

"What do you want me to do—kill him?" Saying it made Jim grip the steering wheel harder. "Want me dragging your husband into that?" He reminded himself he hadn't dragged Ward into anything. For all Ward knew, Vern croaked from a heart attack. And now there was no body. "Ward," he said, wanting his brother to intervene.

"Edie," Ward said.

"Don't 'Edie' me. Don't do that."

Ward slouched in his seat and rested his head back. "Sweetheart, Jim's in hot water with Molly as is, not getting any cash for her and Addie."

"He should be," she said. "He should be in hot water, letting that pervert go. I just don't want you boiled up with him."

Jim was nearing their row house on Vinton. His head throbbed with his pulse and the force it took to shake god-damned Vern's voice from his ears. He'd slowed, but instead of pulling to a stop, Jim hit the gas and whipped the steering wheel toward the stoop. The front end jumped the curb. He wanted his head to stop pounding. He wanted Edith to stop talking. And she did, if only for a second. Jim slammed the brake. "Listen." He eyed her in the rearview. "The only way I pulled Ward into anything is if you yap—you or your old man—telling anybody we were the last people you saw Vern with."

She was serious then, thinking. "So what do I say, then? When people ask."

"Vern's got nobody. Nobody's asking." That should've rung an alarm in Jim's head from the start, Vern having no one. There were good goddamned reasons Vern was alone in the world.

The Ford was parked on the yard. A headlamp lit the brick

column holding up the porch roof. The only people who'd notice Vern was gone were an overworked judge, the Washington County sheriff, Vern's lawyer, and a girl who surely wouldn't mind never seeing Vern Meyer again. Jim couldn't imagine the lawyer stood to make much. "If the Washington County sheriff comes around—guy named Shumway—tell him Vern stopped in. Said he'd blown his terms of release crossing county lines. Had to skip town." He'd been let out on his own recognizance. Of course he had. Nobody would've bonded out the son of a bitch. "He left for the Burlington. Shumway asks who went with him, say nobody. He left by himself."

The heaviness in Jim's mood seemed to shift Edith's. She tried to lighten the air and gave Ward's shoulder a little push. "You want to do something here?" she deadpanned. "He's on the yard."

Ward gave a tired smile. He looked half-asleep already. He opened his door and got out. Jim couldn't see above his brother's waist, only his gesture at Edith, nothing urgent, a folding of fingers.

She got out and shut the door. She paused by Ward, stroked his forearm, then passed through the headlight beams to go inside.

Ward sat back down but left his door open.

"That woman should not drink," Jim said.

"Gilson say he'd help out?"

"Already did. For a few bucks and a favor to Frank."

"Tvrdik. Great." Ward glanced out when a light in the living room came on.

"One favor gets Vern gone for good, it's a bargain."

"Ain't ideal, Jim. Tvrdik's crooked as hell."

"Show me somebody around here who isn't."

"When's the court date? Vern's."

"Next Tuesday. When he don't show, judge'll issue a capias warrant. If Shumway even looks for him, don't just assume Vern took off, he won't come around till he's worn out everything up there—the girl's parents, anybody else in Washington County who'd like Vern better dead. And by now, there's nothing left of him. By now, he's a pile of ash."

Ward took a drag off his cigarette, then looked at it, studying the burning tip. "You know, you ever want a place to stay besides the office, we can figure something out."

"You think I don't sleep now? How would I shut my eyes with a drunk Edith in there? Waiting with a pillow to smother me."

Ward gave a puff of a laugh. "She's feisty, is all."

"Yeah, she's all right. Maybe a little deluded, thinking you're a prize."

Ward patted Jim's shoulder and got out, went in the house.

Jim backed down the yard to the street. He stayed east on Vinton to Twentieth, then turned north toward downtown Omaha. He crossed the viaduct above the railyards, one of the rickety bridges that stitched South Omaha to the city, and tried to remember what the downtown skyline looked like before the streets were graded. Most cities sprawled upward. Omaha had sunk.

The place used to be all hills. Now downtown was one big mound. City commissioners had paid somebody's kid or brother or uncle millions to lop forty, fifty feet off the tallest peaks, drop this street and raise that one. Most politicians claimed they'd carved the place up for cars, but dropping a twelve percent grade to seven didn't do much. Other bigwigs said the hills weren't uniform enough. They were uncity-like. Provincial. Omaha had a neurotic complex about seeming quaint. Which was fair. The place was not quaint. Maybe it wasn't Chicago, Hog Butcher for the World, but nobody was running around with a lifted head, crooning garbage about the pride of being alive. You raised your head in Omaha, you got it slapped with a tire iron. Somebody slit your throat, picked your pockets, and plastered you inside a wall.

He parked on Seventeenth, outside his office in the Henley-Barr Building. He'd paid rent on his and Molly's place through May, but he hadn't slept there in nearly a year. A couple days after the Vern blowup, Jim waited till Molly and Addie left for work. He went to the house, grabbed a tick mattress from a rollaway, and took it to the office. He'd tried to go back again, to sleep at the house after Molly's telegram a week and a half ago. He couldn't. He couldn't be in that place.

Some nights he drank a few swigs of whiskey and knocked out fine at the office. Others, an ancient cadaver of a lawyer down the hall got loud and amorous with a former client's ex-wife. If Jim couldn't take it, he'd have a nip from a bottle of morphine throat syrup he kept in the filing cabinet. Once in a while, if he had a little extra cash and all the bumping and yowling was too much, he'd sleep someplace else. Not Maymie's—he'd told Ward to mention Maymie's because of its notoriety. You couldn't sleep there—it was less brothel than service station. Maymie's had no airs. If it had, you wouldn't have wanted to breathe them.

Sometimes, though, Jim paid for a sleeping room at the Little Underworld, a black and tan in South O where you could drink, gamble, dance. If anybody there asked him what he was, they were curious. Other places, people eyed him sidelong. Guarded. Wanted to know what that black hair and olive-tinged skin made him. Why the hell he was so big. What the hell kind of a name was Beely. Questions Jim had no answers for.

Besides, a sleeping room there was cheaper than any hotel you wouldn't get murdered in. You could use one of the sleeping rooms to do the whole other bit if you cared to, but Jim never cared to these days, which made no sense. He hadn't been faithful to Molly their whole marriage. She'd turned off the spigot when she was pregnant with Addie, and the one industry in Omaha that boomed bigger than packing houses and booze was prostitution. He'd done his part in sustaining the local economy while reminding himself, in twenty-minute increments, that he had a pulse. With Molly gone, he should've been living it up. But she'd managed to pack up any urges he had left and haul those to Spokane, too.

He took the Henley-Barr's back stairwell to the sixth floor. The lawyer's office was quiet tonight, and Jim had almost caught his breath when he reached the end of the hall, the door with mottled glass stenciled BEELY NAT'L INVESTIGATIONS in gold script. He crossed from the brown and cream tiles lined by marble mopboards onto the plain wood floor of the office. At night, with the lights on, the room was pleasant enough. The woodwork was dark glossy brown and the walls were a lighter shade that matched, a color like the fur of a fawn.

He'd have a drink from the whiskey stashed in his desk, unroll the mattress, and try not to hear the echo of Vern's gurgling.

If that didn't work, maybe the echo would lull him to sleep.

4

Jim wasn't out for long, but he slept harder than he had in weeks. Of course he had. Vern Meyer was dead. Better than dead. He was a pile of ash.

Shortly before seven, before the early spring dawn broke, Jim rose from the mattress in his underclothes and stumbled on a box of paperwork he'd been meaning to file. He pushed the light switch and headed for the bathroom, which wasn't a room. It was a couple partitions hiding a toilet and sink. The partitions ended eight feet up, where a transom window opened to the hallway. It was not a good system. After everybody drank a cup of morning coffee, you needed a gas mask to walk through the building.

He relieved himself and took what his ma used to call a whore's bath—pits, feet, and the business district. Then he shaved. He hung his washcloth across the tap to dry, stashed the shaving kit in his desk, dressed, and slipped into his shoulder holster out of habit, like putting on suspenders. He made a mental note he was wearing his last clean suit. He had three. One hung behind a false wall in the coat closet, another he wore, and the third, whichever was filthiest, was always at the cleaners. Frank had said he'd bring Harry Donnegan by, but Jim didn't know what time. Instead of hanging the tick mattress out an office window to dry, keep the straw inside from molding, he rolled and stuffed it behind the closet panel.

The radiator had thickened the air while he slept. He opened the transoms, then the windows overlooking Seventeenth for a cross-draft. The bank across the street was carved from the same mammoth russet brick as the Henley-Barr and absorbed all the morning light at its back. That was about right, that a bank would suck up all the sun to be had. In the shadow between buildings, the sidewalk and street jolted and stopped like a watch popped open and stepped on. It still ticked, but it kept some off-kilter time too hard to track. Cars whipped in and out of parking spaces. People leapt around bumpers and each other, cursing their way to work. Past the end of the block, on Farnam, streetcars rumbled and screeched, and somewhere farther off, a team of horses whinnied, their sound bouncing between brick and pavement. The sound was getting rarer, and for a second Jim memorized it like he sometimes did the voice of a person who was dying. Then he felt like a sentimental jackass, reminded himself he'd be dead sooner or later, too, and made some coffee.

Close to ten in the morning, Frank escorted Harry Donnegan in, then stood at the windows like he wasn't listening, only studying the street scene below.

Donnegan made chitchat and sat in one of the two leather chairs reserved for clients. He could've filled both. He was nearly Jim's height but soft and so white he was pinkish. The top of his bald head was flatter than most, like he'd been shaped from dough and dropped. His face did have an authority to it, some striking quality, but Jim couldn't tell what gave it that. On the rare occasions Donnegan's mouth shut, it rested in a thin-lipped borderline smirk, and heavy lids made his watery blue eyes seem perpetually pitying. The cumulative effect was Donnegan looked mildly clever, moderately devious, and unswervingly condescending. If there was such a thing as fate, he'd shot from his mother's snatch a lawyer.

The Independent Federation candidate who'd hired him turned out to be a guy named Elmer Kobb. Jim only knew him from the papers. Donnegan walked Jim through what Frank already had. Kobb wanted campaign publicity. He'd get it by daring the commission to deny business license renewals to anybody selling booze. "Speaking of, you got anything, Jim?"

"You're not in court. You can say whiskey. Want to keep it legal, don't leave a tip." Jim pulled a juice glass and the bottle from his desk drawer. Donnegan eyed the glass as Jim poured two fingers. When he kept staring, Jim poured one more and corked the bottle. "He's only after booze?"

"For now. He says he'll go straight at gambling later, once he has a commissioner's seat."

"Whole city's a rigged racket, but, sure. Ban bets the commoners might win." Jim looked to Frank. "Omaha without gambling. Didn't that already happen? The pari-mutuel ban?" The state's attorney general put a moratorium on track betting last year. All it'd done was improve the stakes.

"Got horses selling insurance door-to-door now," Frank said, still looking down on Seventeenth. "Hard times." His scrutiny left the window and landed at the back of Donne-gan's flat head. "Prostitution?"

"Doubtful." Harry took an easy quaff, like the booze couldn't strip paint. "Kobb's brother-in-law's Jack Maloney—"

Frank cut in. "The loon?"

Jack Maloney was a weird one, all right. An ex-cop. He was tall and gawky, head too big for his body, but always primped like he was waiting on a casting call. Rumor had it he owed more than a year's pay to every clothing company and tailor in town, so he'd drive out to the sticks, run up a tab in Podunk once a week. He had light red hair that made his eyebrows invisible, so he used lip rouge to draw them on. They jutted up at an angle, two straight lines—cockeyed red dashes that would've looked angry on a cartoon. Maybe that was his intent, to come off stern or serious, but you couldn't take a guy with lip-rouge eyebrows serious. Still, he'd some-how wrangled a job with the cops, weaseled his way up to ser-geant, then busted a trumpeter's lip making an arrest. He got sued, then suspended. After, he'd driven a taxi a few months and claimed he owned the whole operation. He hadn't, but that didn't stop him from joining the Merchants' Associa-tion as company president, which got him fired.

"Ain't he your client?" Frank said.

Donnegan drank and nodded. "He won't serve time for the assault, but he won't be a police sergeant again soon. And since the cab company didn't work out, he's marrying May-mie Strunk."

"Maymie," Jim said. "*Maymie*-Maymie?"

"That some kind of Habsburg marriage?" Frank said. "They starting a freak-whore empire?"

"Kobb's wife needles him about settling Maloney's debts. If Maymie foots the bill, Commissioner Kobb keeps her place from being padlocked and Maloney in those dapper Florsheims."

Frank whistled, impressed or appalled.

Jim wanted to note Maloney's Florsheims were not dapper; they were like everything else about him. Loud. Instead, Jim reeled the conversation back to the matter at hand. "So, Kobb brings city council a list of joints selling booze in broad daylight, makes the police commissioner look bad, nabs his seat. What's the chances it works?"

"Well, it's an odd election," Donnegan said, and it was, even in a city where elections were already convoluted, probably to curb voter turnout. Three-year terms. Voting in spring instead of fall. To top it off, people elected commissioners who made one of themselves mayor. For more than twenty years, minus one spectacularly bad, bad term, they'd picked Jake Berman. But Berman dropped dead three months ago. "With J.B. gone, maybe the city's itching for change," Donnegan said. "Ready to spit-shine Omaha's name a little. Swap out the whole machine."

"And what? Replace it with a slate of cross-burners?" Jim said. "Last time reform took over, we got martial law." That was the spectacularly bad term. A white riot culminated in a lynching and the burning of the courthouse. One headline called it an ORGY OF BLOOD AND FIRE.

"All to Bill Haskell's advantage, of course," Donnegan said.

Jim sighed and massaged a temple. Omaha's version of Al Capone was, allegedly, an elderly white fella in a bowler named Bill Haskell. He'd come to town about the time Jim was born and run gambling in saloons until the city said he couldn't. Then he'd tried his hand at real estate, bred racehorses, did the loan shark bit. Jim once borrowed a month's pay from him—took three years to pay it back. Somewhere in there, Haskell took up political campaigning. Likely because politics had the same appeal as playing the ponies or wagering on Notre Dame football. Ever since, he'd gained mythical status: the city's boss, king of the underworld, head of the gang, one-man political machine. No doubt he'd been a cog, but whether or not he still had teeth and could turn was debatable.

"Harry, ease up on the booze," Frank said.

"I don't know," Donnegan said in the disingenuous, smug tone of a guy who thought he sure did know a thing. "An awful lot of people say Haskell planned the riots so his cronies could retake office."

Jim was getting the headache again—the pulse in his head could pound hard enough to make him see stars. "Sure they say it. Why the hell wouldn't they say it? Blame some villain out of a melodrama for tying half a city's brains to the tracks. Hell of a lot easier than explaining how thousands of bigots lost their goddamned minds—lynched, shot, and burned a cripple, for chrissake."

Donnegan gave Jim the full smirk. "I don't suppose you're cozy with Haskell."

Jim briefly contemplated shooting Donnegan.

"I don't have the clout or the cash to be cozy to Haskell," Jim said. "He snuggles up with bankers and railroads. They tell him which politicians to back, he takes their money and prints up slates telling people how to vote. He's a middle-man. Not even a laundry. If money goes straight from Union Pacific or Ice and Cold Storage to a campaign, that's illegal. Him in between, ain't illegal. Besides, candidates he backs lose as often as they don't."

"And voters with vacant lot addresses? The miscounts?"

"Haskell might try and stack the deck, but no recount's ever overturned ward results."

"Anybody saw that guy's spelling, they'd know he ain't no mastermind," Frank said. "Searched his office for a bomb once, found a shopping list. S-O-P-E, soap. T-O-W-L, towel."

Donnegan ignored him. "If Haskell's not in charge, he sure doles out quite the favors. He's helped more than one man secure gainful city employment."

"The whole city runs on favors and payoffs," Jim said. "It's like a goddamned English estate—cousins marry cousins. Keep money in the family and the rest of us dead broke. You ever buy booze from Haskell? Ever slip him a couple saw-bucks at Maymie's?"

"If I haven't, that doesn't mean bootleggers and madams don't pay into his campaign funds."

"B-E-E-N-S, beans. Not that bad spellers can't be smart at something else, but Christ: B-E-E-N-S, beans."

"Fine," Jim said. "Here's the hundred-dollar question: You ever get a call from Haskell telling you to represent somebody?"

"No, but—"

"No."

"So there's nothing to it. A political machine doesn't run the city."

"Holy Christ." Frank stepped near Donnegan's head and talked loud and slow, hands cupped like a megaphone: "He just told you. The machine is money. Money tells campaign managers and editors who to back. There's the machine. Three parts." Frank dropped the megaphone and smacked the back of one hand into the palm of the other as punctuation. "Money, campaign managers, papers. Ain't quantum mechanics."

Jim steered the conversation back on track. "You never said what's his odds. Kobb's."

Donnegan held his empty glass up, pinched between two pink fingers until Jim poured him a swallow. "The other four on the Federation ticket are no-names. People around here pick devils they've at least heard of, unless the poor devil's police commissioner. He's doomed. I'd say Kobb's chances of filling the seat are better than good."

"Who you think they'll stick with police?" Frank said.

"Well, they hate Kobb. I assume they'll saddle him with it."

"I'd quit," Frank said. He wouldn't quit. "Nah, I probably wouldn't quit. But I'd say I'd quit."

"Politics explains Kobb, not you," Jim said. "Sure, money's money and you don't want your booze cut off. But you go into that meeting as Kobb's lawyer and foul up the case, you come out a jackass. I'm not saying it don't stink already, but what about your reputation?"

"Jim. I'm a criminal defense attorney in Omaha. How would I run out of business?"

It was a fair point.

"Besides, if a lawyer knows one thing, it's how to word a question. It'll look like your operatives bungled it."

"Yeah, and then I'm the jackass for hiring Laurel and Hardy. Maybe Kobb's paying you enough not to care, but this is how I make a living."

"Ah, come on," Frank said then. "You're inscrutable, Big Jim. When reporters ask, you shrug and say rounders are rounders. It'll read like Kobb tried hassling small businesses. That don't win peoples' hearts. Undermine him, you come out the hero."

"The hero." Jim leaned back, elbow propped on the arm of his chair. He rubbed his earlobe, thinking it through. "And why don't Kobb want to be the hero? Go solo. Hire his own investigators. He makes a big enough play, the papers have to cover it. He'd look like the hardest working politician-to-be in town."

"He'd still be a zealot and a bore," Donnegan said, and it was true. In the papers, Kobb talked like an Anti-Saloon League pamphlet. Personality of wet cardboard. "People love me or hate me, but when I'm the headline, they keep reading."

"Who?" Frank said. "Who loves you, Donnegan?"

Donnegan pulled some folded papers from inside his suit jacket. He unfolded and paged through them before handing them over. It was a list. The addresses of every pool hall, cigar store, and soft drink parlor up for license renewal.

"How many?" Jim asked.

"Hundred forty-three."

"Christ." Jim scanned and saw Tony Tvrdik and Pop's places. "You sure this won't backfire, get all these joints raided?"

Donnegan dismissed the idea with a quick shut-eyed

shake of the head. "Too much rental income. Commissioners and friends own more than half the storefronts on there."

Frank whistled again.

"How's it all get bungled?" Jim said. "Specifically."

"No proof. No liquor samples. Give your men the addresses, say, 'Drink and take notes.'"

"That's it."

"That's it. No physical proof, no grounds for formal investigation. No investigation, no charges, no convictions. And without convictions, the commission can't deny permits. Besides, men on that board know shutting down speakeasies is political suicide." That was also true. The state and then the country might've gone dry, but Omaha had stayed crocked from the jump.

Jim asked for half up front plus expenses, thirteen hundred. It was a gouge, but Donnegan didn't even wince. Which meant Kobb was paying a hell of a lot more than Donnegan was worth and Jim should've asked for more. When Donnegan pulled out an envelope and flipped through the cash inside, Jim reached in his drawer and grabbed an agreement. He dated and signed it and slid it across the desk.

"What's this?"

"Standard for cash payments. Skim it if you want."

He looked at the contract, then at Jim, with an earnestness he must've practiced in a mirror. "Are you sure we want a paper trail?"

"Have a look. That agreement goes to court, any decent lawyer can poke a hundred holes through it. You gotta know a decent lawyer or two."

"So why bother? Jim, we've known each other—"

"A hell of a long time. That's why I want insurance. If I'm getting framed up, I want this transaction on record."

Donnegan didn't look happy, but he signed and stood. Jim stayed put. When Donnegan reached his hand across the desk, Jim eyed it, then begrudgingly shook it.

Frank said he'd be back. He'd see Donnegan out.

As soon as Jim was alone, he grabbed his desktop lighter, one the size of an inkpot, and lit the contract. It curled to ash, and he dropped it in the empty wastepaper basket. Donnegan was right; a paper trail was a liability. But him thinking there was one would keep him as honest as a guy like him was capable of being. It'd keep him negligibly honest.

Frank came bobbing back in. If he smelled the smoke, he thought nothing of it. He sat in the chair Donnegan hadn't and leaned for the box of cigarettes on the desk.

"They're stale," Jim warned.

Frank said he didn't know the difference. He lit one and took a drag. "Holy Christ," he said, scorched voice muted in his throat. He stubbed the cigarette out in the ashtray stand beside him. "So? What you think?"

"I think I'd tap-dance to the electric chair before I'd hire Donnegan."

"That Maymie and Jack Maloney thing? So much for attorney-client privilege," he said. "The marriage is all her, right? Maloney didn't think of it. Ain't right in the head."

"Hell, it was probably Donnegan's idea." Jim pulled two slightly fresher cigarettes from an engraved silver case he kept in his desk. He tossed one to Frank and lit the other himself. Molly made him quit fifteen years back, said it was a waste of money. When he'd stopped staying at home for good, he'd made room in the budget for a few here and there. "My brother finds a couple guys for the job, you mind meeting them? Soon as tomorrow?"

"If they're real bums, I probably met them already."

"That's what I'm after. You'd know if they're friendly with anybody I should worry about."

Frank said sure, he'd check them out.

It was reassuring, as was the cash, but Jim was on the fence. "I don't feel good about it."

"What—scared it'll hurt business? You pinched two murderers serving life. Got that coal dealer out of paying alimony. Your reputation's fine."

"Tell that to the *Tribune*. Talk about coal—I'm gonna get raked."

"What'd you do to them, anyway? One week you're 'Agent Beely: Death-Defying Booze Hound Jumps Bootleggers from Running Board.' Next week you're a limerick: 'There once was a man named Big Jim, something-something-something about gin—'"

"That vineyard raid north of town. Knock over some penny-ante bootlegger, you're supposedly bettering the city. Fix it so the Pickards and Henleys can't sip fine wine at the Fontana, their editor buddies turn. Next thing you know, you're out a job." That was another thing Molly hated Jim for. Any job he got was never good enough, and then he'd lose it by going after all the Pickards and Henleys. People with so much money they got protection without paying for it.

"Still got pals at the *Post*?"

"Not sure I'd call a reporter a pal, but I know a couple."

"Well, there you go. They like you all right." He coughed a short laugh on some smoke. "The Pat Crowe bit still gets me."

It was a good bit. A slaughterhouse baron's kid got kidnapped for twenty thousand in ransom. Kid came back fine, but manhunts keep up appearances, and Pat Crowe was the prime suspect because he did it. He never got convicted—no jury would've called somebody guilty for stealing a bag of gold and a brat from a guy whose canned meat had half the city's fingers in it—but Pat did it. The kidnapping was a national sensation. While he was still on the lam, Pat Crowe sightings were a cross-country newspaper joke. In one day alone, he'd be spotted in San Francisco, Istanbul, and Amsterdam. When the *Post* got in on the gag, Jim called. He and Pat were neighbors when Jim lived with Ma out past the beltway. Jim told the *Post* he'd seen Pat a few days before, leaving town. They'd run into each other off Fifteenth, in the alley south of the old Orpheum. Anybody who knew Jim knew it must've been true, but when the *Post* ran his account alongside the rest, the cops couldn't pinch him for withholding information because everything else on the page was a joke.

"Hell of a thing," Jim said. "Plant a little truth in a pile of lies, nobody can tell the difference."

"This town wastes more goddamned paper than New York."

Jim tallied them all. Four dailies, morning and evening editions, English and Czech versions, plus weeklies. "Fewer than there used to be, but I can't say it's better. Imagine if we got down to one."

"Christ. If it was the *Tribune*? Can you picture only having the *Tribune*'s version of everything?"

"I suspect it all gets whittled down one way or another."

Frank finished his cigarette. Then he left for wherever he was headed, back to work or home.

Jim waited until afternoon to call Ward. He'd be done delivering ice and helping at Pop's. He'd have a few drinks in him.

Jim told Ward he needed a couple rounders by tomorrow afternoon. The job was to drink, take notes, and get quizzed by the city commission. Bachelors were ideal. Men who wouldn't be missed if they left town a week or two. After Jim said it, he realized he fit the bill himself. He didn't know how to feel about it, so he didn't. He put the last part bluntly. No use hemming and hawing. "I'm bringing Frank along."

"Like hell."

"Look, he's worked south side and downtown going on thirty years. Either of these guys is a rat—"

"You want him to vouch they're genuine bums."

"Can't hurt."

"You know, if you want Edith to kill you, just ask," Ward said. "The hell are you thinking? Get that office checked for gas leaks."

"Ward."

"Pop don't pay protection. He won't."

"Frank takes money from guys with diamonds on their lapels. Bigwigs. Gangsters with tommy guns."

"Yeah, them and Pete Gilson."

"Oh, come on. Pete deserves a shakedown. When he was coroner, calling every death suspicious? Christ, Ward, half of them were. And his verdicts—sure, four Syrians shot each other at once. All the same time, shot each other and just dropped dead. Suicides that took three, five bullets. Hell, most managed to lose the gun. Even that first wife of his— who forgets they put carbolic acid in some elixir bottle? Pete took county money for inquests, then didn't inquire."

"I guess Tvrdik's a real Robin Hood, then."

"He's a low-paid cop and a Catholic. He's got mouths to feed. I'm not saying he's a saint—"

"He's gunned people down."

Jim shot back, "You killed two gals driving an ice truck." His face burned after he said it, but it was a fact. "There's occupational hazards."

Ward was quiet. "That's low, Jim."

It was low. It was true, but it was low just the same. Both times it happened, Ward was a wreck. He was still a wreck. "I know it. I shouldn't have said it."

Ward was quiet again, angry or deciding or both. "You think you need to bring him by, bring him by. But you tell him: Pop don't pay."

As soon as they hung up, Jim knew he'd put Ward in a bad spot. If a couple rounders didn't come by Pop's, Ward would spend all night tracking them down at rooming houses or wherever else they holed up, all while trying to keep Pop and Edith from spontaneously combusting. Jim hoped there'd be something left of his brother by the time he got there.

5

Jim and Frank agreed to meet at Pop's right after dusk the next day, a Wednesday. Jim went early and waited outside on N Street. When Frank got there, Jim briefed him on what they were walking into. Frank was flippant. Hands on his waist, he blew a raspberry. "I ain't taking no money from that old man. It'll be fine."

Jim let Frank open the door. A fast-moving shadow—a black streak—flew past Frank's head. Jim jumped back and stumbled. The streak bounced off a Pierce-Arrow town car that had no business being parked on Twenty-Fourth and N. Then whatever it was hit the sidewalk with a heavy clank. It was a cast-iron pan. Small-to-middling-sized. You could've brained somebody with it, but you'd need them to hold still for the first hit.

"My sister-in-law," Jim said.

Frank was already inside. "*Hej,*" he called out. "*Godaften.*"

No one answered. Whether the silence was cold or hot, Jim couldn't say. "I'm coming in," he announced. He stepped in ready to dodge whatever flew his way. He was a bigger target than Frank.

Nobody threw anything, and nobody'd drawn a weapon. Edith had a hand on a cocked hip and stared venom at Frank. Ward slouched back against the bar behind her, smoking, not looking at anybody. Pop studied Frank through his spectacles. It didn't occur to Jim until then that Frank was in uniform.

"*Hmf,*" Pop uttered. "*Godaften.*"

"That's all the Dane I got." Frank sat at a barstool in front of Pop.

Edith went to work loudly rearranging glasses and bottles. Pop gripped the counter like it was a ship he was steering through a storm. "I apologize for my daughter. But you've made quite a name for yourself."

Frank shrugged. "Yeah, it's not great." He asked for a malted milk. Pop said he didn't have malted milk. Well, Frank said, he thought Pop ought to have malted milk, but he'd take a Coca-Cola, then. He flicked a dime on the bar. "If you're talking about the shakedowns, I got no excuse besides a family to feed."

"There are many fine professions."

"Like running a soft drink parlor that don't got no malted milk?"

Pop gave a sniff of amusement. "If you're insinuating I run a 'gin joint,' I'll make it plain: I do. And I won't be shut down. The Anti-Saloon League, that Women's Christian Temperance mob, the KKK—they don't give a whit about whiskey or beer. They care who makes money off it."

Frank took a sip of his Coke. "Don't gotta tell me, Pop. I'm a papist and a bohunk. They hate me plenty."

Pop wore an apron. His grip left the counter and his fingers threaded through the ties. He smiled, not friendly.

Intrigued, at best. "So? How do you justify it, then? Uphold-ing a law against Catholics, immigrants, Negroes—"

"Let's head downstairs," Jim said. "Sort out ethics later."

Frank asked Pop, "I ever raid your place?"

Pop didn't blink behind his spectacles. "Not my place, no."

"A cop does more than uphold one bunk law, you know. I quit, what happens? They get some Billy Sunday only cares about booze, he throws a padlock on this place."

"If not for that bunk law, you couldn't collect fees. Fees to let people make a living. To feed their families like you do."

Frank raised his hands like Pop was holding him up. "You win," he said. "I do it. But listen." Frank lowered his arms and leaned in like he was taking Pop into his confidence. Pop stayed vertical. "They kill that law, I'll eat the pay cut. Gladly. Pick up part-time work building birdhouses, installing toi-lets. Till then, anybody you know pays me protection?"

Pop pursed his lips in thought, likely less about the question than about the ramifications of the answer. "No. Nobody I know."

"Anybody I charge, you don't want to know. That fee, it hobbles them a little. Not much, but maybe enough so you, my brother Tony, a few others don't ever got to know them." He took another sip. "Okay, and some I charge because they're pricks."

Pop watched Frank, and Frank awaited Pop's final judg-ment. Pop didn't speak. He plucked up the dime and walked it to the register.

Ward, Jim, and Frank headed down to the basement bar, which was an oddity. South O's saloons didn't set up shop in the basement. Omaha's did, but basements there made sense.

A subway level of tunnels ran under everything, feeding electric lines, steam heat, foot traffic. If a cashier didn't like getting robbed, the lower level made for safer bank deposits. Dreyer's store even decked out three tunnels below major streets—lunch counters, shoe and music departments. But what tunnels South O had weren't extravagant. They were built for trains or leading cattle from stockyard to slaughterhouse. The liquor was served in back rooms, piped down from upstairs, or kept under the bar if the owner said to hell with it, they'd take their chances. And the chances were usually decent, since there was a joint every block. As soon as one got raided, phones at the rest started ringing.

The downstairs bar was makeshift, not elaborate like the main floor's setup. When Jim rounded it, he felt a pull on his jacket sleeve. The sharp end of a nail jutted from the wood, which was scavenged and thrown together in a jumble, pine boards dimpled with mesh marks from a framing hammer.

"Somebody's gonna get lockjaw on this thing," he told Ward, who'd sat with Frank at one of the three tables.

"Keep it down. I don't need Pop hauling the booze back upstairs, Edie out of her head every time he gets pinched."

The old man never wanted to move the liquor down there. He hadn't wanted to take down signs advertising beer for three cents or whatever he'd sold it for when the state went dry. Ward set up shop in the basement because a stairwell connected to a back-alley entrance. He'd done a shoddy job on the bar, but he'd replaced the stairwell doors, outside and in, with panels set flush with the walls. He'd covered them in a thin layer of mortar and sheered bricks. And he'd installed a switch upstairs. If there was a raid or Pop suspected a customer was a liquor agent, the switch lit a red bulb downstairs. Whoever was bartending kept the crate of bottles and barrel on a dolly. If the light went on, they wheeled everything into the stairwell, then shut, latched, and locked the wall behind them.

Jim brought their drinks to the table. Above, Edith was walking louder than usual, her way of saying she knew good and goddamned well they were down here.

"How'd she lose the leg?" Frank asked Ward.

Every once in a while, Jim forgot Frank was an actual cop. It could be tough to square. Then Frank asked a question like that. When something could hold his attention, Frank took it in like a wire recorder.

"Train," Ward said. "Out on the beltway by Ruser's Park. She was deaf a few months from scarlet fever, didn't hear it coming. One of those dummy cars."

"How old?"

"Thirteen."

Frank said he hoped the railroad paid through the goddamned nose, though he was sure they didn't; they never did. Then he changed the subject. "Listen, I know you don't trust me much—I get it. I don't always trust me, neither. But I promise I'm not gonna shake down that old man."

Ward was rigid in his seat. He reminded Jim of a coyote, back stiff-bristled, ready to dart away or snap. Jim decided he wouldn't intervene. Men were just another variety of animal. They'd sort it out or they wouldn't, but you didn't put an arm in between.

"And I know what the papers say about me," Frank said. "If it makes a difference, I never shot nobody that didn't try and kill me first."

"Even the one that didn't have a gun?"

"Hey, he said he did. Ask me, that's a valuable demonstration of the social contract: can't take somebody for their word, we got bedlam." Frank lit a cigarette. "Nah, I shouldn't make light." He waved out his match and flicked it into a dented spittoon by the bar. "My wife, Jennie, she says I scream in my sleep. Hides the gun if I so much as take a nap—and I got the good end of the stick. The one that got to keep breathing."

The door upstairs creaked open. Jim checked the bulb above the bar. It stayed dark. Two pairs of boots appeared on the stairs. The rounders. One of them talked, taking breaks like he was making sure the other listened. Each pause, their boots stopped. The talker didn't sound urgent, more like he was relating an anecdote.

When they came into full view, Jim sized them up. Both wore overalls under their coats, which were the same: gray wool with placket pockets, ratty like they'd been scavenged off dead hoboes, but they could've been hand-me-downs or donations from a mission charity. The younger man, thin like a wick, swam in his. The older was bearded and gnawing on a pipe. His buttons were cupped sideways, ready to pop.

The bearded one was the talker. He'd paused again on the second to last step. " 'No,' says he." Then he muttered a few words Jim didn't catch.

The wick had waited for those last few words, riveted or putting on a show of it. He blinked his close-set eyes twice, then gave a brief wheeze of a laugh, more courtesy than amusement. The bearded one grinned wide and clapped a hand on his shoulder.

Ward released a fortifying breath that said he was used to suffering the bearded jackass. Frank was sitting closest to the stairs, the only one within earshot of whatever was said. His eyes traced the spittoon near the bar, mouth set in a slight, hard smile Jim couldn't read.

The rounders made their way to the table and parked their asses in the two free chairs. The bearded one said Ward's name in greeting. Under the hanging light, Jim was startled to see he'd been wrong about their ages. The wick smiled boyishly, but his lips sank back where teeth used to be. And if the bearded one shaved, he might've been in his mid-thirties.

The latter introduced himself as Gus. He said the emaciated old man was Ole. Ole nodded, gray eyes averted like a shy kid's.

Jim pointed at the men's chests, their coats. The coats were genuinely irritating him, and these two were dumb enough to frisk themselves. "Why don't you just swap?"

They looked confused, first at each other, then him.

"Your coats. They don't fit. If you swapped, they might fit."

They looked to each other again, still befuddled.

"They're the same goddamned coat. Just the wrong sizes."

Gus shrugged a why-not. Both unloaded their pockets on the table: tobacco and matches, change and a pocketknife, a letter. No revolvers, no razors, no dope, and neither had keys. They likely stayed in a rooming house or an idle train car or wherever else would let them in. Once they'd switched coats, each admired the new fit. They were a fine pair of idiots.

Gus struck a match on his bootheel. He'd done it often enough to wear a divot. "Ward says you have work." He puffed the pipe to get it going.

"If you can call it that." Jim told them all they needed to know. "I give you each a notebook of addresses. Split them into four days, go drink." He knew these two shouldn't gamble. They'd lose the whole per diem at the first cigar shop. "Play a punchboard or two if you want—one or two the whole day—no cards or dice. Spread the cash out on liquor. Jot down what you drank where, then show up at Council Chambers next Tuesday. City Hall. Either of you know Harry Donnegan? The lawyer?"

Ole shook his head. Gus said he'd heard of him but never met him. Jim bet that was Gus's answer to most questions and checked Frank to get his read. His expression hadn't changed, but if either guy was a problem, Frank likely wouldn't be subtle about it.

"Good," Jim said. "You'll meet him that day. He'll ask you some questions. Commissioners might, too. Just answer."

"That's it?" Gus said. "No samples?"

Gus must've read the paper or too many detective stories. Cops collected booze in little half-ounce bottles to prove a joint was selling it. "No samples," Jim said. "Notes. Write down what you paid for. When everybody's done asking questions, hop a train. Could be Tuesday after the meeting, could be Wednesday."

Gus cleared his throat like he was readying to orate. "Now, why might that be a good idea? If there's danger involved, we may need a bit more invective."

"Invective?" Frank said.

"Officer Tvrdik," Gus said as a belated greeting. The two had apparently crossed paths. Jim didn't know if that was good news or bad.

"*Do prdele.*" Frank raised his voice like Gus was hard of hearing: "It's *Free*-dik, not Tuh-*ver*-dik, Fritz."

Jim and Ward shot a look at each other. If that was true, they'd said Frank's last name wrong for years.

"The word's *incentive*. Like you need a little incentive to keep your brains in your goddamn head." His jacket had fallen back so his holstered revolver was in view. "And I ain't here. You got that?" He waited until they both nodded.

"You're getting paid plenty," Jim said. "Eight bucks a day wages, ten a day expenses, twenty-five when it's done. You leave town so they can't drag it out, call you back up for more questions. And when you're up there, don't make me the goat. No 'Jim said we should or shouldn't' about a god-damned thing. They ask if you got samples, you say, 'No, I drank it.' I hear one 'Jim said' out of your mouth, you better hop that train and ride till you hit ocean."

Ole said, "Got it." They were the first words he'd spoken, parched-sounding and high-pitched. His fingers trembled on the table. He must've been older than two of Gus's lifetimes. Jim wondered how he'd stayed alive this long.

Ward broke the tension. "Let's get the boys a drink, then." He went to the bar.

Jim made small talk, a thing he enjoyed less than a bout of constipation. But he'd found if he asked people what their line was and where they were from, they'd generally do the conversational heavy lifting. They said they were working construction right now, on a building downtown. Gus said he was from Illinois, which could've been true. Ole said he was born in Omaha, and Jim believed him. Nobody gained anything by lying about it. Ole said he was born in the flats that used to be on Sixth and Pierce. Jim remembered them, packed with dozens of families of dozens of people. In daylight, the mud alleyway in the rear filled with women and kids, infirm grandparents, strung laundry, scraps of food for bony dogs. Chickens, horses, mules. Nothing private in alleys like that.

Ward came back with their drinks. Ole's eyes blinked, baby-like, smiling at something either Ward or Gus said, and Jim had the urge to call it off. Not that Ole wouldn't get paid well enough, and he'd surely survived worse than being paid to drink. Jim just wished something better for an old man than being a rounder who lived in a rooming house or an idle train car, taking whatever labor he could get. At that age, a man should've had a warm apartment. Grandkids darting around to yell at. Kids who'd take care of him.

Then Ole tilted in his chair and farted, easy as a cow.

Frank lit a cigarette while Gus rambled about construction. Frank shook out the match and cut him off. "What's that story you were telling?"

Gus's mouth parted in anticipation or confusion or both. "Pardon?"

"The one you were telling Hans over here on your way down the stairs. I only caught the end."

Gus looked to Ward—a little desperate, Jim saw, but Ward had a curious eye on Frank. As the seconds ticked past, Gus looked to be drowning in the air of the basement. Jim could sense Gus wanted somebody to throw him a rope, but

Jim wouldn't. He wouldn't do it because Gus talked too god-damned much.

"Why, it's only a—"

"Shut up and tell it."

He cleared his throat with two quick huffs, but his voice didn't come out at full volume. He said it was something his uncle said. Gus apparently helped an old bachelor uncle with chores once a week. After, they'd eat, and the uncle told what news he'd heard from a sister in Illinois.

"Yeah?" Frank said. "What'd the old gal have to report?"

Gus took a sip of whiskey, delicate, like a witness stalling on the stand with water. "She says a man out there died of pneumonia. Thirty-two years old. Farmer, I want to say. And tall—six foot and an inch—broad, too, though he'd wasted a bit, last few months." Gus said the family—parents, brothers, a sister—they were Methodists. At the funeral parlor, one of them said something didn't look right. Later, after the grave was filled, someone said, "How tall was John?" They all agreed he was unusually tall. Then one of them said, "How long would you say that casket was?" Then they knew. Somebody said: "Why, that casket couldn't've been no longer than five-five."

The oldest brother took charge. He went back to the parlor and told the undertaker to dig the casket back up. The undertaker said he'd do no such thing; digging was the cemetery's job. When the brother pulled a Colt pistol from his pocket, the undertaker had a change of heart. The two of them went to the grave and dug. When they had the dirt out, the brother jumped down in the hole and pried the coffin open.

Where Gus wasn't bearded, he'd flushed, skin beaded with sweat. He stared a hole into the table's center. "The undertaker, he'd sawed off the man's shins. To save on the casket, I guess. Save on lumber." Gus looked like he could see the body himself right then. "And my uncle's sister, she says, 'Now, there's a lawsuit for you.' But my uncle, he says, 'Nah. No,' he says." He stopped.

Frank's voice was hard and quick. "Why not?"

"Wouldn't have a leg to stand on."

The only sound in the basement was a steady drip of water somewhere, likely snowmelt through a crack in the stairwell. A floorboard upstairs creaked.

"That's funny," Frank said. "What do you think, Ward? Think that's funny?"

Ward didn't say, but the question seemed rhetorical.

Frank said, "Maybe we get Missus Ward down here, you tell it again. See how that goes over."

"I didn't mean any disrespect."

"He didn't," Ole said. "He didn't mean nothing by it— just saw Edith upstairs and thought of it."

"That good enough for you?" Frank asked Ward without taking his eyes off Gus.

Ward gave an almost imperceptible shake of the head, one that didn't mean no, only that he wanted to shake the whole goddamned thing off.

Sensing the unease Gus and Ole were steeped in, Jim let them off the hook. He had to. He needed them for the job. "It's all right, boys. Frank laughs silent. Trick he taught himself getting the jump on fugitives." Jim said he'd get the two another drink.

After he did, he pulled four days' pay and ten per diem from his pocket. He gave each man seventy-two. "No samples," he reminded. "No dice, no cards." He handed them the notepads he'd copied the addresses into. They finished their second drinks a little more rushed, but if either was tempted to skip town as soon as they left Pop's, neither looked it, and Jim knew now they could never pull off a bluff.

After they'd disappeared up the stairs and their boots had crossed the floor above, Jim asked Frank what he thought.

"They'll work. Especially that one can't shut up. Good thing about a guy who talks that much—nobody listens."

"Yeah, well, hopefully you didn't scare them into skipping town with the pay. How'd he know you? The hairy one."

"Picked him up a few times. Nobody's ever in a hurry to spring him. Sleeps it off, gets fined a dollar."

Ward had a shine on his eyes from the whiskey. "You think it really happened?"

"What?" Jim said.

"The undertaker thing."

"Christ, I don't know, Ward." His brother was bordering on maudlin. Ward had a tendency for getting maudlin, and when he did, Jim never knew what the hell to do about it. "Why you got to think about things like that?"

"I don't know how you don't." He turned to Frank. "*Free-dik*? Is that right?"

"Ah, don't matter. Nobody says it that way no more." He'd lit another cigarette. Smoke drifted out on his words. "Beely," he said. "What is that, mick? What are you two?"

"You asked me twenty-five years ago, and the answer's still I don't know," Jim said.

"Ma was a Smith," Ward added, like that'd clear it right up.

"Dad showed up in Hartwick, New York, said his name was Charley Beely. Him and Ma had thirteen kids, got run out of state on bad debts, landed here. He disappeared in eighty-seven. Probably wasn't a real name." When he'd first started Beely National Investigations, Jim made a perfunctory effort to find Charley. "No evidence he existed before showing up in Hartwick and marrying Ma. He was hardly around after he did. Stopped by now and then, knocked her up, claimed he'd taken work out of town. She always thought he had another family holed up somewhere." Jim didn't know why anybody else would've had him. Ma thought she had to. Her parents died on a county poor farm, her sister worked as a prostitute to feed her kids when her husband didn't come back from the Civil War. Ma figured Charley Beely was her least rotten option. Still, the way he'd left, disappeared on her—Jim decided if the old man was still alive, it was best the two of them didn't cross paths.

"Came from nowhere and went back to it," Ward said. That'd been Ma's line whenever the subject of Charley came up. He didn't come up much.

"Maybe it don't matter. Knowing where you come from," Frank said. "Everybody headed nowhere in a hurry, may as well travel light." He picked up his glass and offered Ward a cheer.

Ward hesitated, deciding, then clinked his against it. Both downed the dregs.

6

By the time the commissioners' meeting rolled around six days later, Jim had taken on and finished two jobs. For a cumulative two hundred fifty dollars, he'd reunited a bank teller with his stolen car and a housewife with her missing underwear. Finding the car took two days of driving around town. The underwear required three phone calls and an afternoon of shadowing the woman's husband, who'd been stealing her unmentionables and giving them as gifts to a woman living in a Council Bluffs hotel. The mistress was half the wife's size, and the underwear might've been twenty years old. That the husband gave the things in earnest, that the mistress accepted them as flattery, and that the wife hadn't suspected an affair were, collectively, a testament to humans' capacity for either optimism or delusion. Jim suspected there was a lot of overlap.

He decided he'd stalled as long as he could for Gus and his notebook. Ole had slid his through the mail slot Sunday night. Jim had typed up the addresses and what he could make of Ole's scrawl. He'd made eight copies on the mimeograph downstairs and took four to Harry Donnegan's office. Jim went before dawn to avoid the smirk and slipped them under the door. Then he'd gone back and waited, ready to chew Gus out. He never showed. Maybe Frank had scared him into skipping town.

With ten minutes to spare before the meeting, Jim put on his hat and overcoat. If Gus was at Council Chambers, Jim would throttle the loudmouthed jackass there.

Outside, the air was biting cold, but the walk was short. City Hall was the next door west of the Henley-Barr, across Farnam from the rebuilt courthouse.

City Hall was an architectural study in confusion. Half church, half bordello. Conical turrets, pointed gothic windows, a bell tower missing half its wood slats—every other month, one flew off and nailed a pedestrian. There'd been a sixteen-foot, six-hundred-pound replica of Lady Liberty up there for a while, but the place was made of sandstone brick. It was bad enough when chunks of that fell off and brained somebody. Lady Liberty would've crushed a streetcar. A city safety director had the sense to yank her the hell down off of there.

The sunlight was blunted by soot from warming businesses and hotels, and wind from the east blew in yellow haze from the lead-smelting plant. The haze drew the sky low, like a foggy bedsheet draped over the buildings and streets. Jim yanked down his brim and wove his way through the crowded sidewalk. A horse gave a panicked neigh as a streetcar rumbled by, barely missing an older-model Cabriolet that darted from around the corner.

Jim hustled up the steps and under the massive archway

that was probably no more trustworthy than the roof. The inside of the building was as busy-looking as the outside and made Jim woozy. Layers of diagonal staircases were piled atop each other, so done-up they looked like lace. The whole goddamned building was probably held together by twine.

Down the hall, outside the entrance of Council Chambers, Jim found Ole shifting his weight from one leg to the other and twisting his flat cap in his hands. He stared at the tile like an alarmed rabbit. Jim looked around for Gus, expecting him to be nearby, tipping his hat theatrically. In a less grubby life he would've been a shoo-in for a commissioner's seat.

"Where's your pal?" Jim asked Ole.

"Oh—Jim," Ole eked out, high-pitched. "Ain't seen him."

"When's the last you did?"

"Sunday night?" Gus had done the job, then. Or at least the part that involved drinking.

Someone poked Jim's shoulder. Jim turned to see Donnegan's flat pink head. Donnegan asked if this was one of their friends.

"Harry Donnegan, this is Ole. Other one's a no-show."

"He hasn't been back to work," Ole said.

"That normal?" Jim asked.

Ole rubbed his hat between his hands like he was drying his palms. He shook his head.

"Oh, that's all right." Donnegan clapped Jim's shoulder. "Who knows? May be better."

Jim had been a little touched by Ole's concern for his pal, even if his pal was a jackass. Then Donnegan came along with his Oh, that's all right. Who knows, may be better. Jim wanted to smack him.

Donnegan said he'd head in, probably to gladhand the commissioners and give clients in the gallery a sly wink.

"Remember what I said?" Jim asked Ole.

"No samples?"

"No making me the goat." He pulled a flask from his overcoat and handed it over. There was only a swallow, enough to calm the old man a bit. Ole swigged and handed it back.

Walking into Council Chambers, Jim was always repulsed. The joint reminded him of a newspaper advertisement, a cartoon pig in horn-rims and top hat above a banner for something called Miracle Powder. Jim didn't get why a pig. Not much was less miraculous. A lot of human time and effort had gone into making a sentient being born to be slit open and bled out for bacon. The ad usually ran near news briefs from Magic City, a nickname South O got from growing so fast. Like it'd all sprung from nothing. Miracles and magic. Miracles and magic sure sounded a hell of a lot better than *slaughterhouse* did.

The room was like that cartoon pig—all horn-rims and top hat on a grotesque bit of business. The place was all graft, ceiling to floor. Pillars and arches were beveled, chandeliers layered in gilt. The mezzanine had a parapet straight out of some Viennese opera house. The only honest-looking thing in the room was under the horseshoe of desks—carpet pocked with cigar burns and ink that never made it to paper.

Nobody was on the mezzanine, but the main-level gallery was nearly full. A couple reporters, both white fellas, flanked the left. The pair scribbled down names. Jim could guess how the columns would read: "an array of colorful underworld characters, including Yano Catalano, Jack MacFarland, Marv Klein, Ruth Lisling, Joe Dahir, and Arch Sims, Negro." Flanking the crowd on the right were reporters from the colored papers, the *Omaha Weekly* and *Standard*. One was Mrs. Teagarden, a widow close to Jim's age. He knew how the *Weekly* and *Standard* columns wouldn't read: "Yano Catalano, naturalized Sicilian; Jack MacFarland, white, likely Scotch or Irish lineage; Marv Klein sounds Jewish; Ruth Lisling, homely blonde—probably English; Joe Dahir, of Syrian descent; and Arch Sims."

Jim tried to catch Mrs. Teagarden's eye. They'd talked some, during an election dustup years ago, when a sore loser paid Jim to shadow the guy Jim voted for. The client wanted evidence of election rigging, which was alleged to have taken place where reformers always said it took place, in wards that had more people than dollars. There'd been no evidence of cheating, only of poll workers who'd gotten drunk, piled up ballots by winners and losers, and played the country carnival game of guessing how many corncobs were in the stock tank. The recount was different, but a taller pile was a taller pile. The reformers still made a stink, and because laws were like Hydra—cut off one, two more sprout up—the state nullified one statute and passed four more. Added the office of election commissioner to ballots nobody wanted to count.

Mrs. Teagarden was intent on her notepad. She'd been none too impressed by Jim back then, and he'd admired her clarity. He'd had nothing to be impressed about. He had even less now. Mrs. Teagarden struck Jim as cold and dispassionate, and Jim admired a cold and dispassionate disposition. He also admired her face, which was the shape of a heart—wide at the cheeks, delicate chin. Her hair was finger-curled, with a shine like polished gray granite.

In the last row of chairs behind her, far corner, Frank was in uniform, reading a paper. Behind the chairs, near the middle of the room, stood that odd duck Jack Maloney. He didn't have a business license. He must've had nothing better to do. His light red hair was so slicked with pomade it looked wet. The cockeyed, lip-rouged dashes for eyebrows were too high to look stern. They just hovered on his forehead. Jim couldn't stomach staring long enough to interpret their intent. What mood they were meant to convey. Jim told Ole to go sit by Donnegan. Then Jim sat in the row before the gallery.

The three commissioners who'd apparently lost a bet and been assigned to license renewals today were the heads of Parks, Streets, and Public Improvements. None of them was considered mayoral material when Jake Berman died. Streets was occasionally effective but universally disliked. Parks and Public Improvements were both generally liked but ineffective. All three bore a resemblance to bleached-white toads in suits. Public Improvements was asleep.

Sitting by Harry Donnegan was the Independent Federation candidate Elmer Kobb. Jim recognized him from an old grainy newspaper photo taken back when Kobb was booted from a job as sidewalk inspector because somebody's in-law needed work. He'd blamed corruption and nepotism and sworn to raise all hell campaigning for prohibition. Campaigning and raising hell weren't paying jobs, which meant he hadn't needed one to begin with.

Jim studied him. In person, Kobb was best described as

nonthreatening. He was thin and pasty, with thick hair that probably went white before he was twenty. The giveaway was his brows, which were still dark. They sloped downward from the bridge of his nose and gave him the look of a sad beagle. His chin was a little knot, his head a tied balloon that narrowed into his shirt collar.

Christ. Kobb did have a decent chance of getting elected. He had a full wallet and a natural look of persecution. That kind of man got away with anything.

City Attorney Cy Pospisil was there, too, reading and paying no attention to anyone. He likely had actual work to do. Being city attorney made Pospisil deputy county attorney, which made him deputy county coroner by default. Politicians set up these rat-fucks to give a relative two or three salaries. The arrangement stuck till somebody called foul and made the commission change the law. Cy Pospisil was the youngest of the batch, in his mid-forties. If he'd had a milder temperament, he could've been mayor or run for state senate. He was black-haired, slender, had a strong jaw—he caught everyone's eye and couldn't have cared less.

A commissioner called the meeting to order, and since everybody knew why that wet blanket Kobb was here, he quickly ceded the floor to Donnegan, who gave the opening soliloquy. It was everything to be expected. He wanted to cast no aspersions on those in the gallery, many of whom he was grateful to call friends, but he felt it his duty to his community and to his conscience, as a man who knew the damage of drink, to make good on the promise he'd made his wife and his dear departed mother, et cetera.

When Donnegan was through, Kobb called Ole to the

podium, which faced the commissioners' horseshoe of desks. Past that, at the far end of the room, a raised box with inlaid panels got the best view. It was for reporters. They were already seated and scribbling.

The two commissioners who were awake peppered Ole with questions unrelated to booze, questions meant to chip away at credibility Ole didn't pretend to have. They were stuck on gambling, on what game of cards Ole played someplace. Jim had winced when he'd typed it. He'd told Ole and Gus not to mess with cards, but of course they had. Maybe that was why Gus gave the slip. At least Ole was honest about it.

"Rummy," Ole said. "I lost twenty-five cents on rummy."

"You know that's illegal? Gambling on cards?" a commissioner said.

"But I was getting paid for it."

"If you got paid to murder somebody—you think that's legal? So long as you're getting paid?"

"If I was a copper, it'd be legal. Ain't that legal?" He said it sincerely, but the gallery erupted with slapping knees and elbows, voices repeating him. The newspapermen up front got a kick out of it, too, and rushed to write it down. Mrs. Teagarden didn't crack a grin.

Kobb stared down at the list of joints, knit-browed, pen in hand. "Gentlemen," he said, presumably to the bleached toads and Donnegan, "upon inspection of this list, we need to withdraw our allegations against several establishments."

"Why?" a commissioner said.

"The addresses. The way they've been altered. Some of these are incorrect."

Jim knew he should've shelled out for a stenographer.

Since he hadn't, he'd fixed a handful of typos in pen. It'd been late, and he'd had a few drinks, but he couldn't have screwed them up that badly.

"You mean what's typed above the mess? Above what's x-ed out?" the commissioner said.

Jim hadn't x-ed out anything. He didn't know what the hell they were looking at. But he also knew better than to seem like he didn't. He leaned his cheek on a fist and gazed out a window facing the Henley-Barr. Looked bored with the whole deal.

The commissioners went back and forth, poring over the addresses: "Say, this one's my sister-in-law's bakery."

"Oh for chrissake. Line ten's an empty lot."

"Fifty-three's right here—City Hall!"

The gallery behind Jim erupted again. At the podium, Ole twitched, tapping a foot.

"I hope you're proud," a commissioner roared at Ole. "You've wasted the time of every man in this room." The voice turned on Jim then. "Whichever of you made this mess."

Jim shrugged.

City Attorney Pospisil didn't look up from his work. "Whole thing's a waste of time. Ordinance says you renew permits for anybody not convicted of a crime in the last year. Allegations aren't grounds for permit denial."

"Taxpaying citizens deserve to know the character of the people you're handing out licenses to," Kobb interjected.

"So write a letter to the editor. Hand out flyers. For permit renewals, ordinance has a process," Pospisil said.

Kobb turned to Donnegan. "Speaking of process, how were these notes transcribed?"

Donnegan stood and looked at Jim. Jim looked back, with a stare that said Jim planned to make that flat head flatter. Donnegan was stupidly undaunted. He told Kobb, "Why, I received the lists of business owners from the clerk of the district court. I gave them to investigator Jim Beely, who hired two operatives, one of whom is at the podium. And he's been—if I may say so—treated very roughly today. It's my understanding the operatives visited each establishment and noted what they bought. When I received these notes from Mister Beely, I delivered them to you." Donnegan turned to Jim again with a feeble attempt at looking sorry. "Jim?"

"Mister Beely," Kobb said, "would you discuss the procedure used in transcribing this list?"

Jim felt the crowd behind him staring. "If you're insinuating what I think you are, probably I wouldn't." Jim didn't know precisely what was being insinuated yet. But he knew he was being goddamned framed up.

"Listen," a commissioner said. "If it was one or two addresses, we could chalk it up to a bad stenographer. But every address on here's been messed with."

"You must know what that looks like," Kobb said.

"Go ahead and spell it out," Jim told him. "If I'm being accused, I'd rather hear it straight."

Kobb sounded almost good-natured then. "No one's accusing you of anything. That's why I asked about the procedures."

The commissioner wasn't so good-natured. "It sure as hell looks like whoever mucked this up was trying to get in good with the gallery here."

Jim considered the situation. It was a committee meeting,

not a grand jury. Nobody was under oath. Jim could lie without perjuring himself if he wanted to. But he didn't want to. Omissions and skirting answers—he could do that all day. Outright lying was different. About the only thing Jim disliked more than outright lying was being framed up, and he was being goddamned framed up.

He walked them through it: he got the list of addresses from Donnegan. He copied them into notebooks he gave the operatives. Ole here brought back his with notes.

Jim decided he'd lie about having a steno, solely because an office without a steno sounded like a penny-ante operation. Sure, Jim was penny-ante, but he wasn't about to advertise it. Besides, a make-believe steno was a decent goat if it came to that. He said he'd made copies and took them to Harry Donnegan's office. "You want to subpoena the stenographer, waste more of everybody's time when the city attorney says you don't got just cause, be my guest."

A whoop rang out from the gallery behind him.

"Where's the other man?" Kobb wanted to know then. "You said there were two. Only one came to the hearing?"

Jim made a show of searching the room from his chair. "Looks like."

"Well? Where's the other?"

"Hell if I know."

"Is that customary? Hiring men who don't appear at hearings and meetings?"

"Sometimes I hire women. Look, it's customary to hire rounders when you need evidence rounders know how to get. Maybe you don't know, but drunks ain't too reliable. It's why you hire more than one."

Kobb approached, studying the paperwork. "Would you mind taking a look at these lists, Mister Beely?" He handed them over.

They were altered, all right. They'd been goddamned vandalized. Someone had x-ed out street names and typed others above them, then typed over street numbers. Sometimes threes and zeros were made to look like eights. Other times, the digit was blotted out. Jim studied the type. The top bubble of every capital P was missing, so it looked more like a lowercase r. The lowercase b was missing part of the circle, too, so it looked more like a capital L. The list was a copy, not an original.

Jim was accustomed to scenes like this, usually in grand juries and court trials. But he'd always been the choreographer, not one of the chorus girls. He supposed this was overdue comeuppance. He didn't have to like it, but it was fair enough.

"Did the stenographer make these adjustments? The changes to the addresses?" Kobb stared at him. He might've had a soul of wet cardboard, but his eyes were dark gray flint.

"Couldn't say. We do a lot of paperwork, people in and out all day. Could've been the janitor."

"Are these the addresses you dictated?"

"I look like a city directory?"

Kobb gave a slight smile. Subtle amusement. But his eyes didn't change, and Jim saw he wasn't stumped. He'd been trying to look it while studying the pages, and from the distance of the gallery, he'd probably pulled it off. Up close, Jim saw Kobb knew exactly what was going on. And he'd shoved it in Jim's face. If Kobb had a neck, Jim would've wrung it.

Kobb walked past the podium, to the center of the horse-shoe of desks. Kobb's back was turned to the gallery and Jim, ensuring those in the press box heard loud and clear. "Gentlemen, I apologize for this misuse of your time. But if we've established one thing, it's that the criminal element has a stranglehold on this city." There it was. The talking Anti-Saloon League pamphlet. "Independent investigators and their operatives are hindered, some even failing to appear before you today. Perhaps, as Mister Beely suggested, that failure is dereliction of duty. Or, perhaps, his operative came down with what the 'street-wise' call 'a case of cold feet.' And perhaps that fear is justified." Paperwork dramatically half crumpled in his grip, he pointed to Donnegan. "After all, when one of the most visible and ardent advocates for a cleaner, safer Omaha performs an earnest inquiry and is re-paid with a knife to the back, one cannot help but wonder: Who is safe? Thwarting an inquiry of this breadth requires a powerful and threatening machine. One whose reach—"

A commissioner cut in. "We get enough of your god-damned ticket campaigning in the papers. You want to stop wasting city time, can it." Somebody in the gallery applauded.

Jim slapped on his hat and stood. He walked to the podium, where Ole still trembled, and told him to come on. The two of them headed to the Burlington on foot.

Other than saying he hoped Ole didn't take that thing about rounders personally, Jim didn't talk about what'd just happened. Jim wasn't sure what the hell had just happened. Jim was sure he planned to toss a lawyer and a cop and a politician or two down those layers of staircases back at City Hall, but that was about all Jim knew at present.

He bought Ole a ticket to San Francisco. That way the old man could get off anywhere along the way if he wanted. Jim slipped him an extra two hundred from what Donnegan had paid and said to be careful out there. He didn't ask Ole if he had any family or plans. Jim just waited until the old man was safely boarded westbound, then marched back to the Henley-Barr.

7

Jim thoroughly winded himself taking the stairs to the sixth floor and drew a breath that felt like razors in his lungs. At the far end of the hallway, his office door was open. Frank and Donnegan both sat facing Jim's desk. A surging current swept through him. He charged down the hall, barreled toward them both.

Frank stood before Jim's shoe crossed the threshold. He stepped between Jim and Donnegan. "No, no, no, no, no, now—now—take it easy, big fella." He held up a flat hand like he was directing traffic. Jim rammed straight through it. Frank hopped back.

Jim grabbed Donnegan's bow tie in one hand, a lapel in the other, and pulled him to his feet. "What the fuck was that? I make you mad with a contract, you turn around and frame me up? Or was that the plan from the start?"

Donnegan's face was an inch away, but his eyes wouldn't meet Jim's. "Frank," he said. "Frank—for Christ's sake— show him."

Frank grabbed some paperwork from the chair he'd been

sitting in. "Listen, I about rang Donnegan's bell when the meeting let out. Grabbed everything on him."

Jim had twisted the bow tie between two knuckles so Donnegan's pink face flushed red. Jim let go with a push. Donnegan landed in the chair.

When Jim could pry his eyes off Donnegan, he checked the paperwork. It was the address list he'd typed with Ole's notes. It was a copy Jim made, no x-ing, no changes. "And that's all this conniving son of a bitch had."

Donnegan had caught his breath but didn't look up. "I saw your copies yesterday morning. I kept one and took the rest to Kobb. Hand-delivered them myself."

Harry Donnegan's single redeeming quality—the only goddamned good thing about him—was he was a bad liar. Not that he didn't try, but he'd never once won a case through persuasion. He won through trickery and witnesses who parroted whatever testimony he drilled into them. Jim knew Donnegan was telling the truth, but that truth wasn't much. He'd hand-delivered some copies to Kobb. That was all Donnegan had admitted. "Get out." Jim kicked Donnegan's foot. He shouldn't have. The corn on his toe seared. The pain shot straight up his leg and back and into his head. He gritted his teeth.

"Now, hold on," Frank said. "Before we chuck him out a window, maybe he can explain this garbage."

Jim was careful not to limp when he rounded his desk and sat. His head pounded and he was seeing stars. His blood pressure was up. He pulled the whiskey and a glass from the drawer, poured himself three fingers, and took a gulp.

"So, what, then?" Frank asked Donnegan. "Kobb changed the addresses? Why?"

Donnegan studied the floor and shook his head.

Frank was wound up and pacing, thinking through it. "It'd mean Kobb wanted the whole thing to go screwy, too."

Jim remembered the look in Kobb's eye, the lack of puzzlement. That neckless prick. "He was putting on a show back there, I could see it. But it's a hell of a lot of trouble. Pay Donnegan to pay me to sink his own crusade? The hell does he get from that?" He turned the question to the dough-man. "Donnegan? Pipe up."

"Another minute of campaign time? Assured headlines from the fiasco?"

Frank asked Jim, "Was Kobb trying to discredit him?" He turned to Donnegan. "You defending anybody he don't want off the hook?"

"Frank, half the city's had me on retainer. Another quarter I've traded for favors or publicity."

Frank thought for a second, then looked pained, like a bad nerve in his back had flared up.

"What?" Jim said. "What are you thinking?"

"Publicity. Maybe the case ain't happened yet."

"You know something I don't?"

"Nah, but it's election season. Who knows what the hell's coming down the pike?"

"Christ," Jim said. "You talk to Feffer lately?" Walt Feffer owned a cigar store and bookmaking operation. He made a windfall every election. Took bets on which slate would get pinned as being in Bill Haskell's pocket, which ticket would pull the Catholic vote by printing up KKK endorsement flyers for the other. Standard election-season tactics.

Frank said he hadn't.

"See what he thinks—what bets are going—who'll smear who and how." The skin at the back of Jim's neck tingled. He and Frank shouldn't have been talking in front of Donnegan. But so long as the son of a bitch was still in the room, Jim asked, "Did Kobb know we weren't bringing samples to the commissioners' meeting?"

"I said they'd testify, have notes—"

"Shut up. Shut your mouth. Pay me what you owe me and get out."

Donnegan finally looked up. "Mind if I?" He pointed to Jim's whiskey.

Jim ignored the hot poker in his foot. He stood, rounded the desk, and pulled the flat-headed smirker up by an armpit. Jim flipped open Donnegan's suit jacket and found the envelope full of cash. He threw the money on his desk, put the envelope back, and shoved the glass into Donnegan's hand. Jim pushed him to the door. "Take the cocktail with you." Jim tossed him out, shut the door, and waited to hear his steps shuffle away. When Jim was sure the bastard was out of earshot, he turned on Frank. "You ain't in the clear, either, Tvrdik—framing me up in this goddamned horseshit."

Frank looked at him, eyes soft like he had feelings capable of being hurt, head tilted like a confused dog. "Big Jim. You know I wouldn't."

Jim couldn't take looking at him like that. "Let's say, for one goddamned second, you didn't know you were framing me up."

"Jim, hand to God."

"Shut up." Jim thought out loud. "Donnegan wasn't talking. He was parsing. Answering questions with questions and maybes, leaving things out."

Frank mulled it over. "If he knew—if Donnegan knew Kobb screwed up the list—then Donnegan knew he was supposed to look duped. He was getting positioned that way. To look duped."

Kobb's speech landed on Donnegan being backstabbed, but Jim didn't know what Donnegan could've gained from it. "For what? Why?"

"For whatever's coming? Hell, I ain't clairvoyant." Frank apparently didn't care that he was in uniform. The whiskey bottle was uncorked on Jim's desk. Frank grabbed the neck and took a gulp. Then he winced and gave a quick, sharp exhale. "Swear to God, somebody ought to make elections illegal."

8

Jim didn't take morphine as a habit. For one, he knew better. For another, he couldn't. He had a finite supply in liquid syrup form, prescribed for a sore throat eight or nine months back. But after the commissioners' meeting turned into a farce and he'd kicked Donnegan with his bad toe, all Jim wanted was to knock off early. A nip of morphine, a whiskey chaser, and the sleep was warm and buzzing. It ended abruptly after midnight, when the cadaver of a lawyer next door and his former client's ex-wife started going at it.

Jim lay on the cot mattress in the dark and wondered if all that thumping and alley cat yodeling were what had lopped off his libido. The woman was so overly insistent about the grand time she was having. Every *ooh* and *aah* always played out the same. At this point, Jim even knew how long they'd screw: eight minutes. About twenty minutes later, they'd do it again. Jim didn't know how. He didn't know how the old man could get it done that quickly, much less start right back up again. What Jim did know was if the woman enjoyed it at all, she didn't enjoy it to the extent she let on—that noise bouncing through the corridor was all artifice.

Maybe she thought she'd get a chunk of his money. But even if the lawyer wrote her into his will, he was a widower with three kids, one of whom was the locally famous "Lady Lawyer from Ceresco." If Jim had to screw an old man for money, he'd like to think he'd pick one whose kids weren't lawyers.

Another night, Jim would've stuffed gauze in his ears. He kept some within reach. It never helped him sleep, but if he was sufficiently exhausted, the gauze blunted his rage at being awoken. Tonight, as soon as the *ooh*s and *aah*s punctured the morphine, he was keyed up, pulse racing. Waking like that meant he wouldn't sleep for hours—he'd lie there angry about not being asleep. And he was in no mood for the Little Underworld. A certain amount of drinking and talking was customary before you asked for a sleeping room where you wanted to actually sleep. All Jim wanted was some rest and a clearer head so he could decipher what the hell that commissioners' meeting was about.

He got up and took a leak, dressed, slipped into his holster and overcoat, and headed for the elevator so he wouldn't pass the lawyer's door. If he didn't pass the lawyer's door, he wouldn't pound on it and yell, *THAT'LL DO, FLOOZY.* Besides, this time of night, most of the building was empty. He wouldn't be pressed to exchange pleasantries.

The Ford was parked where it always was, around the side of the building on Seventeenth.

His head was still a little cottony, his legs warm from the

morphine, and being outdoors calmed his pulse. He drove to the house he still technically rented, on Twenty-Eighth off Leavenworth Street. He pulled up to the curb, let the Ford idle, and killed the headlights. The narrow cottage was grafted onto another that was identical. The pair was built before Omaha's row houses and apartments, before *duplex* meant buildings people lived in. The conjoined houses looked embarrassed at not being separate—so embarrassed they'd overcompensated with affection. The roofs were steep-pitched, and the woodwork beneath the eaves was all pierced and scrolled. Someone had slathered it all in paint that'd peeled and pulled away like it wanted to bolt. Molly hated the place, said it was old-fashioned. She said the joint couldn't decide if it wanted to be gaudy or shabby and did a piss-poor job at both.

The house was dark, like it would've been if she'd been inside. Back when he slept here on occasion, he'd pull up hoping she'd gone to bed and left the front room lamp on. Never happened. Not once. When she went to bed, she switched the light off and let him grope and stumble through the dark. If the light was on, that was worse. It meant she was still awake, angrily darning socks on the fainting couch that'd come with the house. He'd peer through the drapes to gauge her mood. There was never any point. Even before Vern, Molly's primary mood was seething. She'd married Jim like Ma married Charley Beely. She'd thought he was her least rotten option. Jim had knocked her up. He'd figured she'd come around once they had the baby, but she'd lost the first one. He suspected she stayed married to him afterward as some kind of penance.

Sure, they had their good moments. Mostly when the two

of them laughed. But if he ever got too comfortable, she reminded him he was dirt. He never made enough money, he never had a job she wasn't ashamed of, and he didn't know what kind of people he came from. She even added an *e* before the *y* in Beely whenever she gave anyone her name.

Whether Jim went in that house bold or meek, if Molly was awake, she chewed him down to size just the same. He'd hang his hat and coat on the entryway hook and dread the silence. If he talked first, she blew her top. If he waited for her to say something, she'd simmer to a boil, go from teakettle to factory whistle to the howl of an oncoming train. There was no winning.

That could've been just the thing to have carved on Jim's headstone: THERE WAS NO WINNING.

Driving here was pointless. Even if she'd been inside right now, angrily darning a sock, and Jim could say he'd killed Vern, made sure she and Addie would never see him again, made sure the pervert could never put his hands on another kid, Molly would say it was too little and too late. And she'd be right.

He couldn't go in that place. When the lease ran out, the landlady could keep or sell everything Molly had left behind.

He switched on the Ford's headlamps and pulled away from the curb. Down the street behind him, another car pulled out.

At the end of the block, Jim made a left, and the headlights followed. He noted it, but it wasn't unusual. The car was likely making its way back to Leavenworth like Jim was. When he made the next left and the car followed again, he assumed that was the case. He turned right at Leavenworth. The car followed.

To be cautious, he pulled over before he reached Seventeenth, outside Maymie's. The car passed, then slowed. It was a black Packard Six. The driver might've braked to keep an eye on Jim or was just leery of the road's grade. Leavenworth dropped hard like a carnival ride below Sixteenth.

He squinted to make out the plate. In stark white numbers against black, it read 1–1743. Then the Packard disappeared. It sank past the intersection.

The annoyance over potentially being tailed scraped at the warm morphine cotton. A tail meant sifting through the past month and deciphering which miserable son of a bitch he'd pissed off this time.

There was today's date, he guessed. Vern was scheduled to appear before a Washington County judge this morning. The trial was supposed to start. But a sheriff from another county had no reason to come looking for Jim. Not yet, anyway. First Shumway would assume Vern ran. Then he'd figure out Vern had no relations to run to. He'd check in with the girl's father and mother and anyone else near Kennard who might hold a grudge. And then, if and when Sheriff Shumway ever came for Jim, he wouldn't be a sneak about it.

Jim checked up and down the block. The night was quiet, not a lot of foot traffic. If the Packard had been following him, no witnesses were nearby, none close enough to stop the driver from putting a few slugs in him. Not that he knew of anybody who'd want to kill him right now, tonight, specifically. There was always a general risk that somebody he'd questioned once, or a relative of somebody he'd sent to prison, or some rich former client he'd gouged could be lying in wait, sure. That would've been smart, for somebody with a grudge to wait a few years or ten, then kill him. But people generally weren't that bright, and grudges had expiration dates. People got over it, died, or moved.

A comforting thought struck him. Maybe the comfort was only one of those temporary moments of warm, buzzing clarity that came with a little morphine, but it was soothing anyway: the nice thing about having nobody and nothing was it significantly reduced your chances of getting murdered for anything you had.

He'd stay put a minute, let the Packard either circle back or get some distance. Through the Ford's window, music drifted down from Maymie's. She had the two floors above Monte C's all-night restaurant, which was dead. Jim knew the record, Duke Ellington's "East St. Louis Toodle-Oo." The song had just started, a dirge with carnality woven through it. Like a sexy funeral. The trumpet gave over to bumbling joy, then tipped topsy-turvy in a way that made Jim's palms sweat. It was the sound of being in a basement bar with a fella who was drunk and high on cocaine and who'd taken out his pistol for show. When the song went back to the sexy dirge, before it even finished, a muffled voice upstairs told someone to play it again. Jim would've liked to stay and listen, but he didn't. If the Packard was a tail, it hadn't circled back, so he put the Ford in drive and headed to the office.

He lapped the block, eye out for the black Packard. City Hall and the business tower behind it were closed, and the night's last movie at the Palisade, behind the Henley-Barr, let out before eleven. The few cars lining the streets were spillover from diners and clubs and the Daisy Dancehall. No Packard.

Jim parked on Seventeenth and got out, shut the car door. He sifted through the left-hand pocket of his overcoat for his watch and checked the time. Twelve after one in the morning. At least the party in the lawyer's office would be over with.

When he reached the curb, footfalls slapped behind him.

Before he could pull his revolver, before he could even turn around, a jolt rang the back of his head. The sidewalk rose. Jim recognized the sensation but couldn't place it—like the time he'd messed with wiring at Ma's old place out on Center. In the moment he'd been frozen by electrical shock, he couldn't say what was happening, only that it felt familiar.

Now, by the time his right cheek hit the pavement, Jim knew what'd happened—he'd been hit. By what he couldn't say, not until he saw the fella—an exceptionally tall fella, Jim's height or more—holding a length of pipe in a gloved hand. Over his head was a burlap sack with eye holes cut out. The holes were big enough Jim could see he was pasty white and had no eyebrows to speak of. The corners of the bag jutted up like cat ears, and when the guy raised a gaudy, black-and-white, square-toed Florsheim, one with extra-fancy perforated broguing, to step on Jim's head, Jim saw a nickel-sized hole worn through the sole and couldn't help it—he smiled at how bizarre it was. The clown was Jack Maloney. Maloney didn't like the smile, apparently. He pressed down hard with his shoe.

"Maloney," Jim said. "What gives?"

Maloney's voice was a put-on. He forced it low and gravelly. "This isn't Maloney. I'm not Maloney," he said, then coughed. "It's good you screwed up the addresses. Next time you come after the gang, we'll fill you full of lead."

Even with his head ringing and pinned under the guy's foot, Jim had to pucker his mouth hard to look serious. The gang. Fill you full of lead.

Maloney didn't wait for an answer. He raised the pipe with both hands. Jim shut his eyes and waited for the next blow. But it didn't come. The shoe left Jim's head, and Maloney took off at a weirdly straight-backed and high-kneed sprint.

Jim rolled like a flipped turtle till he could get his footing. When he stood, he saw stars. They were likely from standing too quickly, but the back of his head throbbed, too—it'd been a decent hit, and Maloney knew where to aim, high enough not to knock Jim out. Jim jogged to Farnam. A truck was passing. He stopped and bent, rested his palms on his knees to catch a breath. In the second the truck blocked Jim's view, Maloney and his burlap cat ears disappeared. He must've made for the alley behind the Carmody Building. If Maloney had half a working brain, which was a sizable unknown, that was where he'd parked.

By the time Jim got there, he was gone.

9

Satisfied he'd survived worse blows to the head, Jim took a smidge more morphine and napped in his office chair. He awoke to pounding on the door and daylight's glare through the open shades. His pocket watch read seven-thirty. He couldn't see through the mottled glass, so he called out, asked who it was. It was Frank.

Jim didn't answer. He could ignore Frank henceforth. With Vern Meyer turned to ash, their business was done.

"Come on," Frank said. "Hand to God, Jim, I didn't frame you up. Want me to slash off one of Donnegan's ears? Bring it to you? I'll do it."

Jim ignored him.

"Honestly, I'll probably do it anyway. Even if you don't want it. The ear."

Jim walked over and unlocked the door, then went back to his desk.

Frank was in uniform, a newspaper tucked under his arm. He stopped at the edge of the mattress Jim hadn't moved. Frank either decided it wasn't noteworthy or had the decency not to ask. He walked around it.

"You starting the day or ending it?" Jim asked him.

"Ending. They got me on overnights."

"Foot patrol?"

"Nah. Motorcycle."

"So, you pissed somebody off, but not enough to make you hoof it."

Frank sat in what had become his chair as of late. "Jennie's making you some kind of soup. I would've went home for it, but I figured I'd check on you first. What the hell happened to Fritz?"

Maybe Jim took a harder hit or more morphine than he'd thought. He didn't understand eighty percent of what Frank just said. Soup? "What? Why am I a charity case?"

Frank pursed his lips and eyed the mattress.

"Oh hell," Jim said. "I lived with Molly. I've seen worse years."

"Know who did it?"

"Did what?"

"The guy that beaned you."

Jim stilled in his seat, unsure whether or not he was dreaming. "How'd you know about it?"

Frank pulled the paper from the chair beside him. "How hard you get hit?" He scanned down the front page, folded the paper in quarters, and tossed it on the desk. Jim read the headline:

COMMISSION QUIZ:
"GANG" RETALIATES
Masked Man Bunts—
Beely's Head the Pill

The article took up less space than the headline, and nobody was quoted. The gist: ex-morals officer and current private detective Jim Beely took a beating outside the Henley-Barr Building in the early morning hours. The masked assailant remained at large. Suspected motive of the attack was under-world retaliation. Yesterday, Beely had a role in Elmer Kobb's unsuccessful campaign to deny business license renewals to establishments allegedly selling liquor. " 'Ex-morals officer.' They love to throw that in. 'Suspected motive.' Suspected by who? I didn't call the goddamned *Tribune*."

"Shit." Frank looked like he'd taken a punch himself and was shaking the daze. "If you ain't seen the papers, you don't know. That loudmouthed Hun turned up dead."

"What?"

"Fritz. The Fritz you hired to go around and drink. The prick."

"You mean Gus? You need less confusing slurs. Fritz is a real name."

"Sounds like a cat sneeze. *Fritz*," he said, like it was a cat sneeze. Frank picked his teeth with the wood end of a match.

"When and where? What happened?"

"It's in there." He gave a wave at the paper. "Unidentified fella, three, four nights ago. One they found down below Fourth. Streetcar coal pile. Says O'Neill and Dietz found him, says he was all shot up. He's been sitting on ice, down-town station. Guess they're backed up? Usually they'd've tagged him John Doe, did the inquest, put him in the ground already."

Getting shot was only a matter of time for Gus, but the news was unsettling. Jim's first thought was Ole. He hoped the old man stayed the hell on that train pointed west. "Who IDed him?"

"Rooming house gal. Saw the description, hadn't seen him, figured the worst."

"When?"

"Had to be after evening edition got printed. Yesterday afternoon. Pospisil called for an inquest. Got a jury together." If Pospisil had the reins as deputy, the county attorney must've been tied up or out of town. "They meet three o'clock at Gilson's. Guess they still throw ol' Pete a bone when it's bound for Potter's Field." Frank lit a cigarette.

Throw Pete a bone. Jim shut his eyes and shook his head. "Seen Feffer yet? Ask if he's heard any election wagers?"

"Said the same thing Donnegan did—odds say Kobb nabs the police commissioner's seat. Putting money on any other Federation candidate's pissing it away. Ain't heard nothing else. Say, how's your noggin? You ain't said what happened."

Jim was reluctant, but if he knew one thing, it was that Frank wouldn't mix himself up with that loose screw Jack Maloney. Jim said what he knew and what he'd reasonably deduced, that Maloney, in a black Packard Six, had tailed him from at least the house to the Henley-Barr. Just as likely Maloney was tailing him when he left the office. Jim didn't mention the morphine, only that he hadn't been paying attention. He told Frank about the burlap cat ears, the no-eyebrows, the Florsheims, that voice Maloney put on—all the garbage about the gang and filling Jim full of lead. "He's got a weird run. Fast, though."

"Good he's got that one talent. Everybody should have something. Why the hell did he hit you?"

Jim stroked the bump at the back of his head. "Well, we know he's out of work. Somebody probably paid him. Kobb's my first guess, but I'm biased. I'm still sore about the god-damned commissioners' meeting you snared me into." He paused to let that resonate. "And Kobb's guilty by associa-tion. Maloney's brother-in-law."

"But Kobb played it like you backstabbed Donnegan. Wouldn't that mean you're in league with 'the gang'? Why's 'the gang' gonna attack you?"

"Donnegan." Donnegan was the answer, but Jim didn't know the question yet. He thought through it. "He was here when you said maybe the whole farce was about 'publicity.' For a case that ain't happened yet. Or something election-related. If any of those guesses was even close, Donnegan leaves here, calls Kobb, says you and me are onto them. Kobb gets Maloney to knock my head around, throw us off. Make us think I did cross some gang by snooping around joints."

"That's goddamn insulting."

"Then they go to the papers. An article saying I got jumped and warned about 'the gang' makes it sound like a gang exists. Makes the police commissioner look more worthless than he already does, helps Kobb's campaign." The knob on the back of his head throbbed from speculating and likely getting ahead of himself. "I don't know. Could be somebody has a grudge. Saw the papers—stuff about the commissioners' meeting—used the excuse."

"Nah. Anybody that motivated, you'd be snuffed."

Jim checked that Kewpie doll head for subtext, but there was none. Frank was right, which meant Kobb most likely paid for the bunt. "Nobody else was milling around. No witnesses. Maloney probably hit me, drove off, and called the paper himself." Jim remembered checking his watch. "I got hit twelve, thirteen minutes after one. Anybody at the *Tribune* you can call and sweet-talk? Find out what time they got the tip?"

Frank had taken a deep drag of his cigarette and tilted his head back. Smoke rings pulsed from his raised jaw toward the ceiling. He let the rest out in a stream. "I don't sweet-talk nobody, Big Jim, just say who I am. Gimme your phone."

Jim slid the phone toward Frank and went to the mattress, which was dry, at least. He rolled it up, head throbbing when he bent down. While Frank called the *Tribune*, apparently got an "I don't know," and snapped, "Then find the hell out," Jim moved the mattress to the closet. Frank didn't thank anybody when he hung up.

Maybe Molly was right. Even if Jim being a cop wasn't good enough for her, maybe he should've tried harder to stay one—not gone after all the Pickards and Henleys. Not held a grudge about scraping by in a city fixed so if you weren't born ahead you couldn't catch up. If he'd stayed a cop, Jim could've hung up phones without thank-yous. Saved years of breath spent on chitchat and empty formalities.

Frank said a guy called ten minutes till one, not a minute later.

That was twenty minutes before Jim got beaned, when Maloney had been on his tail. "Somebody's confident in that jackass."

"Or they wanted the story in before morning edition went to print. Let me check out the car. See if Maloney or Kobb, any their relatives got a black Packard Six."

As long as he was checking, Jim could make it easy. He jotted down the plate number and gave it to Frank. "Got time to pay Pete Gilson a visit? Take a look at Gus before the inquest gets botched?" The county attorney's office was prone to botching inquests. Botched inquests closed cases. The system was efficient.

Frank said he had time.

"You go first, in case I still got a tail."

Frank saluted and took off. After he had a head start, Jim paged through the *Tribune* Frank left. Jim found the state-wide news and spotted the article. The judge in Washington County issued the capias warrant for Vern's arrest. Failure to appear. A continuance was granted for Tuesday, April 15. That gave Sheriff Shumway a couple weeks to track down Vern, and he'd likely realize Vern was nowhere in Washington County within a day or two. A day or two more, he'd find out Vern had no relations. Then Shumway would decide Vern skipped town and either let it go or keep looking. Jim would deal with Shumway if and when.

Jim left for Pete Gilson's. Neither the Packard nor anyone else followed him. He took detours through potholed alleys to make double sure. When he got to the funeral parlor and saw Frank's motorcycle out front, Jim pulled around back and parked between the hearses. He was surprised both hearses were there, then surprised he was surprised. He guessed he'd assumed if it was daylight, somebody was getting hauled around in a hearse. That both were sitting here gave him a waft of relief that left as soon as it came. Death was the only numbers game with sure odds.

Jim knocked. Pete did the bit with the peep window,

then opened the door. He was wearing Vern's tie with the painted horseshoes. The sight of it sent Jim's innards through the laundry mangle again, but Pete had toned down the pomp and circumstance from last week. The old man was distracted and irritable and had something that looked like tallow swiped below his nose. "I don't know why this fella's so golldang popular, but if you need to see him, you'll want this." Jim caught a draft of Gus thawing out right as Pete handed over a handkerchief. It was soaked in a mentholated concoction a hell of a lot sturdier than chloroform.

Frank's nose and mouth were wadded in fabric, too. He was over by Gus—or what had been Gus—the beard was the giveaway. He was naked, and the rest of him had gone gray-translucent like an uncooked sausage casing, trails of veins and arteries everywhere. There was something honest-looking about it, Jim thought. That was all anybody was, a great big dream packed inside what amounted to a sausage casing.

Gus had four bullet holes drilled into him, close range. One in the right thigh, one beneath his lowest right rib, one below the same side's clavicle, and one dead center above his heart.

Frank's voice was muffled by the cloth. "You strip him?"

Pete cupped his ear and shook his head to mean he hadn't heard.

Frank mumbled a "For fuck's—" and pulled the cloth from his face. "I asked if you stripped him."

Pete said he had and gestured at the other gurney. Jim wondered which one Vern was on, the night Jim got himself mixed up in this garbage. He reminded himself he needed a new tarp.

Gus's clothes were cut longways and laid in two flat layers. Frank lifted the overalls and coat to give himself and Jim a backside view. Four holes, one for each shot. A few traces of blood but no gushers. He hadn't bled out. Meaning he'd been dead first, then shot. Not the more customary sequence.

"Ain't that a pip," Frank said.

Jim thought to check Gus's coat pockets for the notebook, but the cops would've turned everything over to Pospisil.

He gestured at Frank and Pete to follow him toward the back door. Once they were outside, he took a menthol-free breath and asked, "They bring anything else with him? Bullets? Personal effects?"

Pete said they hadn't. Jim said thanks and gave back the handkerchief. Frank did the same and added, "We weren't here," with a wink. Pete smiled then and gave an eager wink in return. For a guy who saw people after they couldn't give one shit anymore—about as intimate a view as views got—Pete apparently wasn't accustomed to being taken into anyone's confidence. He went back inside.

Jim told Frank to get in the Ford with him. They'd be hidden between the hearses. When they were in the car, Frank offered a cigarette and Jim took it.

"You're a pal," Frank said, "but I ain't digging in a coal pile for bullets shot through a dead guy."

"I'm sure they already have them, but I can't see the point. How cold was it Sunday night?"

"Cold enough." Frank lit both their cigarettes. "No telling. Could've been anything killed him. Bad heart, bad booze, fell asleep and froze to death. Only thing it wasn't was gunshots."

"How well you know O'Neill and Dietz?"

He considered, lips jutted like a duckbill, and reached a quick verdict. "Ain't notable. Young. Lick boots enough to stay on the payroll but no ambition."

"You trust them? O'Neill and Dietz?"

"Not on your life. Only thing less trustworthy than a guy with ambition is a yes-man with a gun." He was struck by a thought, one that made him smile, and he looked at Jim without turning his head. A Kewpie grin. "That's why you and me make good buddies, Big Jim. No ambition, no yessing."

"Sure." Jim thought it through. "Guess anybody could've shot him. Kids out shooting rats. Found a dead guy, wasted some bullets."

"Yeah, could've been my mother, but I doubt it. Who all knew you hired him?"

Jim was halfway through the cigarette and light-headed. It was a relief. "Likely anybody who'd listen. He's lucky he died. That mouth would've got him killed."

"That's dark, Jim." Something dawned on him. His face straightened. "Before Maloney got axed from the department, O'Neill was his partner. I got no idea what it means, but it's a hell of a coincidence."

"Maybe. Around here, whole lot of uncanny coincidence boils down to garden-variety nepotism."

"Only law Omaha enforces."

"You know you're a cop?" Jim took another drag. "With the county attorney's office backed up, they'll cut corners, close the case. If the inquest gets bungled, think Pete could dig around in there after, see if he can tell what happened?"

"He will if I say to."

"Say to." Jim told Frank to call when he'd heard from Pete.

Frank nodded but didn't open the car door. "What do we tell your brother?"

"Christ." Jim didn't know how Ward would take the news about Gus. Ward wasn't soft, and Jim could tell his brother wasn't fond of the jackass, but Ward had those moods. If he was drunk enough, he could unravel like somebody'd tugged the wrong string. He might blame Jim. He might blame himself for putting Jim and Gus in a room together. And then there was Edith. If Edith was tipsy, she didn't need much excuse to bludgeon Jim to death.

Frank seemed to get the picture without Jim sketching it. "Let me get a nap, find out what Pospisil's jury says, what Pete finds. Then I'll call you, we can meet at Pop's." He gave Jim an extra cigarette to take with him. "The Fritz getting used like a clay pigeon ain't our fault, but if blame's going around, I'll take the heat with you."

10

After inspecting Gus's corpse at Pete Gilson's, Jim went back to the office. Two phone messages from the Henley-Barr's answering service were slipped under the door. One was from Art Silver, a reporter at the *Post*, the other from some fella at the *Standard*. The messages weren't explicit, but they didn't need to be. They were following up on the *Tribune* article, itching to know more about Jim getting plunked in the head last night.

Deciding what to say should've been a carefully calculated decision, probably. Jim was locked into a chess match, most likely with Elmer Kobb. But Jim didn't know where any of the pieces were or how many were left on the board. And even if he had known, Jim had played chess just enough times to know he was bad at it. He'd stare at the pieces, play out every option in his head, predict how the other player would react, picture his next move, then theirs. He'd get too far ahead of himself. His opponent would do something Jim hadn't counted on, and the whole goddamned thing fell apart.

When he couldn't make precise calculations, he went

with instinct. For him that usually meant throwing dynamite at a thing that could've been plucked with tweezers.

He called Art Silver first because the two of them had rapport. Art was twice divorced and no doubt working on a third. Art didn't like women that way but insisted on marrying them, and, as was the case with most reporters Jim knew, Art drank like a rounder. Jim would rehearse, hash out the details talking to Art. Then he'd call Mrs. Teagarden at the *Standard*. Jim didn't know the fella who'd called, and, while Jim and Mrs. Teagarden didn't exactly have rapport, they'd spoken. Jim would give Mrs. Teagarden the fine-tuned version. He suspected she had perfect pitch.

Art was gruff. "Why'd you call the damn *Tribune*?"

"Come on," Jim said. "I didn't. You know I wouldn't."

Art was either waiting for Jim to elaborate or he'd passed out.

"You there? Your next question ought to be, 'Who did call them?' and the answer's I don't know. But whoever it was called twenty minutes before I got hit."

"What? You're hurting my head."

Jim walked Art through it. About ten till one, somebody called the *Tribune*, said Jim had been attacked. Twelve after one, a clown in a burlap bag—Jim didn't say who—knocked him down with a lead pipe, said Jim shouldn't have messed with "the gang," then ran off. Nobody was around and Jim hadn't called anybody. He didn't even know he was in the paper until somebody pointed it out.

Art chuckled. "The hell you make of that?"

"It's a frame-up, but don't print I said it. I'll sound like a kook. You hear about the commissioners' meeting yesterday?"

Art said sure. General consensus was Jim changed some records to keep the commission from denying licenses.

"Sounds like something I'd do, except I didn't. I'd guess the son of a bitch who changed the records hired the guy to hit me and mention 'the gang' or 'vice elements' or 'the machine.' Now, who do you guess would do a thing like that?"

"An ambitious politician?"

"I didn't say it; you did."

"Any speculation about which one?"

"You're not getting me sued, Art. You want to sell more papers, buy a newsstand. Quote me as saying it's more of the same, all politics. And the only gang in this town is the Independent Federation."

After they hung up, Jim called Mrs. Teagarden. She picked up on the third ring. He said who he was and met a gap of silence. He hoped it was more surprise than irritation. She asked how she could help him.

"I know you didn't call me—" Jim had the impulse to say he'd phoned because he admired her disposition. If he said that, she'd think he had psychosis. Maybe he did. Even if her husband was dead, he couldn't tell Mrs. Teagarden, a cold and dispassionate editor of a newspaper, that he admired her. He landed on "We're acquainted. I don't know if you remember."

"I remember, Mister Beely."

He tried to wring some comfort out of the way she said it but came up dry. "Please," he said. "It's Jim. I meant to say hello at the commissioners' meeting." Every sentence was worse than the previous.

She was decent about it, though, and cut him a break.

"Well, it was a raucous meeting, even by city commission's standards."

"Say, I don't want to seem forward in calling. It's just I saw you there and we've talked before."

"That's fine," she said, though he could hear the strain of tried patience in her voice. Paper shuffled and voices called out to each other in the background. She said she'd asked her reporter to follow up on this morning's *Tribune* article, but since she and Jim were already on the phone, she could do it just as easily.

Jim started telling his version. He left out the lawyer and the floozy but said he'd been late at the office and went to check on his house. "My wife left me a few weeks ago," he heard himself say, and he fought the urge to punch himself in the face.

"That's—I'm sorry."

He forced a chuckle and asked her please not to print that. He apologized and went on. He hadn't told Art about the Packard Six or knowing Maloney was Maloney, and he left it out now. They were details he could sandbag on the off chance somebody'd slip up and show their ass. Besides, the press was best used to steer the bunk. That and let whoever'd hired Maloney, presumably Kobb, know that throwing Jim off would take more than knocking him over with a lead pipe. Jim told her about the timing of the *Tribune* call, about checking his watch, how it didn't add up.

"How do you know what time the call was? To the *Tribune*."

There it was—that perfect pitch. Jim couldn't mention Frank. For one, he'd be publicly associated with Frank. For another, something like that could snowball, get Frank suspended. Even if Jim was on the fence about Tvrdik, he didn't want a husband and father of six kids chucked out of a job. "I know I'm the one who called you, but is it too late to say no comment?"

She gave a quiet, amused sound. A little *chk* of air. The sound was a relief to him, like a scalpel tip to an abscess. He said he'd had a friend call, an official—he guessed Frank was officially something—but if she could maneuver around that bit, he'd appreciate it. She said she could. He told her what he'd told Art: the attack was political and if anyone wanted to know who the real gang was, look at the Independent Federation slate. Then he thanked her.

"You're welcome, Mister Beely. Take care." She paused, either waiting for him to say goodbye or debating saying something else. If it was the latter, she didn't. They said goodbye and hung up.

The mattress was rolled up in the closet and Jim was in his suit, but he lay on the floor anyway. He rested his head to the side, avoiding the walnut of a bump, and he smoked. While he waited for Frank's call and dreaded how the news about Gus would go with Ward, Jim wondered what Mrs. Teagarden might've debated saying, right before she hung up. It sounds like you've really kicked a hornet nest, or, You should get that head of yours checked out, or, I'm sorry again, about your family situation.

The first was trite, and the second was obvious. Mrs. Teagarden was too astute to be trite or state the obvious. That made the third more likely, which meant she'd felt sorry for him, which meant he'd sounded pathetic.

Maybe everything he'd said on the phone wasn't a lapse into psychosis. Maybe, he thought, that was loneliness. Jim wouldn't have known loneliness because he'd never had it and never understood it. He'd silently ridiculed anyone who ever complained of it. He never understood how people deluded themselves into thinking they weren't always alone, every single millisecond of their lives.

Now that he'd had a dose, he assessed what he thought about it. He couldn't say he felt more sympathetic. He felt like a twit.

He was a twit for feeling lonely, and he was a jackass when it came to admiring women. Mrs. Teagarden had always been unimpressed by him. Molly had always been unimpressed by him. Indifference was like goddamned catnip, and if there was one thing he should've learned by now, it was to stay the hell away from women who were apathetic about him. At best. Disdainful, more likely. He was a goddamned sucker for disdain.

He sat up. He'd work on the box of filing he'd ignored for months and wait for Frank's call about the inquest.

The phone rang a quarter after four.

"Homicide: no suspects," Frank said, which meant the file was essentially closed. Aside from tidying up paperwork, the ruling served only one purpose. Prosecutors and cops could throw anybody they suspected of something else in jail a couple nights. Manufacture some far-flung connection between them and a "homicide: no suspects" case.

"How?" Jim said. The county attorney's office might've been backed up and wanted to close the file, but homicide was a hell of a leap.

"I don't know. Pospisil's no dummy. Police surgeon's no dummy. It don't make sense. Pete said the whole medicine show was done in a half hour. Five minutes after the jury let out, Pospisil and the surgeon left. Pete dug around in there like I told him. There's something wrong with a guy who can dig around in that stink. Still can't get it out of my goddamn nose."

"Pete say what killed him?"

"Yeah, upchucked and suffocated on it. The upchuck."

"Christ."

"Guessing Fritz went to the coal pile to nab a few rocks, drunker than hell, took a stumble, snoozed on his back."

"Between the booze and the cold, you suppose—Pete think he suffered any?"

"Nah, he wasn't feeling no pain."

Jim surprised himself by asking, "What do you think?"

"My hypothesis? Somebody found the Fritz dead and thought he'd be more useful a different flavor of dead. And Pospisil's gotta be in on it somehow, so eight-to-one odds we're better off not knowing. I hear now's a good time to visit San Diego. How about it? You, me, a whole bucket of post-cards to get stamped and prove where we were."

"Maybe later," Jim said.

Frank shouted syllables at somebody. Probably one of his brothers. They were talking Czech. Jim knew roughly eight Czech words and no doubt said them wrong. All the Czech he'd picked up he'd learned from waiting at the Hinky-Dinky deli counter. There'd be a back-and-forth until the guy wearing the bloody apron figured out what a customer wanted. When he got it right, the customer nodded, said,

"Pro-seem," and got handed a chunk of meat. The customer said, "Dee-kay," maybe added, "Ahoy," before walking away. The times Jim worked cases and asked if somebody spoke English, he'd get, "Neh," or they'd start talking English. He'd gotten "neh" enough to finally ask someone what "yes" was. "Ah-no." Which still sounded like no. So five words. A quarter of the city talked like that all day, there was a newspaper written in it, and all Jim knew was how to say, "please," "thanks," "bye," "no," and "yes." All the Czechs in Omaha could've been plotting Jim's murder, for all he knew.

While Frank gave whoever the what-for, Jim thought Frank was right. They'd be best off skipping town and knowing nothing more about Gus. And anyhow, why should Jim care if somebody made Gus more useful dead than he'd ever been in his life? Why would Jim need to know why Maloney hit him or what Kobb and Donnegan were up to? Jim had killed Vern—he'd killed a guy—and come out of it looking no worse than he always did, with more money in his wallet than he'd ever had at once. Jim had no reason not to let the whole thing go. Blow his cash on postcards in San Diego.

Hell. Now that he thought about it, Jim had no reason to do or not do anything.

"Ah, *jdi do píči*," Frank snapped. Jim couldn't have repeated it if he tried and didn't know what it meant. He knew it wasn't amicable. "You still there?" Frank asked.

"Yeah, I'm here." That was about all Jim was. Here. He said he was headed to Pop's.

"I'll bring soup."

It was afternoon, so Jim picked up copies of the evening editions. He didn't look at the headlines, just grabbed one of each at the newsstand outside the Henley-Barr, tucked them under his arm, and took off. Ward had surely seen the morning news about Gus, probably on his lunch break. Whether or not he'd read about the coroner's findings depended on if he'd seen the latest edition and, potentially, how drunk he'd gotten after reading the morning's.

On the way to South O, the traffic was stop-and-go and every streetcar took its sweet goddamned time, but no black Packard Six or anything else was trying to follow. Jim swung a right on N, parked, and got out.

He walked inside Pop's. Before his eyes adjusted from the outdoor sun, something slammed the base of his sternum. He doubled over and heard a clatter. He couldn't get a breath in. Getting the wind knocked out of you was the most worthless mechanism in the human body. It served no goddamned biological purpose.

He'd crumpled to his hands and knees by the time he could pull air into his lungs. In the middle of the room, Ward had Edith in a bear hug from behind, raised off the floor. She kicked and tried to peel off Ward's arms with her fingers. When she realized she wasn't getting anywhere, she made a *fthoo* and lobbed a wad of spit at Jim. It was short by half the distance between them. Jim searched the floor to his left, where he'd heard the clatter. He pushed himself to his feet, bent over for his newspapers and the cast-iron pan, walked back to the front door, opened it, and threw that goddamned pan, hard and high as he could to clear the Ford. He didn't care if it hit a car driving down the street. That pan was somebody else's problem now.

"Hey!" Edith's voice pierced the air behind him.

Jim turned to her. Each syllable came punched out of him, short and even like a series of Morse code dots, no dashes. "You don't get no more goddamned pans," he said. "You cook with something else now."

"Edie," Ward said to her. "Edie, I'll let go when you calm down. Jim, get the hell outside. Give us a minute."

Jim went outside. He was fine with going outside. He would've goddamned left if he didn't need to talk to Ward. He stood in the shade of the awning. He couldn't make out what the voices inside said, only the tones. Ward's was level. Edith's was all hotheaded staccato.

"Big Jim," he heard coming down the sidewalk. Frank carried a lidded vat. "It ain't soup." He said it was something that sounded like *fleech-key*. It was probably made of barn swallows and ox ass.

"Better not be hot. Anything food-related, Edith's using as artillery." He listened for the voices again. Edith wasn't calmer, but she'd lowered the volume.

"Waiting for the coast to clear?"

"Waiting for Ward to come outside. I ain't going in there again."

"Ah, come on," Frank said. "You don't, she'll think you're scared. Can't let women know you're scared of them. They smell it. Go for the throat."

"I think that's dogs."

"What's people? Dogs that think they're not, wearing clothes, walking on their back legs for a little mutton. Get the door."

Jim thought maybe the metal vat would be decent armor. He opened the door for Frank but stood back, out of range if Edith fired anything their way. Instead, Ward filled the doorframe, apparently ready to walk out. He stared at the giant lidded pot. "What's that?" His eyes were bloodshot and slick looking.

Frank said it was ham and noodles.

Ward hesitated. He didn't say anything, but he stepped back, let Frank by. Jim followed. Frank asked if he could put the pot on the bar. Pop said sure in an uncharacteristically chipper way. Jim hadn't seen Pop when he'd tried to go in before, but Jim had spent most of that time on his hands and knees.

Edith was at the end of the bar. She washed and dried glasses again, slamming them down on a clean towel. "So, what—you think you can bring some stinking bohunk food in here and all's forgiven? Get a guy killed, bring some goulash?"

"Edith," Pop said.

"'Edith,'" she said. "Sure. 'Edith' me like I'm hysterical." She aimed her wrath at Jim. "First, you bring this one here—a cop the whole town knows takes protection. You bring him into my father's place, you get somebody we know killed, my husband's a drunk mess over it, and then you come back here when there's gangsters out to kill you. You throw my goddamned pan in the street—"

"Okay, okay," Frank said. "But eat."

"Smells good," Pop said, like nobody'd been yelling or throwing anything.

"Try it," Frank said. "Big Jim, you throw this lady's pan in the street?"

Jim said he sure as goddamned hell did.

"Make nice. Go get it."

Jim went outside. Cars were swerving to miss the pan. He plucked it up as a coupe cruised by and honked. Jim yelled—told the coupe to go fuck its mother.

When he went back in, Frank was ladling noodles into bowls and talking about Gus. "Nah, it wasn't like that. Here, get some ham. Guy was already dead. Jim and me seen it. I know what the paper says, but it's wrong. Didn't bleed out. Hardly any blood."

"He'd been shot," Ward said.

"Yeah, sure—but not till after he was dead."

Jim hadn't looked at the papers yet. Now he scanned for articles about the inquest. All three said Gus died of gunshot wounds. All three said Gus had been carrying a notebook related to Elmer Kobb's licensing protest, and all three said Gus was hired by Jim. The *Tribune* had called Kobb for comment and quoted him multiple times: "more proof the criminal element has this city in a chokehold," "stark evidence Omaha needs new leadership," "certain parties who profit from vice have used the interim mayorship opportunistically, to organize and strengthen their grip." Certain parties. That was code for Bill Haskell, supposed Overlord of the Underworld, but Haskell had sued papers for libel more than once and won. And Jim supposed the phrase worked to Kobb's advantage anyway. Vague. A wider umbrella. Jim could hear Kobb saying it all to the press box at City Hall and wanted to pop that balloon of a head.

He scanned for his follow-up articles about Maloney beaning him. He didn't have to look far—both the *Post* and the *Standard* printed them right alongside the ones about Gus. The positioning was nice: one column claiming there'd been a gangland murder, the next saying the Independent Federation slate was the gang.

"This is good," Pop said of the fleech-key. Frank said it was all Jennie. Pop told him to thank Mrs. Tvrdik for him.

Frank explained why the lack of blood meant Gus had been dead beforehand, how attorneys and cops used "homicide: no suspects" cases to hold somebody they thought was guilty of something else when they didn't have evidence to charge them yet.

"So, anybody could go to jail right now, accused of killing somebody," Edith said. "That's rich."

Frank shrugged. He asked Pop, "You really like it?"

Pop had a mouthful, so he nodded.

Ward was quiet, leaned back against the far end of the bar. Frank told him to get a bowl. Ward said no thanks.

Jim walked over to talk to him. "Listen—"

"No, now—no." Judging by the assertiveness, Ward hadn't unraveled, and he didn't sound maudlin. His voice was quiet but firm. Jim got the impression he'd prepared a statement. "You getting jumped last night, I'd wring the guy's neck if I could. And I know it was only a matter of time for Gus. It didn't help he was working for you when it happened, and that's on me. I gotta live with that. But whatever you're mixed up in now—with him—" He nudged his head Frank's way. "I don't know what it is, and I want to keep it that way. I don't want it coming down on Pop and Edith. I don't want it coming down on me, neither. They need me."

"Ward, you know I'd never—"

"I know you'd never. I also know if you'd seen what was coming before you let Vern Meyer in your house, you would've locked the door and shoved a dresser against it."

Jim couldn't look him in the eye. He nodded at his cheap shoes instead. "We'll clear out."

Ward reached across the bar and planted a hand on Jim's shoulder. "You can handle yourself. I got them to think about. They're family."

Then the hand dropped. Jim checked Ward's expression— to see if he'd meant Pop and Edith were his only family now. To see if Jim was really getting the kiss-off from his own brother. But it was Ward's turn not to meet Jim's eyes. Ward looked toward the other end of the bar, where Pop and Frank joked. Even Edith had warmed up enough to eat. Ward had meant what he'd said, but he was Ward. He was moody.

"I'll tell him something," Jim said. "We'll get going."

"Nah, let them finish first."

11

The sun set in a haze behind the Ford as Jim and Frank drove northeast to the Henley-Barr. Frank had walked from his house to Pop's with the fleech-key, which they'd left there. Frank said he'd go back for the pot when Jennie nagged him enough. He had the night off, and since his sleep was switched around from working nights, he said he was awake whether he liked it or not. So was Jim. His mood was heavy over the way he'd left things with Ward.

At the office, Jim and Frank had a drink and smoked. Frank related Pete Gilson's full account of the inquest. Pete had been rankled, of course, that a lawyer—not even the county attorney but a deputy county attorney—was doing a job rightfully left to a man intimately familiar with corpses. "Only a lawyer could get homicide out of that," Pete had told Frank.

"He's right, but do me a favor. If you're nearby when I keel over, don't hand me off to Pete."

Frank looked struck by a thought. "Say, that's a puzzler. Bohunks die, they go to Kucera or Kava. Coloreds die, they go to Bristol or Thomas. Micks die, they go to McKutcheon or Haney. Syrians go to Shada, Italians to Golizia or Salvio, Jews to Blumenthal—where the hell's a Beely go?"

"Wherever's running a special."

"Ah, I'm ribbing. Hell, I ain't even bohunk. Folks came from Moravia. Don't matter. Over here, your last name ain't got enough vowels, you're bohunk."

"That don't bother you?"

"Nothing wrong with bohunks and not my business. They got to peg you as something, let them peg."

"But you call yourself a bohunk."

"Convenience. You oughta try it. Beely sounds mick, say you're black Irish." Frank finished his drink and poured another. "Can I ask you something else?"

"You can ask."

"Why you sleep here? Don't you still got a house?"

"It's paid through the end of the month." Jim did some quick ledger-balancing in his head that had nothing to do with finances. He couldn't say the place reminded him of what Vern did. Even if Frank wasn't suspicious, even if he would've thought killing Vern was justified, Frank was a cop. Jim wasn't about to give a cop a motive to mull over. Besides, that was only part of the reason Jim couldn't go back there. "Place reminds me of Molly. I don't got to tell you. You met her a couple times."

Frank chewed a corner of his mouth, likely thinking of how to put his response. "She's spirited."

"She's goddamned mean." Jim refilled his glass. "We were a pair of old maids. Never planned on marrying. I took her out a few times, knocked her up, got hitched. I thought she'd come around with the kid, but she lost it. We stayed married, had Addie—she never did come around." Jim knew he wasn't being fair. "Wasn't always so bad. Not all the time. She was damn funny when she wanted to be. Anybody that naturally miserable can be damn funny."

"That's the bitch of it, right there. Bad all the time's one thing. When it's good once in a while, good feels like best."

"Sure. Somebody prying your fingernails off with a pair of pliers—feels great when they stop a minute. Then Vern happened, she threw me out. Can't blame her. My fault he was there. He was out of work, I was an easy mark."

"Nah. It's what you're supposed to do. Give people a roof when they need it." He took a drink. "So, you been sleeping in this joint, what—a year? More? And paying rent on a bedroom, all because of the pervert? If he wasn't dead, I'd kill him."

The mention of a dead Vern flipped the conversation ledger into the red. Jim forced a shrug. "He was what he was. No use hating a squirrel for being a squirrel." He changed the subject. "Take Gus. Doubt he paged through a catalogue and picked 'rounder.' Especially the kind that gets shot after he's dead."

"Thing I don't get's Pospisil," Frank said, and Jim knew he'd rerouted Frank like a railyard switch-tender. "He's a prick, but crooked? Can't see it. And he ain't stupid."

"Maybe somebody's got something on him."

"Can't see that, neither. Pospisil's the kind of guy says, 'What of it?'—'You eat that pickle off the sidewalk, Pospisil?'—'Yeah, what of it?'" Frank finished his drink. "Let's go find Maloney. Pick up a couple burlap sacks. Lead pipe."

It was tempting, but Jim needed to smooth things over with Ward. Jim thought he'd shielded his brother from knowing too much, knowing what he'd done to Vern, then turned around and asked Ward to find a rounder who wound up dead. "Think I'll retrace Gus's steps. See if anybody knows anything." The addresses with Ole's notes were still on his desk.

"Yeah, all right," Frank said, answering a question Jim hadn't asked. "I'm half crocked. Might as well get full crocked. I'll tag along, keep you out of trouble."

"You've done a hell of a job this far." Jim decided some company might not be so bad. Besides, Frank could be a decent cop. Even when he was dirty, he was decent at it.

Since Ole had last seen Gus the final night they'd made the rounds, Jim and Frank would start backward, from the last address on the list. All the joints on the final page were between South Thirteenth and the river. Tony Tvrdik's pool hall wasn't last, but it was on the last page, so Frank talked Jim into stopping for the free drink.

"You're already soused." Tony served Frank a beer. Frank protested in Czech. Tony shot back some consonant-riddled epithets. While they bickered, Jim drank a whiskey and noticed only three pool tables. Maybe there was no minimum for a place to be designated a pool hall.

Apparently, Tony was through arguing. He ditched the Czech. "I don't need Jennie coming in here with a switch. Drink your fucking beer."

Frank did and described Gus and Ole, asked if Tony remembered them. Tony said Gus wouldn't shut the hell up and the old toothless fella couldn't get a word in edgewise.

When Jim asked what Gus was going on about, Tony only said, "Who'd listen?"

Jim and Frank left on foot to make the rounds. The proprietors at the last four joints said they hadn't seen Gus, only Ole. The next three on the list said they weren't sure about either, but Jim sensed they were being mum. Maybe Frank was the problem. If Jim came back without a cop, especially one that was a Frank, maybe they'd be more talkative.

The address eighth from the last was Yano Catalano's, which was licensed as a soft drink parlor. The entrance was on the alley side of the house, a basement door to a windowless brick storefront beneath a wood-frame house. Frank went in first. The door creaked open to a dimly lit hallway. Jim heard a loud snap and reached for his pistol grip. Frank was undeterred. He was either accustomed to the noise or so lit he didn't care what they were walking into. Then a cymbal hissed and a bass drum throbbed a few times. The snap was a snare.

The hallway opened up to the right. The glow from the wall sconces was dim, but across the room footlights lit a short stage. At the back, silver tinsel dangled from ceiling to floor. In front, a drummer sat behind a small kit. Her bobbed black hair nearly touched her shoulders. Nobody sat at a nearby piano.

"What can I get you?" The voice was muffled, a reedy baritone. It came from off to the right, a bar with no one behind it. Then something scraped the floor and Yano stood. He must've been moving a barrel or keg. "Frank," he said in greeting, then, "You Jim Beely?"

Jim never knew whether or not to admit it but said he

was. Frank went to the bar and sat on a stool. Jim followed but stood. Yano told him to sit, sit. They hadn't said what they wanted, but he poured them both whiskey.

Frank paid. "You got entertainment now?"

"Got a lotta goddamn noise." He said the girl was his kid sister, which explained the resemblance. Their complexion was a shade darker than Jim's. They had the same narrow nose that came out and down at an angle. Yano said his ma was upstairs cooking rabbit, if they wanted any. She'd come down eventually, tinkle the piano. "They got it in their heads I'll pay them." He raised his voice so his sister could hear. "For what? For driving everybody out with that goddamn noise."

She rolled her eyes, dropped the sticks on the snare, and disappeared behind the tinsel.

Frank lit a smoke. "Hear about a guy the cops found all shot up Sunday night?"

"Nope."

"I didn't ask if you shot him. I know you didn't shoot him." Frank described Gus, said he was a Fritz with a bushy brown beard, smoked a pipe, wore a gray coat that looked like it came off a dead hobo.

"Loudmouth? Come in with an old guy, no teeth?"

"That's him," Jim said.

Yano finished scooting the barrels and gave the empty a kick to free it from his path. He rested a forearm on the bar. "That was never gonna end well. Old man all right?"

Jim said he'd skipped town.

"Good. I should've skipped this town, too. Stayed on the train, got off in Denver."

Frank asked if Yano remembered anything Gus had yammered about.

"Indiana, Illinois, Iowa—I don't know. Wouldn't shut up. Saw he had a notebook, told him stick with writing poems and shut his mouth. Somebody else made a crack—'You know how to write?' He got miffed, said it was work, said he was a detective. Didn't say police or private, but neither's good news. No offense," he told Jim.

Jim thought to say he was an investigator, not a Pinkerton, but only gave a quick shake of his head to say none taken.

"So I snatched the notebook, saw it was a list of joints, saw which he hadn't gone to yet, and threw him out. Told the old man he could stay if he wanted. Sweet old man." Yano had let Ole finish his drink. "Then I called every place the loudmouth hadn't been to yet. Said he called himself a detective. Didn't know if it was true, but I said, 'You let him in that door, he won't shut the hell up.'"

That explained why nobody who'd seen Gus would say so. Jim wished he'd asked Ole more questions about Sunday night, but judging by the handwriting, Ole had been too drunk to remember much.

"You send that guy in here?" Yano asked Jim.

"Sorry."

"Nah—it's a relief. I was at the commissioners' meeting, getting my renewal. Here." He scooted half of Frank's money back at him. "His is on me."

Jim and Frank thanked him, finished their drinks, and started for the dark hallway.

Yano called out, said wait a second. "Don't know if it

makes a difference, but I called Mickey's, too. Wasn't on the list, but it's only a couple blocks, so I warned him." They thanked him again, and when they shut the door, a quick rat-a-tat-tat came from the snare again. Yano yelled something about the goddamn noise.

"Who's Mickey?" Jim asked.

Frank wasn't paying attention. His cheeks glowed red from the booze. "Dumb Fritz tells Yano Catalano he's a detective. For all he knows, Catalano's in the Black Hand."

"The Mafia," Jim said. "Because he's Sicilian?"

"Ah, lighten up, Beely." Frank was drunk. "Yano's on the up-and-up. Ma making rabbit, sister plays drums. Think his dad was a grocer. What'd you ask?"

"Who's Mickey?"

"Hold on." Frank had sudden purpose and urgency. He gripped Jim's overcoat sleeve.

"Don't puke on me."

Frank shook his head but gave a closemouthed burp. "Mickey's place wasn't on there? Come on."

The alley ran east-west, south of Pierce, and it was steep. Frank moved fast, letting the downhill grade carry him. Jim felt like he was sprinting to keep up. They took Pierce east to Sixth and headed north. They passed one brick row house after another packed with people upstairs and down. The air was thick with onions sauteed in oil, some kind of meat marinated in red wine. They passed a corner store, then modest houses and an old saloon turned into a butcher shop.

Before the cobblestones hit the train tracks, Frank stopped.

He pointed at a squat brick building with a high false front. Under the streetlight, Jim made out the numbers above the door: 1905. For a second he thought he'd gotten turned around, that they'd gone south instead of north. Then he realized 1905 was a date. The door said 1104.

Jim scanned the list for 1104 South Sixth. "It's not on here."

"Oughta be. Cigar store, sells liquor. License would've been up for renewal." Frank looked satisfied about something, peering across the street into a darkness punctured by scattered streetlamps. "And you know what's over there?"

"Power plant, the yards." Shit. "The coal pile."

Jim read the addresses again, constructed a mental map, pushed little stickpins into the grid. The pattern wasn't tough to make out. If the building had made the list, it would've been second-to-last.

If the three joints after Yano's wouldn't let Gus in or threw him right back out, it made sense he'd give up, not bother with the last four, and, seeing this place wasn't listed, blow the last of his per diem here on a nightcap. Even though Yano had called Mickey and warned him about Gus, Gus could've shown Mickey the list, pointed out the place wasn't on it. Mickey might've let him stay so long as he kept his mouth shut. Then Gus could've left, trudged over to the coal pile to pocket a few rocks for heat at the boardinghouse, and passed out.

Frank thumped Jim's chest with the back of his hand like he had an extra blue punch line coming. "It's Mickey *O'Neill*'s place," he said. "Brother of Police Detective Pat O'Neill, former partner of Jack Maloney." He smiled, a little manic.

Jim's head hurt again, not from the bump Maloney gave him but from trying to picture pieces on a chessboard.

Goddamned chess. If that chessboard had ears, he'd tell it to screw. "Think Mickey called his brother, said Gus was here?"

Frank shrugged. "All guesswork after Yano's. Fritz could've just wandered that way. Streetcar yards are O'Neill and Dietz's beat."

"Do we go in? Ask?"

"You got two more yous under that coat?" Frank said. "Nah. Mickey's place ain't that rough. But if he knows anything, he ain't gonna spill on his brother. Worse, he'll say we're asking around. Let's get back to the car." They'd left it at Tony's. "Then let's pay Harry Donnegan a visit. Have a chat about this list."

12

Jim had never been to that louse Donnegan's house and didn't know where it was. He didn't want to. He saw enough Donnegan in Council Chambers, courtrooms, and the papers. Jim would've liked to see a hell of a lot less Harry Donnegan. Besides, the last time he talked to Donnegan, Jim got beaned with a lead pipe afterward.

Frank yapped and smoked and gave directions.

Before Jim knew it, they were headed south on Twenty-Fourth. "Sure you know where he lives?"

"What—think Donnegan's got a place in West Farnam?" West Farnam was a cluster of mansions at what was once the city limit. Omaha had crept west since then, built over farms and roadhouses that'd been built over encampments that'd been built over whole civilizations.

"Wouldn't've figured Donnegan for South O."

"Eh, carpetbagger. I only know where he lives from tracking down a client he harbored."

Donnegan's house was on the east side of Twenty-Fourth, two blocks south of Pete Gilson's parlor. The place was all right, two stories and an attic with a couple dormers. Better than a tick mattress on the floor of the Henley-Barr but nothing special.

He must've heard them pull up or seen them coming. Donnegan had the front door open before they could cross the porch. "What's this?"

Frank's footing was surprisingly sure, given he'd drunk his volume in liquor. "You and us need to talk about some addresses."

"Come in," he said. "Come in off the porch. But keep your voices down."

The front room was nothing special, either. It was tidy, and somebody must've liked crocheting. Doilies on everything.

"Frank, I can smell the booze with your mouth shut," Donnegan said. Then he turned to Jim, tried to look concerned. "I read about the attack. Frank here gave me the impression that you might've suspected Maloney was somehow involved."

In Jim's experience, the degree of a guy's guilt matched the number of words he used to say a thing. "Forget it. My bell just got rung. I was goofy. Got any idea why Mickey O'Neill's place wasn't on the renewal list?"

"What?"

Frank enunciated it, loud: "You got any idea why Mickey O'Ne—"

Harry hushed him. "My wife's got a migraine. I heard you. You have it? The list?"

Jim handed it over. Donnegan asked what the street number was and scanned the addresses. "The clerk of the district court gave me these. They came straight from him. Say, hear the news about his kid? Assistant DA. Soon as the diploma's signed."

Frank poked the papers with his middle finger. "And you got no reason to leave one or two joints out."

Donnegan flipped back through the pages and landed on an address. "Here, look." He pushed the sheet in front of Frank. "My ex-wife's place. I pay alimony. When her business is good, she leaves me alone. If I wanted to scratch an address, don't you think I'd pick that one?" It was goddamned art, the way Donnegan could avoid saying yes or no.

Jim knew he wouldn't get a straight answer but asked the question to gauge Donnegan's reaction: "Got any clue how Pospisil ties in?"

"Pospisil?" Donnegan looked genuinely surprised, which meant he was. "He barely tolerates everyone and everything. I think he's only stayed in town because his mother's still alive. I assume he'll leave as soon as she's dead."

"You know where Maloney's at?" Frank said.

"I think you'd better sober up before you go looking."

Frank was slurring a bit—that delayed effect of drinking too fast and the buzz catching up. Still, he sounded quietly menacing. "You gonna tell me to sober up, Harry?"

"Let's go." Jim grabbed Frank by the arm and led him to the door.

Before they were on the porch, Donnegan gave Jim a look of gratitude. "You might try Maymie's."

"*You might try Maymie's,*" Frank mimicked.

Jim and Frank got in the car. "Bob Wright. Clerk of the district court," Jim said. "First thing out of Donnegan's mouth at the committee meeting was he got the addresses from clerk of the district court. Old-time reformer, thick as thieves with Kobb."

"So who do we beat with a lead pipe, then? Wright?"

"Can't touch Wright. Can't touch guys like him or Donnegan or Kobb. You do, they pay somebody to chop your brake line. Make a few calls, get you evicted and pinched as a vagrant. Get their toadies at downtown station to link you to a 'homicide: no suspects' case."

"Yeah, if we're lucky. Wright's on the Insanity Board. We'd get railroaded into the booby hatch."

Jim didn't want to see Maloney any more than he'd wanted to see Donnegan, but he was their best option. "Maloney ain't untouchable. You can shove a guy like that's head in a toilet till he fesses up. And since his ex-partner found Gus, he might know why Gus got shot after he was dead."

"Even if he don't, we get to shove the loon's head in a toilet."

The drive was three miles, fifteen minutes, give or take. Halfway there, Frank said he was sobering up, like it was a bad thing. Jim reminded him Maymie would have plenty. They puttered north on Twenty-Fourth, past homes and corner stores and the Polish-Catholic church. They crossed the viaduct over the railyards. By the time they reached Leavenworth, Frank had nodded off.

Jim made the right to head east. He did it without thinking, then realized he'd lost the instinct to make a left. To head toward the house, toward home. Even after he'd stopped sleeping there, the left turn was automatic. Now the house had been empty a few weeks, and the instinct was gone. The sensation of having lost it wasn't good or bad, only a blank spot. Like there was slightly less of him. But he was still here, driving, breathing, digesting whatever he last ate. He was functioning. He guessed that meant whatever he was missing wasn't vital. The notion unsettled him more than picturing himself without lungs or arteries.

Jim could see well enough on his own, but he said, "Frank. Wake up. Help me find a spot." He passed Eighteenth and looked for a space. Monte C's was busy tonight. Jim pulled in near the end of the block. Frank was alert again, shaking off the grogginess.

They got out and made their way around one corner then another to the alleyway. Smack-dab in the middle of the block was a complicated maze of stairs and landings that led upward, all pale pine. The fire escape had gone up in flames three times Jim knew about, the brick building never damaged. Jim would've thought after one fire Maymie might've replaced the wood with iron. But maybe she wasn't sure an investment in wrought iron would pay off. She must've made a lot of money, but if she trusted the universe as much as Jim did, she could've thought a permanent fix would be a jinx. As soon as the last seam was welded, the place would collapse or her door would get padlocked.

Jim and Frank made their way up the stairs and Jim avoided looking down. Frank said, "This thing made of matchsticks?" and shook the pine railing.

"Knock it off."

"You can't be scared of heights. You'd be walking around scared all day."

At the second landing, they passed two closed, draped windows before they reached the door. Jim rapped it with a knuckle. The landing shook with approaching steps. Jim gripped the doorframe.

He shouldn't have been surprised to see Maymie open the door herself. He'd been here enough to know the place was Maymie's domain. Jim supposed he'd girded himself to confront Maloney and forgotten Maymie was more intimidating.

If beauty were defined as "delicate," Maymie didn't have it. She had a round white moon of a face, and her nose ended in more of a dollop than a tip. If you caught her smiling, chances were high the joke was at your expense, and a pair of gold incisors lent a tinge of threat. She also had deep brown eyes that seemed to cut straight through your clothes, your skin, your bones, and let you know whatever she saw there, at the center of you, left her indifferent. Beauty or not, of course Jim found her attractive.

She looked past him and found Frank. She called him Frankie and said to come here.

"Nah, I ain't going to hell. Not for whatever's in that snatch."

She sized Jim up, swiped her eyes across his face till she'd IDed him. "Beely," she acknowledged. She stepped back from the door, as close to an invitation as she'd offer.

For a "disorderly house," a phrase as Victorian as "morals squad," slapped on any joint prone to vice raids—gambling, booze, prostitution—Maymie's was neatly curated. The Victrola that'd played "East St. Louis Toodle-Oo" the night before was cranking out a Ruth Etting tune. A girl dressed like she could've been a switchboard operator slumped beside the horn in a green chair. She looked to be asleep, cheek leaned on a fist. Next to the Victrola was a matching green couch beneath a window that must've been nine, ten feet tall. The top was arched with panes leaded together like a fan's flattened folds.

As for the people on the clock and their customers, they must've been off in the rooms. Jim made a point not to listen for anything but the record, and he was glad all he smelled was the piney scent of gin, a mix of cigarette and pipe smoke. A trace of rose water crept in when Maymie stepped close and past him to finger Frank's shirt collar.

"No chance," Frank said. "You got a drink?"

She dropped the hand that was flirting and looked at him. The look was skeptical, long, and unblinking. "You, too?"

Jim didn't know she was asking him if he wanted a drink until she glanced up. "Sure," he said, to say something.

Next to the couch, the other end from the Victrola, was a fully stocked liquor cabinet. A front panel was folded down like a secretary desk. She used it to pour two drinks and said have a seat.

"Maloney here?" Jim asked.

"*Pfft*. No." She gave an arched brow. "I said sit."

Frank took one end, Jim the other. She sat across from the couch on a footrest covered in red tapestry. "What'd the crackpot do now?"

"Heard you're marrying that crackpot," Frank said.

"Jealous?" She bared one of the gold teeth. "That plan's all Donnegan. Who's an idiot. Occasionally useful, but an idiot."

"He says it keeps a padlock off your door." Frank had sobered up quickly. Maymie seemed to put him on guard. He was even alert enough not to drink. Whatever Maymie had served them was not gin. As best Jim could tell, it was grain alcohol with a splash of port. The smell could've sliced his skin off.

"Donnegan gets off on damsels in distress. But I do just fine. Haven't jimmied a lock yet."

"What's your secret?" Jim had said it—he'd heard it come out of his head, anyway. He'd taken a drink before he'd known better.

She tilted her head back and to the side—more scrutiny. It was laced with a little insolence that gave Jim a warm electric jolt. "You really want to know?"

He thought about it. "Probably I don't."

"Probably you don't." She gave a thin smile, no teeth. "Donnegan thinks I'll pay that crackpot bum's tabs. Maloney wants to dress like a strumpet, he can rent a room like anybody else here. You gonna say what he did?"

"We want to talk, is all."

"I guess a loon makes better conversation than a tree stump. Tell you what—promise to kill him, I'll say where he is." She waited, and if she didn't mean it, she did a fine job not showing it. When there were no takers, she shrugged. "Give it some thought. He's at the Hotel Fontana. He's muscle—if you can call him that—at some Federation fundraiser."

Jim checked the level in Frank's glass. He hadn't sipped any more, and Jim was relieved. "Let's head down," he said.

Maymie laughed. "Think you'll get in? A cop and—" She raised and lowered her hand, palm up, in front of Jim. "You? What is that, anyway? Beely. Sounds Irish. Your mother Syrian or something?"

"She was a Smith."

"Well, whatever you are, you're giant. Not real nondescript. And last I heard, they hate you down there."

She was right. Jim was not nondescript, and the Fontana pricks did hate him. The Fontana was a posh hotel, headquarters for the wealthiest sect of anti-labor robber barons. Nominally, they were Republicans, but that didn't matter much. Materially, they were bankers, real estate men, railroad magnates. Pickards and Henleys. People whose nephews never got shot in the back on the sixteenth green of a golf course for allegedly stealing gas. Around the early aughts, Jim made a hobby of pissing them off. He ran for low-level offices, register of deeds and the like, to split their votes. He'd filed a restraining order once, kept them from handing out slates that looked like sample ballots, printed with corporate money. Other people went to church or played high five for jollies. Jim gave the Fontana a taste of what mortals lived like. Endless goddamned hassles.

"Know anybody could get us in?" Frank asked.

"Sure—Prince Gordon's the cook."

"Prince Gordon?"

She shrugged. "His name. Think it's safe to say if it was a title, he wouldn't work for a living." She told them to go to the service entrance in the alley, by the loading dock, and say she sent them.

The Victrola had finished playing, and the needle was grinding static. The girl dressed like a switchboard operator didn't seem to mind. She was still sound asleep beside it. Jim thanked Maymie for the tip, and Frank ducked and dodged when she tried to plant a kiss on his cheek.

They made their way back down the pine stairs and

around the corner to the car. "She's sure sweet on you," Jim said, glad to have something to needle Frank about.

"Nah, she's being cute. Thinks I won't take protection from her because I'm too good for the joint."

"Why don't you?"

"I'm too good for the joint. Hell, I don't know where those dollars been."

"Well, she likes you better than Maloney."

"There's a compliment." Frank lit a cigarette and flicked the match. It burned on the sidewalk before it went dead.

The Fontana was six blocks north but felt like a city away. As the Ford passed beneath the crosshatch of trolley wires and rumbled over the tracks, buildings grew taller, their shadows darker. Residential hotels and basement cigar shops gave way to business towers, banks, and the center of city and county government. Just past the courthouse and City Hall, the Fontana shared a block with the new Elks building, the Masonic Lodge, and St. Mary Magdalene. The combination made obscure sense: one concentrated block of abstraction, a center of symbols and rituals and cloaks. Secret languages and initiations. If there was an underworld in Omaha, Jim thought, that was it.

"I hate this goddamned joint," Frank said when they found an open spot on Eighteenth.

"You been in?"

"A maid cut the hell out of a porter once. Slashed him faceless. Other time, an old biddy thought housekeeping stole her jewelry. Wound up it was in her purse."

They got out, and the Fontana loomed plain brick up to

its top two stories, which were white. The windows up there were framed in gothic curves and points, and a row of jagged spires lined all four sides of the roof. The spires looked a little like white evergreen trees, a little more like pikes awaiting decapitated heads. Jim and Frank slipped into the alley between the Fontana and the Elks.

There'd been no rain or snow, which meant the puddles glinting in the moonlight had leached from barrels and bins of kitchen garbage. Jim dodged the juice, grateful the night wasn't warm enough to make the air riper. They found the loading dock and the door beside it. Jim pounded and tried not to breathe through his nose.

A woman old enough to have been his mother answered, bibbed apron smeared with whatever hadn't leaked out to the alley yet. Her cheeks were flushed, likely from steam— she held a soapy dish. Jim asked if Prince was here, said Maymie Strunk sent him. The woman asked if he meant Hamlet or Eddie. She was so curt about it, Jim didn't catch the joke until she'd given up. She yelled out for Prince and told Jim and Frank to get inside, keep the goddamned stink out.

Jim didn't know what somebody named Prince should've looked like, but he didn't know what the hell a Jim was supposed to look like. It was like Frank said. Everybody got pegged as something. This Prince looked like he could've actually been one, in someplace ancient Jim should've read a book about but hadn't. Prince looked like a statue carved from walnut wood and brushed in a sheen of gold dust. He was all angles and no slack. Maybe being a cook gave him a grudge against food.

The kitchen was busy, and Prince was brusque. Jim said they were looking for a guy. They needed to talk to him but couldn't afford the price of admission.

"Fuck anybody who can." Prince said to hurry up and follow him. They dodged line cooks and waitstaff to a door. It opened into what looked like a room-sized pie-cooling cabinet. An ornate, perforated metal grille gave Jim and Frank a view of the meeting. Prince said it was the closest they'd get and shut the door.

They stood in the darkness and peered through the grate. The main event was on a platform off to the right. Elmer Kobb, with his bright white hair and sad beagle eyes, stood at a podium. Tepid laughter gave the room a hum that sounded obligatory. Seated to his right and left were the other four Independent Federation candidates, plus Clerk of the District Court Bob Wright. You couldn't miss him. Wright had a head shaped like a giant aspirin capsule. It was as without contour and color and nearly as bald. As a clerk, he openly pocketed fees for anything anybody filed with the district court: cases, licenses, naturalizations. He was unapologetic. Proud, even—he'd found a loophole that made pocketing fees legal. If you had a problem with it? Good luck in the booby hatch. Next to Wright was his pimpled, bespectacled son, then the DA and the state's attorney general.

"Jesus," Frank said. "Hoover here, too?"

Jim took in the room past the grille. The place was more grotesque than Council Chambers. Chandeliers hung from gold chains. The lights were long octagons, glass shades marbled and striated like glowing mother-of-pearl. Columns stretched from floor to ceiling, and at the top of each was what looked like a family crest—ornate gold, like filigree. At the far end of the room, under a lamplit painting of what looked like rocks and water—Jim wondered why the hell anyone would paint it, much less spend money lighting it up—two cops guarded the entrance. Neither was Maloney.

"Know those two?" he asked Frank.

"Left's Dietz. Right's O'Neill."

Aside from ears that stuck out like a pair of boat sails, Dietz was the lucky one on looks. He had a head of thick black hair and eyes like Valentino's. O'Neill was unfortunate: light hair that didn't know if it was blond or brown, a face that came to a point like a rodent. He looked like he was trying to swallow his chin, and his haircut did him no favors. He'd gone in for a half-crown shaved up to the temples. What was left on top he'd slicked flat with Vaseline or kitchen grease.

Jim scanned the attendees. Those he recognized were the usual suspects, the modern and rich Know Nothings. The men owned everything; the women were Temperance Union, DAR types who hosted brunches for out-of-town speakers and sent their kids to Europe, which they probably called the goddamned Continent.

Kobb had introduced the attorney general, who approached the podium to warm applause.

"Let's check around front," Frank said.

Jim told him to hold on. So long as they were here, they could get a peek at the Federation's angle in the upcoming election.

"Ah, hell," Frank said. "Same garbage every time. Conspiracies, invisible governments, political machines, the gang."

He was right, but at some point reformers had to see dropping the word *reform* and repackaging the same material over and over didn't get their slate elected. "Just hold on."

The AG thanked the crowd before launching into his pitch. They had reason to believe, he said, that a vice syndicate, a "ring" of liquor, prostitution, and gambling interests, had not only formed in the city—it was being protected by members of the current administration, from top to bottom.

"Yeah, all right," Jim said. They hadn't even repackaged anything. They'd left the wrapping paper on and switched out ribbons.

As he and Frank made their way toward the door, feeling along the wall in the dark, Frank knocked something over. The handle of a mop or broom smacked the floor. The AG stopped talking. For an instant, Jim froze. He pictured his and Frank's heads up on those pikes lining the roof. He whispered to hold on again, stay put.

The AG still stood at the podium, and no one in the crowd looked toward the grate. But Dietz was on the platform now, in the AG's ear. The AG gestured to Kobb, and the men consulted with one another, looking grave.

"Ladies and gentlemen," the AG said, "I urge you not to panic, but we've received news of several bombings, one at the home of Elmer Kobb."

13

The Fontana was chaotic after news of the bombings. Jim told Frank to go wait in the Ford and took advantage of the confusion, checking entrances inside and out for Jack Maloney. He wasn't there. A porter said he had been but left a couple hours ago, when the bigwigs arrived.

As Jim crossed the street to the car, he heard a voice call out, "Mister Beely." He turned. Kobb stood on the sidewalk outside the hotel. Jim took his time walking over. Kobb said he was surprised to see Jim at the Fontana.

"You oughta be." Jim said he'd been walking past, seen somebody he knew, and stopped to chat.

"You haven't heard, then?" Kobb grimaced.

"Hell if I know."

"Our homes," he said. "Both our homes were bombed."

Initially, Jim thought Kobb meant his own family had two homes and both got blasted. That wouldn't have surprised Jim. He was sure Kobb could afford two houses, and if Jim wanted to bomb a couple, Kobb's would be at the top of the list. But the wince on Kobb's face, a look as phony as the puzzlement he'd worn at the commissioners' meeting, clarified what he meant. Jim didn't let a muscle in his face twitch. "Any word from your family?"

Kobb thanked him for asking. Yes, thank God, he'd spoken with his wife—she and his son were fine. The damage was limited mainly to the porch. "I've heard matters are much worse at your house."

"Well, it's a rental."

"I hope—fervently—your family escaped danger. Would you like to phone? There's a pay phone in the lobby of the Fontana. Do you need some change?"

"They're out-of-state." Jim ignored Kobb's offer of spare change and kept his tone hard and flat. "Visiting relations."

"Well, that's a relief."

"Sure."

"Who's that you're with?" Kobb squinted into the darkness across the street. Frank must've lit a cigarette. A puff of smoke crept from the passenger window of the Ford.

"My brother."

"Of course—Ward Beely. He's an ice man, isn't he? Married to the daughter of—what's the gentleman's name—Daddy?"

"Pop." Which was what Jim wanted to do to that goddamned balloon head of Kobb's.

"That's it. Pop Nelson. Distinguished old Danish gentleman, with the soft drink parlor off Twenty-Fourth."

"I get it. You know who's who in my family."

Kobb smiled. "Well, Omaha's a great big small town. Hard to keep secrets."

Jim stared at him, assessing his expression, reading his eyes to see just how many secrets Kobb thought he knew.

"Say, I nearly forgot—I'm sorry to hear about the attack

last night. It's been one thing after another for you." Kobb tilted his head downward. An expression of pity. It was not a good look on him. "But listen, I read your response in the *Post* earlier, and I'm afraid you're wrong about the gang. About who's who."

Jim stared at Kobb's head that tapered into his shirt, at his shock of bright white hair, his sad beagle eyes. After he popped it, Jim wanted to run over that head once or twice with the wheels of the Ford. "Anything else?"

Kobb looked mildly affronted. "No," he said. "Only that I'd be careful, Mister Beely. It seems you've upset some dangerous characters."

After Jim was in the Ford, he watched the mirrors until Kobb left.

"The hell was all that?" Frank said.

"Fucker had my place bombed, too."

"Want to kill him?"

"He read what I told the papers. About his slate being the real gang. Bombing my place alongside his makes me look wrong. Like we're on the same side. And sends me a warning as a bonus."

"For a politician, seems efficient."

"He saw somebody was in the car and I said you were Ward. He says, 'The ice man, married to Pop's daughter?' Made sure to mention he knows where Pop's place is."

"Eh, let's kill him."

"No good. Kill one politician, another shows up in the same suit." Jim said he'd drop Frank at home. As they drove, Jim mentioned what the porter said about Maloney being at the Fontana earlier.

"Fifty says he's your bomber."

"Odds that short wouldn't cover the ticket."

"You see Pospisil wasn't there?"

Jim remembered Donnegan's surprise at hearing Pospisil's name. But that didn't make the inquest less suspect. "Not sure it says anything. He works alongside people he hates all day. Might not want to eat dinner with them."

They pulled up to Frank's place on Twenty-Second, the street's bricks a humming rumble beneath the car. Jim said he wanted to run by his house, check out the damage. Frank asked if he wanted a place to stay. Jim looked at the white clapboard one-story where Frank and Jennie made room for four daughters and two sons. "I'm fine at the office."

"You sure? We got room on the roof, looks like."

Jim told him to get some shut-eye, and Frank got out. Jim waited, idling, till Frank waved from his front door.

When Jim saw what was left of his and Molly's place, he circled the block twice, eye out for Maloney, a Packard Six, anything suspicious. But even that loose screw Maloney must've been bright enough not to stick around.

Jim parked alongside the curb and got out. He stood in the wet grass and weeds, under the light of a streetlamp. The fire crew must've made record time dousing the place, which was blown open like a kid's dollhouse along the north side.

The duplex might've been built before row houses, but the layout presaged them. Inside the front door, you could stay on the main level, pass through the living room to the kitchen and bath, or you could go up to the bedrooms. Some of the stair treads were intact, others blown off or dangling.

Jim hadn't exactly taken inventory the time he'd tried to

come back—he'd had tunnel vision, couldn't catch a breath. But now he saw Molly had left everything. The furniture, quilts, all the pictures on the walls. Anything she took must've been hidden away to begin with, in closets and drawers. And the radio. It looked like she'd taken the radio. She'd left the bulkier Victrola.

He looked up at her vanity dresser. The mirror was intact. The chair she sat in while she brushed her hair or powdered her face was upright and unmoved, as if to make a point, as if to say not even a goddamned bomb could topple it.

Right then, he missed her. He wasn't stupid about it—he knew if she materialized here beside him, he'd enjoy her company for eight or ten minutes before she reminded him how much she hated him, and that'd be followed by the ache of everything that ever had and hadn't panned out. Still, he wished like hell she could be here for those eight or ten minutes, standing here, looking at this absurd mess, this blown-open dollhouse they'd tried to live in. She'd love seeing the place blown to goddamned shreds. She'd finally love something. And she'd laugh, which would make him laugh, hard and long, until they both were light-headed.

14

Bombings weren't that uncommon. There'd been a few in the aughts and teens. What was uncommon was anybody getting pinched for one. Bombings generally worked the same way "homicide: no suspects" cases did. If somebody wanted to blame unions or anarchists, with the bonus of, say, inflating the cost of a county courthouse by half a million dollars, bombings were too useful to solve. But in lieu of an assassinated president or a grisly double-murder-suicide involving incest or mutilation, a bombing had solid odds of grabbing front-page headlines. Tonight's would get top billing and read like "gang warfare"—Kobb would make sure of it—so Jim decided to sleep through the morning edition. When he was back at the office, he took the phone off the hook, closed the shades, stuffed gauze in his ears, chased a sip of morphine with the last of his whiskey, and sacked out.

He awoke to pounding at the door. Daylight filtered in around the closed shades, and Jim marveled at how well he'd slept. He hadn't needed to take a leak, he hadn't turned or shifted because of a sore joint—he even had dried drool on his cheek, like he was a little kid. If he'd known sleep like that was still possible, Jim would've murdered Vern and blown up his and Molly's rented duplex every day of his life.

With the shades shut, the office was dark enough he could make out Ward's silhouette through the mottled glass and hallway light. Jim was relieved to see him, even if Jim couldn't tell him anything new about Gus. And nothing Jim could've found out would've changed things. Gus wouldn't have died when and where he did if Jim hadn't hired the guy to go drink. Jim realized there'd been no point in retracing Gus's steps all night. Not so far as Ward went.

Jim got up and let him in, then quickly and quietly shut the door and locked it.

Ward had Frank and Jennie's clean fleech-key pot on top of a crate. He set both on Jim's desk, then surveyed the room. "I been trying to call," he said. "What'll you do about the house?"

"Good riddance." Jim said he'd leave it. Once the lady who'd rented them the place figured out she couldn't make him pay for it, she could pawn or sell off anything salvageable. The landlady and the papers were why the phone was off the hook.

"You just wake up? Christ, Jim—it's lunch."

"Guess I'm catching up. Haven't slept like that in ages. What's in the crate?"

"Whiskey. Edie made you a cheese sandwich."

"Tell her thanks." Jim didn't want to roll up the mattress and slide it over by the closet, but he felt pressed to keep up appearances. He asked how Edith and Pop were.

Ward snapped then. "Jesus Christ. Everybody's goddamn fine." He wadded up his cap in a fist. "Jim, a guy working for you's dead, you got jumped, and now your goddamn house got blown up."

Jim wanted to point out what he had to Kobb, that the house was a rental, but Ward was too worked up. "Look. I know Gus wouldn't have died like he did if I hadn't paid him to drink. But he didn't get murdered. And the house blowing up, the guy that hit me—it's election-year antics. Hell, that pan Edith winged at me hurt more than the pipe did." Jim sat down at his desk. He eyed the receiver and considered hanging it up. He didn't.

Ward stayed standing. "Even if that's true—even if all that's right—none of it would've happened if you never made a deal with Tvrdik."

"Yeah, well." He didn't want to say the next part out loud. Aside from telling it to Frank last night, Jim had avoided saying it out loud, like not saying it could make it less true. "If I hadn't been such a goddamned easy mark, I wouldn't've let some down-on-his-luck mechanic who turned out to be a pervert stay in my house. Like you said—I would've locked the door and thrown a dresser against it. Then a whole hell of a lot wouldn't've happened."

That wasn't it, though. That wasn't all there was to it, and as long as he was saying it, he'd say all of it.

"And maybe if I hadn't married somebody who was incapable of being happy, of being goddamned content, maybe I wouldn't've had a kid whose life could get ruined by me being an easy mark."

Ward sat down and seemed to mull it over. Or he mulled

over what there was to say about it, which couldn't have been much. "Don't say that." He didn't look Jim in the eye. "You don't regret Addie."

Jim didn't know. Maybe he did.

There was a lot there to regret. He knew it the first time he saw that wad of flinging arms and jerking legs, eyes rolling around, taking in everything. It wasn't beautiful, that squirming wad; nothing about babies was beautiful. But Addie was something, all right. Something stupidly fragile, idiotically vulnerable, spat out into the rotten half of the world. Jim guessed it was more than half, the rotten part, so Addie's odds weren't great to begin with. He'd looked at the miniature fingers gripping his and wanted to say, I'm sorry, kid. I'm sorry life's hard and bad, and I'm sorry I can't do shit about it. You see terrible, senseless things. Terrible, senseless things happen to you, and then you die. And for most people, you having been there or not won't matter. To everybody but me and maybe your mother, you might as well never been born. You'll give people what they want, all of it—your time, work, thoughts—and it's wasted on math that's rigged. Sometimes you trick yourself into thinking there's better for you out there, some kind of break, but I can tell you there isn't. There won't be. You'll work and hurt till you get snuffed out or used up.

Jim guessed he could've said it. She wouldn't have understood it. She'd been a goddamned baby.

But he couldn't say it now, not to Addie and not to Ward. Jim couldn't say it any sooner than he could tell Ward he was lucky his own first kid died before he could fail it. Before the world could fail it. Jim couldn't tell Ward he was only slightly less lucky his second kid caught a glimpse of it all. Jim couldn't say it because saying it would be the one thing worse than what Ward had already been through.

So Jim said nothing.

Ward stood, set the pot aside, then yanked the lid off the crate. A bent piece of straw came up with it. He pulled out the sandwich. Edith had wrapped it in wax paper. "Eat." He tossed the sandwich in front of Jim. Then he said he needed to get back to work and left.

Jim did eat. The sandwich was fine.

After he'd eaten, he took his ticket to the cleaners and exchanged a dirty suit for a fresh one. Then he picked up the morning copies of the papers because he supposed the story was getting told whether he read it or not, and he was in it. So long as he was still upright and breathing, he might as well know what it said. He trudged back up to the office.

Kobb had sent a post-bombings letter to the *Tribune* and *Post*. The *Standard* said they'd "acquired a copy." All printed the righteous screed in full. He said the attacks were ordered by the king of the underworld, "a name everyone knows but dares not say, for fear of retribution." Jim wondered if Bill Haskell could sue anyway. Jim bet if Haskell's lawyer was good enough, he'd have a case. Kobb claimed that more nameless figures, ones in the current administration, were complicit. He said the bombings were a response to the attorney general being in town to express concern about a vice syndicate. Kobb said if nothing was done to curtail these dark forces, Omaha would soon be as dangerous a city as Chicago.

Jim ran the figures in his head. Sure, Chicago was more dangerous if you didn't adjust for population. The place had three and a half million people. Omaha had about two hundred thousand.

But Jim wondered how often a Chicago coroner ruled a death a suicide when the body was found in an outhouse with twenty-seven stab wounds and a slit throat. He wondered if Chicago ever had an ongoing "nuisance" involving out-of-towners stepping off trains and turning up corpses stuffed under porches. He wondered if the Cook County sheriff's wife ever drowned a drifter and never saw a day in court. He wondered if any mass graves were uncovered when a school got razed in Chicago's vice district. If you wanted to kill somebody, Chicago had the edge on options. If you wanted to get away with it, Omaha was a safe bet.

Jim turned to the statewide news. There was nothing about Vern being at large. The only Washington County news was from Blair. A longtime resident, George Shumway, had died while visiting a daughter in Omaha. There was nothing in the paper about a funeral, only that the body would be buried in Blair. Pete Gilson's undertaking rooms had him. Frank was right; the city still threw Pete a few bones. After he was axed as coroner, some gentlemen's agreement ensured Pete's place was used for inquests, and he got to drain and prep most of the city's runoff bodies, ones bound for Potter's Field or another city or state. The paper said George Shumway was survived by his wife, three daughters, and two sons, one of whom, John Shumway, was sheriff of Washington County.

A dead Shumway wasn't necessarily cause for concern. These things happened. Elderly relatives dropped dead during visits. It was what elderly relatives did. And the daughter in Omaha might make all the arrangements: have Pete doll the old guy up, drop him at the house for a family service, then leave.

And even if not, even if Sheriff Shumway made the trip to Gilson's to retrieve the body, Pete might not be wearing Vern's tie, which was just a tie, anyway. It was hand-painted, but that didn't mean it was the only tie like it. Sure, Jim knew if Vern wore a tie to his preliminary hearing it would've been that one. Jim had never seen Vern wear any other. But the sheriff might not have gone to the preliminary hearing. And if he did, he might not have noticed the tie.

As soon as it was dark again, Jim unrolled the mattress, pulled one of the bottles from the crate, and opened a book he'd had a few years and never managed to finish. A former client had left it, the coal dealer who hadn't wanted to pay his ex-wife alimony. Jim held on to it because of Edith and Ward—the broad who wrote it was named Edith Wharton. *Twilight Sleep*, it was called, and combined with a stiff drink, it generally worked as advertised.

He awoke to more knocking. He checked his watch, but it wasn't ticking and read 6:58. He'd left the light on, so he couldn't make out the silhouette. He reached for the pistol in its shoulder holster. He kept it between the mattress and the wall when he slept. He called out, asked who was there.

It was Frank. Jim let go of the revolver, got up, and let him in.

"Operator says your phone ain't working."

"I took a day off." Jim asked what time it was.

"So did I, I guess." Frank said it was half past four in the morning.

Jim was confused. Frank was in uniform. He looked distracted. Jim set his watch and asked Frank if he wanted a drink. He said he did. Jim poured him one and asked what happened.

"Hell if I can figure out. Yano's sister-in-law—wife's youngest sister—shot one of the other sisters' husbands. Didn't kill him right off the bat, but he'll be dead by lunch."

Jim tried to understand. "Yano's sister-in-law shot Yano's brother-in-law—but not the one she was married to?"

"Sounds right."

"That's too bad."

"Nah, guy was worthless. That's not the weird part. O'Neill and Dietz show up, I get pulled off the scene." He took a drink and replayed whatever happened in the air in front of him, trying to sort it out. "They say, 'Cap wants you back at the station.' I get there, Cap's got no idea. Didn't say no such thing."

"Did you go back to the scene?"

"Nah, I was too hot. Thinking about Dietz and O'Neill, the Fritz, about Maloney beaning you. Would've killed them both, not known why. I got a desk at the station. Sat and tried calling you the last four hours."

"I'm skirting the landlady and the papers."

"The papers," Frank said. "What time they get to the newsstand?"

"*Tribune*'s earliest. About five."

Frank must've decided five was close enough. He ran out, presumably to grab a copy. Jim didn't want to be awake, but he was, so he washed in the bathroom sink, dressed, and warmed water on the hot plate to make coffee.

Frank came through the door cursing in Czech.

"Teach me some of that so I know when you're talking about me."

"Gangland. Says it was a gangland killing. Yano's wife's sister's sister's husband."

"What?"

"Don't make me say it again." He threw the paper on the desk, and Jim read the headline: GUNS BLAZE IN LITTLE ITALY: STRBA SLAYED BY RUM SYNDICATE. Jim skimmed. A booze syndicate was suspected in the slaying of Yano's brother-in-law, Hal Strba. O'Neill and Dietz were called to the scene, no mention of Frank or even the sister-in-law. Strba was found shot three times. The attending physician said the outlook was grim. The inspector of detectives said the would-be slayer was at large. O'Neill and Dietz had received information about Strba's involvement in a liquor hijacking scheme. One that went against the interests of a newly formed vice ring.

Bill Haskell had the other big headline, offering a thousand dollars for a picture of Kobb's bomber—the implication being that Kobb ought to send Haskell a picture of himself, collect the reward, and get his porch fixed. Haskell was funny now and then. Or his lawyer was. Given what Frank said about Haskell's spelling, there was no chance he wrote the letter himself.

"Do like I did yesterday." Jim put a bottle of whiskey into the empty fleech-key pot. "Take a day off."

"Nah, soon as I fall asleep, Jennie's got me up fixing half the house while the kids wreck the rest."

"You can stay at my place, if you don't care about walls." Jim's mattress was still on the floor. "Want to stay here?"

"What am I, your honeydew? 'Just make me a pallet on your floor,'" he caterwauled in his best Ethel Waters. His best Ethel Waters was subpar. He looked around and gave a tired smile. "Nah, this place is a little depressing, Big Jim."

15

Later that morning, Jim caught up on the books and contemplated hanging up the phone. Donnegan had paid enough to tide Jim over a while, but he'd need work eventually—in part to pay for the phone, which was how most jobs came in. While Jim added and subtracted, three messages came slipping under his door. The first was the landlady, the second Art Silver at the *Post*, the third Yano Catalano. Yano's said, "Come by at your convenience." Jim decided now was convenient. He hung up the receiver and left the office. It felt like a compromise.

Since the message wasn't urgent, Jim walked. He'd clear his lungs, if not his head. He couldn't clear his head around here. Too many associations. He crossed Farnam and passed the alley where the Packard Six was most likely parked the other night. He hustled past the eight-story building where that flat-headed smirker Donnegan's office was. He passed a Scandinavian-owned café with a German name whose ad in the paper read, "A Man's Place to Eat: IN THIS MAN'S TOWN." Molly used to rattle the line off at full volume when they walked by.

At Howard, where Seventeenth also met St. Mary's Avenue, in an intersection so broad it looked like a stage set and so complicated it was a deadly public hazard, he went left, east, and refused to look across the street at Quivira Court, a joint that was like an ornate trinket in a jewelry shop case—a bauble with no price tag and if you had to ask, you couldn't afford it.

He'd never been in. The society column showed the place off plenty, and what it showed was goddamned offensive. One square block crammed with tea rooms, gift shops, furriers. Some milliner pounded out thimble-shaped women's hats. A handful of apartments housed rich small-*b* bohemians: philanthropists and artists who liked being big fish in the bucket of Omaha. If you passed the west side of Quivira, you could see the courtyard—all bushes and flowers, stone paths, fountains, pools—and a thick iron gate that reminded you where you stood.

There'd been more houses and shacks downtown years ago. Now there were a few residential hotels, and they weren't the Quivira. They were boardinghouses minus the food. If you said you lived in one, you'd get pinched as a vagrant.

He headed downhill toward the river and darted through intersections, between cars and streetcars, pedestrians, the occasional horse. On the sidewalk, he dodged bodies of shoppers bustling in and out of drugstores, barbers', and cafés serving chop suey or hamburgers. The closer he got to the Missouri, the bustling bodies were workers dragging pallets of tomorrow's garbage: mattresses, drapes, ladies' hose. The street was shadowed by smokestacks and brick- and iron-fronted buildings.

Jim made a right on Tenth, where the closest ware-house advertised oysters at wholesale. In Omaha. Oysters. The place stank to high heaven. He crossed the viaduct high above the railyards, where workers cobbled together a new Union Station, a $3.5 million replacement for one the city leveled because why the hell not. Across the tracks was the busy Burlington, and ahead, trees and neighborhoods sprouted. The sight let him breathe a little. Jim trudged up to Pierce and made a left. He didn't know if Yano's place would be open the day after a sister-in-law shot a brother-in-law, but Jim would try the back entrance first.

The alley was steep the day before yesterday, but the climb felt vertical in sober daylight. He'd sweated through his overcoat when he reached the brick basement. He tried the knob, and the door opened. Inside was dark like it'd been last time, and Jim braced himself for the snap of a snare. Instead a radio played Merle Johnston and His Ceco Couriers. Jim called out for Yano, who called back, said to come on in.

The stage was lit but there was no sign of the little sister, and Jim didn't smell anything cooking upstairs. Yano leaned an elbow on the bar and read a book. He didn't look jovial. He flipped the book over and started pouring Jim a drink.

"I got your call," Jim said. "Sorry to hear about your brother-in-law."

Yano paused, mid-pour. "What'd you hear about it?"

"Not much. But I heard it different from what the papers said."

Yano scrutinized him, then must've decided whatever he saw was okay. He finished pouring and gave Jim the drink. "Strba was a no-account. Had it coming. But it wasn't no syndicate shot him. O'Neill—Mickey's brother, the cop—and that partner, one with the ears, come by last night afterward. 'What do you know about the syndicate, Yano?' Asked if I gunned him down. I should've, the no-account, but they know I didn't. Frank knows I didn't, but those two sent him packing. Don't matter anyway. By the time they ask, they already decided. If I had any brains, I'd skip town now. Ten-to-one I get Sacco and Vanzettied or deported."

"Why you?"

Yano laughed. "Make that my epitaph: WHY HIM?" Jim thought about telling him his: THERE WAS NO WINNING. Maybe when private investigating and running soft drink joints dried up, they could go into business together writing epitaphs. "An Italian accused of being in a syndicate? Ask Capone and Luciano how that's working out."

He grabbed something from under the bar. A police notebook. It was standard-issue, cover emblazoned with a badge. "Reason I called. I caught O'Neill messing with wiring outside. Couple hours after they came by and hassled me. It was early. Still dark. He was up a pole, far end of the yard. Waited for him to shimmy down, saw this on the ground before he got there." He handed over the notebook. "It's got my address in it. Thought you might know what it's about."

Jim asked if the wire was still there. Yano said he'd clipped it after O'Neill left, but a strip of it was still hanging.

They went outside, to a phone pole at the southeast corner of the property. Even with the sun in his eyes, Jim made out the wire was wrapped around a bolt. "He was tapping a phone. Yours, I'd wager, since your address is in the notebook."

Yano was heated. "That's illegal. I'm naturalized—I got rights." For that second, he seemed to believe it. Then he apparently heard what he'd said and shook his head with a snort.

"State says it's illegal, but there's a fed loophole." They walked back down the alley and inside the bar. When Jim sat with his drink again, he thought about what the AG said at the Fontana fundraiser. "The 'liquor syndicate' thing—'vice ring'—there's nothing to it, right? You heard anything?"

Yano shook his head, irritated. "Nah, this town runs wide-open. Laws are for show. Only reason there's cops is to make people who got nothing to worry about worry less. Joints help each other out, sure, but it ain't no ring. Anybody gets robbed or raided, they call, warn everybody else. Other than that, booze is a business same as a grocer. Wholesalers and retailers. If that's a 'ring,'" he said, looking around the room, "we got barstool rings. Billiard ball rings. Light bulb rings—"

"No, I know," Jim said. "I know. I shouldn't've asked."

"Nah, it's all right." He rubbed down the bar with a towel. "Just ain't slept yet, sick of hearing it."

Jim flipped open O'Neill's notebook. The last few pages were address after address next to phone numbers and initials. Lines were drawn through dozens, and beside them all was a *D* or *O*. Next to *YC*—Yano Catalano, the last on the list without a line through it, was *O*. For O'Neill. It wasn't a tough code to crack. Two addresses down was a *D*—Dietz— next to *PN*. It was Pop's. Of course Pop's was on there. Kobb made a point of saying he knew right where Pop's was. "He'll come back for this," Jim said. He pulled his own notebook from his overcoat. "You got a pencil?"

Yano gave him one. O'Neill wrote with a heavy hand. Jim laid a blank page over the back of O'Neill's and rubbed the lead. It made a good print. Backward, but legible. He did the same with each page of the list.

"Put this out where it was." Jim slid O'Neill's notebook to Yano. "Doubt he'll come back till dark. He works nights." Jim told Yano to keep an eye out for wires on that pole and be careful what he said on the phone.

"What they after?"

"Proof there's a syndicate. And if they listen hard enough on half the phones in town, they'll find it, whether it's real or not."

16

Jim could've caught a streetcar at Thirteenth. The Kansas-Albright line ran practically to Pop's doorstep, but the streetcar stopped every block, and Jim didn't take streetcars. Maybe when there was a streetcar union, Jim would take the streetcar. Until then, let anarchists come and blow the goddamned things sky-high.

As soon as he got to the Ford, he hightailed it to Pop's. From outside, the place looked closed. The blinds were shut. But the door was unlocked, and when he opened it, Jim stood back in case anything flew at him. Nothing came. Instead of being behind the bar, Pop, Edith, and Ward sat at one of the tables in front. Jim couldn't tell if they'd stopped talking when he came in or if they'd been sitting in silence. They were somber. Or sheepish. Jim wasn't sure what they were. "What happened?"

They exchanged glances he couldn't read.

"Listen," he said. "Cops are tapping phones. I got the numbers, and this place is one of them."

"Yeah, we got one." Pop sounded grave.

"A wiretap?"

"A cop," Ward said.

"What do you mean, you got him?" As soon as Jim said it, he wished he could reel the words back in. The longer he didn't know, the longer whatever had happened hadn't.

"He's dead," Pop said. "In the basement."

"Christ," Jim said. "Lock the goddamned door, at least." He reached back and locked it himself.

Edith said she'd heard someone on the basement stairs, but nobody'd been down there today. When the steps creaked close to the door, she whipped it open with one hand and used the other to smack the guy with an empty bottle. Jim wondered where the cast-iron pan was. She said the cop flew back. Most of him hit the concrete. His head hit the pile of loose bricks. They were left over from when Ward covered the panel door. Then Pop had gone downstairs with his pistol.

"Head stoved in. He wouldn't have lived but a few hours," Pop said. "I couldn't leave him like that."

"We should've just called," Edith said bitter and low, more to herself than to her father.

"Called who?" The way Pop said it, Jim sensed the conversation had been repeated. "Who do you call when a half-dead policeman's broken into your basement full of liquor?"

"Why was he on the stairs?" Jim asked.

"It was my fault," Edith said. "I guess the lock didn't catch when I dumped the trash last night. The cop must've been in the alley, seen the crack in the wall. He'd run the wire through the stairwell. What the hell was he thinking? He'd camp out in the stairwell? Ward was on the phone with an order—cop must've snuck up to listen, make sure he had the right line."

"You cut the wire yet?"

Ward said he had. "Badge says Dietz. Dark hair, great big ears."

"Listen." Jim knew his next words might land the table on him. He set his feet shoulder-width apart. "Let me call Frank."

"Jesus Christ," Ward said.

"Jim," Edith said, like his name meant Come on, now. Be reasonable.

Ward stared down at his hands. "I know you think Tvrdik's all right." He was searching for a way to say what was on his mind. Jim could guess but didn't. Ward steeled himself. "You know better than anybody. You don't got a great track record. Of judging character."

"It's true." Edith sounded distinctly un-Edith-like. She was almost soothing. Jim was more jarred by it than if she'd screamed. "Just look at Vern."

Jim drew a breath against the mangle that mashed his innards anytime that goddamned name came out of somebody's mouth. But the crushing wasn't from the name, or what Vern did to Addie, or what Jim did to ensure he never had to see that weasel's face again. What pressed all the air out of him with a burn in his chest was the possibility. Because they were right. Jim had been a piss-poor judge of character. And Jim had once trusted Vern more than he'd ever trusted Frank Tvrdik. If Jim had been wrong—that wrong, about Frank—he shut his eyes and got the spins, like he'd drunk too much and tried to sleep too soon.

In the darkness behind his closed lids, he heard Pop say, "I trust him."

Jim opened his eyes and searched the old man's expression. He had that look of a carved marble bust, decided, authoritative.

Ward and Edith stared like Pop had chirped or mooed.

"What?" she said.

"I said I trust him. I trust that Frank."

"How?" Ward said. "He's crooked. A crooked cop, for chrissake. He takes protection."

"He's honest."

Edith talked like her father was a kid with a fever. "Pop, he's not a good man."

"Don't be simple," he snapped. "Show me a man who calls himself good, I'll show you a man with no brains. Or a tyrant. And tell me: What the hell use would a 'good' man be right now?"

Jim called Frank. He was half-asleep and Jim was vague. Kobb was right that Omaha was a big small town where secrets were hard to keep, and holding the lid on them was getting a hell of a lot harder. Jim didn't know if anybody was listening, but Frank's house was on the list of taps with a line through it, next to an *O*. That wire was already run.

Before Frank showed, Jim was still uneasy. What Ward and Edith said had him rattled. But when he unlocked the door and Frank strode through rubbing the sleep from his eyes, that purposeful bob in his step, Jim knew Pop was right. And so was Ward. Frank was crooked, and he was the first to admit it.

Jim didn't bother pulling Frank aside to brief him. Everybody in the room was up-to-date. Jim showed him a page copied from O'Neill's notebook. He told Frank about O'Neill running a wire at Yano's, then Dietz trying the same thing here. Jim told him Edith hit Dietz, Dietz fell down the stairs and caved in his head, and Pop put him out of his misery. "It's not good. I know it isn't. But who the hell were they supposed to call?"

Frank must've sensed the heaviness and alarm in the room. He tried to make light of it. "More like a little hassle," he said. "Saves me the trouble of killing him later, probably. I'll take care of it." He took off the button-down he was wearing, so he was in an undershirt and a pair of thick work khakis.

"Here," Pop said. "Let me get some coveralls."

"You got a tarp, some rope?"

Pop said he had a quilt.

"Make it one you ain't attached to—it ain't coming back."

Frank added to the list: some towels they didn't mind losing, a bucket, bleach, a wire brush, a pillowcase. Edith went to gather it all. Frank asked Jim for the keys to the Ford.

"I'll help," Jim said.

"Nah—no. Dead cop," Frank said quietly. "Anything goes wrong, you get the chair. I got a chance. To talk my way out of it. You take care of Pop and your brother and Edith. They're shook."

When he had everything he needed, Frank told them to close shop, go get some supper. "Get a malted milk," he told Pop, and flipped the old man a quarter. Frank said to go to Carl Ziske's place. Ziske ran one of the few real soft drink parlors in town, two blocks south on Twenty-Fourth. When Frank was through, he'd ring there once and hang up.

The four of them left. Outside, the sun's glare felt nonsensical—all this happening in broad daylight. Once they were seated in a booth at Ziske's, Jim tried to read the menu. The kitchen didn't serve much besides soup and sandwiches from cold cuts, but Jim wasn't hungry. Nobody was. They ordered anyway and picked at their plates to stall. Pop got a malted milk, chocolate, and told Carl he enjoyed it. Carl talked about the versatility of malted milk like he was on malted milk's payroll. He said you could add vanilla, almond, peppermint—even clove. Ward and Edith were silent, their eyes pinned to objects on the table. Things that were solid. Ward's spoon trembled against his coffee cup when he stirred in a little cream, and Edith looked wired from being worn out. Jim wondered if the last of the adrenaline was wearing off and dread was setting in. Jim had felt it, the day Molly said what Vern did to Addie. Jim wouldn't tell Edith the dread didn't let up. It seeped in so you stayed waterlogged with it.

Two and a half hours passed like that. Then the phone rang once. Pop was on his third malted milk. Everyone else stopped picking at uneaten food, stopped breathing. Carl answered the phone, waited, then shrugged and hung up. Jim took the lead. He went to the register and paid the check.

Pop's storefront was like they'd left it: the blinds closed, the door locked, the BACK SOON sign's clock hands set to 9:08. The same time was always on there and never meant anything. If Pop's was open, it was open. If it was closed, it was closed.

When they went in, Frank was wearing his own clothes again and drinking a Coke. Jim saw he'd left a dime on the bar. Frank asked Pop his size and said he'd get him a new pair of coveralls. They'd had to go.

"Is he—" Edith started to say. "Nobody can find him?"

"No him left to find," Frank said. "Never happened."

Pop walked to him. Jim expected the old man to thank Frank or shake his hand, but he didn't. Pop wrapped his arms around him and rested his forehead on Frank's shoulder. Frank held him like that. They stayed that way while Pop's shoulders shook.

17

The quilt had done its job—the backseat of the Ford was as clean as it ever was. Frank was in the passenger side, silent as they crossed the Twenty-Fourth Street viaduct into Omaha proper. They were headed to Jim's office. To get Frank talking, Jim asked what he'd done with Dietz. Frank had taken him to Pete, said to cremate him. Then Frank threw anything that might not burn off the Douglas Street Bridge, into the Missouri.

"Anybody see?" Jim asked.

"Toll taker maybe. Couldn't know what I tossed. Put Dietz's badge and wedding ring in a tied-off sack with half a brick, along with some tools, spools of wire." He went quiet again. "That Pop's a good guy."

Jim didn't explain Pop's philosophy on good men, only nodded.

Frank had kept Dietz's gun. "Might come in handy." He showed the revolver to Jim, then swung open the cylinder. "The hell's this?"

"What?"

"Round-nose lead, steel-jacket, copper-jacket, steel-jacket;

he's got soft-nose, round-nose, hollow-point—got a flea market in this thing." He swung it closed. "Shit. He had a watch. Dietz did. Wasn't in the sack."

"Pete probably burned or pilfered it." Jim pulled out his notebook and handed it over. "Should be handy, too. Who all they're tapping. You're on there."

Frank flipped through it. "All these lines—who listens in?"

"Morals, feds, other cops—no matter which, O'Neill and Dietz can't cover it." Jim caught a glance of Frank lighting a cigarette. He still had dried blood under his thumbnail.

Frank studied a page and gave a short chuckle. "There I am."

Jim pulled into a spot on Seventeenth. They got out and climbed the stairs to Jim's office.

When they'd sat down and Jim caught his breath, he read through the pages he'd copied. "Remember that mass indictment in Chicago last year?"

"Sure—forty-some defendants?"

"This many taps, think the AG's serious about working the syndicate angle. Government won't pay for a hundred trials, but they'll shell out for a conspiracy case with a hundred defendants."

"Yeah, but wiretaps. Illegal. Phone company didn't let them do it, so the feds didn't sign off."

"Could be for show. 'Wiretap' sounds G-man enough for the DA to dangle it in a speech, make a mass indictment sound like it's got teeth."

"But they can't use what they get." Then Frank said, "Shit. Sure they can. Grand jury."

"And if a grand jury says a trial's justified, and any evidence from the taps is worth using, it won't matter the state says they're illegal. Prosecution'll find some fed to sign off, backdate the order."

"Goddamn racket."

It was. It was a goddamned racket.

"What keeps them from slapping a phrase from one phone onto another?"

"Not much," Jim said. "They'll write up what they hear. Transcripts. They mishear something—they even want to mishear something—"

"Wait. All this goes way past Kobb getting a commissioner's seat. Grand jury and trial, that many defendants? We're talking a year, two years out."

Jim tossed the notebook across the desk. Frank picked it up and glanced through addresses and initials again.

Jim remembered what he could about mass indictments in Detroit, Chicago, New York. "You see *BH* on there? Bill Haskell?"

Frank skimmed. "Nah, but Haskell don't go near prostitution. Or gambling no more. And he ain't no bootlegger, heard he don't even drink."

"Mass indictments always got a ringleader. For headlines. Hell, they'll probably tie Capone in somehow. Haskell's obvious. Why ain't he on there?"

"Because it's all horseshit?" Frank threw the notebook on the desk and leaned back, threaded his hands behind his head. "Well," he said, "I, for one, am glad they got me on here. Sure, it's for taking protection—helps the 'conspiracy' angle—but at least somebody else's gotta listen to Jennie's ma. Yelling about her gout every goddamn day and night." His eye caught something on the notebook he'd tossed. He picked it up. "*CP*," he said. He rattled off the address. "Don't Cy Pospisil live on Nineteenth?"

Jim flipped open the city directory and found Pospisil's address. It matched the one on the list: 613½ South Nineteenth. "Why you think he's on there?"

"Maybe being tapped clears him, maybe it don't. Let's pay him a visit. Feel him out."

Jim said it'd be worth a try, but another thought was more pressing. "What happens when O'Neill figures out Dietz is AWOL?"

Frank thought, eyes scouring the space between himself and Jim's desk. "Lot of names on that list. It'll take a while. For O'Neill to figure out where Dietz left off." He looked up, an urgent glint in his eye. "We stall him. Let's get some wire."

Frank said O'Neill wouldn't be on patrol for a couple hours, when Frank would be clocked in, too.

They sped to Frank's and dug around in his garage. They couldn't be seen buying wire at any hardware stores, which meant pickings were slim. There was no wire identical to what Dietz had used, but Frank had two spools of a narrower gauge with the same black rubber coating. It'd have to do.

Climbing phone poles at dusk was not a thing Jim was made for, but Frank was light on his feet and didn't seem to mind the exercise. Jim served as lookout. They went back to Pop's and rewired the bolt, then ran lines at five more addresses scattered on that page and the next. They picked places that were easy, where they wouldn't be seen. They made the work look as earnest as they could, running lines into empty upstairs offices, abandoned sheds, wherever a cop could plausibly hole out and snoop, like Dietz thought he could in Pop's stairwell. Whenever O'Neill came looking for his partner, he'd see a few places were skipped and assume there was a reason—a homeowner outside working on a car, a dog yapping and drawing attention.

When they were low on daylight hours, Jim and Frank tracked down Pospisil's place. It was between the Quivira and Maymie's to the west a couple blocks. Pospisil's half address, 613½, was an upstairs flat in a beige-brick building.

They were halfway up the concrete stairs when Pospisil came out. They asked him for a minute. He said make it quicker. He was surly. He said he needed to catch a streetcar and get his damned mother. She was nursing some old Greek. Pospisil suspected the Greek was faking stomach cancer to get her attention and half Pospisil's paychecks.

Frank must've been accustomed to being the most abrasive person in a room. He reciprocated Pospisil's lack of cordiality. "First off, your phone's on a wiretap list. You're welcome. Second, how'd you get homicide out of that inquest at Gilson's?"

"Wiretap?" Pospisil wasn't worried, only more irked than usual. "Why?"

"Start with the homicide, maybe we'll say," Frank told him.

"It's in the paper. Get somebody to read it to you. Guy was shot four times."

"You know how blood works? Guy was dead first. Then shot."

"The fuck are you talking about? Guy bled out his thigh and heart."

"The fuck am I talking about? The fuck are you talking about?"

They were like a pair of goddamned roosters. Jim shoved himself between them so he faced Pospisil. "We saw the body before the inquest. Four bullet holes but only traces of blood."

"I don't know who or what the hell you saw, but the back of that guy's clothes was soaked through. Fair amount pooled in front." He rattled off the wounds: "Left chest. Right collarbone, abdomen, and thigh. You want to dig him up, I'll sign the papers. Quit hassling me. Go bug the police surgeon. Somebody on the jury. Not like it was just me and Gilson there." He leaned around Jim to yell at Frank. "Who the hell's tapping my damned phone?"

"Couple cops," Frank said.

"We think the AG's building a conspiracy case. Vice ring." Jim didn't mention Kobb, Wright, or Donnegan. For one, the list of participants was getting too long. For another, if Pospisil was in on it and playing dumb, Jim needed to play dumber.

Pospisil threw his head back and rolled his eyes. "More syndicate shit."

Frank said, "Sounds like they're working up a mass indictment. Pinch the whole town." Then he added, "Heard Bob Wright's kid's getting assistant DA. Probably prosecute the whole deal."

If he was testing the city attorney, seeing what Pospisil knew, it worked. "That pimpled little pissant. He even pass the bar yet? Fuck this town."

"You didn't hear it from us," Jim said. Maybe word had traveled, but if it hadn't, the assistant DA detail drew a straight line from Harry Donnegan to Frank and Jim to Pospisil.

"I didn't hear it at all. Those bastards want to build a phony case to get me out? Watch. Tomorrow I'll get a telegram about a job in Los Angeles. Put in my notice. I got a sister out there. We'll move for Mother's health." He checked the time and shot past Jim and Frank down the stairs.

He was halfway up the hill to Leavenworth when Frank yelled, "You're welcome."

Without turning back, Pospisil flipped Frank the middle finger.

Jim said, "Pleasant fella."

"He's a goddamn prick, but he's telling the truth."

"Yeah, but how? We saw that body with our own two eyes."

"Four." Frank was distracted, thinking something through.

"What?"

"You said our own two eyes. You and me, collectively, Big Jim, we got four." He pinched his bottom lip in thought. "Pospisil don't play nice with nobody. He don't do no favors. He ain't buddied up with nobody tapping his phone, and what's he get—fixing the Fritz up like a murder? No. That guy—" Frank's eyebrows lifted like he was impressed and even a little astonished. "That is not a guy who pays off a coroner's jury to agree with him. He ain't just a prick. He's a grade-A prick." Frank pulled out a cigarette and lit it. "Shit," he said. "Shit, shit, shit. Big Jim. This ain't good."

It was not good. It was bad. "Pete staged it?"

"Who else got regular access to gallons of blood, seen

thousands of crime scenes? Misses politics. Always happy to make a dirty buck."

"And we just handed him a dead cop. One who's in on the whole syndicate sham." When Jim had taken Vern to Pete, Pete held up his end. Frank bringing in Dietz—Pete might've had incentive not to. "Did you see him do it? Cremate Dietz?"

"Christ." Frank shut his eyes and pinched the bridge of his nose.

The streetlamps lit on Nineteenth. It must've been near seven o'clock. Jim asked if Frank had time to go by Pete Gilson's.

"Give me a bit." Frank said he'd run home, change, and check in early at the station, say he couldn't sleep. Then, so long as Pete hadn't called the captain right after Frank dropped off Dietz, so long as Frank didn't get pinched for killing a fellow cop when he reported for duty, he'd swing by Jim's office.

When they reached Jim's Ford parked by the curb, Frank asked, "You know how to work a crematory if we need to?"

18

After Frank apparently checked in at the station and wasn't arrested for a murder he didn't commit, he showed up at Jim's office. He said he'd double-checked the schedule. O'Neill and Dietz were supposed to come on at nine, about thirty-five minutes from now. Before Jim and Frank could leave for Pete Gilson's, Frank pulled a slip of wadded paper from his pocket and tossed it on the desk. Jim unwadded it. It was the license plate number of the Packard Six with "Mary E. Maloney" written underneath. "His ma's car," Frank said. "Real resourceful."

"Well, it tells us one thing."

"Sure. He's a loser—borrows his ma's car to commit assault."

"That and he's got no fear of being caught."

"So he's a birdbrain, or he's got nothing to lose?"

"Maybe he knows he won't get pinched. I don't know what it means." Jim felt like he was staring at a single brick in a wall, red and pocked and grainy. He needed to take twenty steps back if he wanted to see the building.

They drove the Ford to Pete Gilson's. Jim slowed to a putter and made a loop around the block with an eye out for anyone coming or going. Frank not getting arrested or even asked about Dietz was a good sign, but there was too much they didn't know. They didn't know if Pete had cremated Dietz. They didn't know how deep Pete was in with whoever benefited from Gus looking like a homicide victim. Jim parked a block west, on Twenty-Fifth. If worse came to worst with Pete, at least the Ford wouldn't be in the back lot or sitting curbside for a bystander to see.

The tenements across the alley from the mortuary were dark and quiet. Everyone must've been working second shift, sleeping off first or third, or drinking at a nearby bar to cope with lives that whirred by in shifts. Jim and Frank shut the car doors as quietly as they could. They crept around the apartment building and through the alley, keeping to the shadows.

Jim tapped the steel door. The peep window shifted and Pete welcomed them in before locking the door behind them. Jim scanned the room for both Dietz and a dead George Shumway, father of the Washington County sheriff. The only person who was out in the open, dead or living, was Pete. And if Pete had any idea what hell he was about to catch from Frank, his face didn't show it.

Jim didn't feel good about that. Even if Pete planned to double-cross Frank, and thereby screw Pop, Ward, and Edith, Jim didn't feel good looking at Pete's slack-jawed grin, at those unsuspecting bug-eyes of his, at the way his belt was cinched tight and tied off because he'd grown too thin to use the first hole. He was wearing Vern's hand-painted horseshoe tie again, but instead of squeezing Jim's innards, the tie stilled them like an omen. A terrible inevitability. Jim knew Pete wasn't frail—he couldn't be frail and maneuver lifeless bodies all day—so what Jim felt had nothing to do with Pete being old or helpless. Nor did Jim suddenly fancy Pete a saint. He was a person, and as such, he'd done rotten things. He'd likely back-stabbed Frank, he'd almost definitely poisoned his first wife, and he'd made an ugly living off death, bilking mothers and fathers and kids in the moment they were rawer than they'd ever been, overcharging them to primp people they loved for burial. For years, he'd stolen tax money those same people couldn't afford, promising answers he never bothered looking for and justice that wasn't possible. Justice that wouldn't have changed a goddamned thing if it had been.

Still, here was Pete, a person, with memories he mourned or conjured to get through the everyday of living. And he was about to catch hell. Jim didn't know how literally Pete might catch hell, but Pete was in for it.

"What can I do you for?" he asked them, hands on his shrunken waist. Jim eyed the perforated drain. He'd let Frank take the lead.

"Anybody in the cooler tonight?"

Pete was surprised by the question, but he probably wasn't asked often. "Right now? Why, it's empty."

"You sure about that?" Frank walked to the cooler.

Before he could open either door, Pete made a fuss. "That top latch sticks. Just leave it. I'll never get it closed. Say, Frank, what's this all about? The fella you brought by? I took care of it. That's why it's so damn hot in here."

The room was hot as hell, all right.

Frank opened the top compartment, then the bottom.

Both were empty, and Jim felt a cool relief. He'd fully expected Dietz to be stashed in there, but even the dead Shumway was gone. Jim had been at the office all day yesterday and in and out today. If the sheriff had picked up his father's body, seen Vern's tie hanging from Pete's neck, and thought it meant anything, thought it connected an Omaha local to Vern's disappearance, Jim had motive and wouldn't have been tough to find. There would've at least been a message.

Frank looked relieved, too. He was taking a long breath and leaning a forearm against the wall by the crematory. Its door was open. Jim hadn't studied the door before. It was thick, the interior lined with brick. Frank asked how the thing worked. Gas, Pete said.

"You gotta get it going, warm it up ahead of time?" Frank was making small talk, Jim sensed, stalling for time to think.

Pete said, why, yes, he did need to warm it up. He was eager to tell how it worked in great detail, likely because it was the kind of accumulated knowledge nobody else wanted to know the first thing about. He said it didn't take too long to heat. Cremating time depended on size, of course.

Frank pulled a cigarette from his shirt pocket. "Pete, we stopped by because I'm troubled." Pete lit a match for him. "The fella we came in about Friday—one shot after he was dead." Frank puffed a few times to make sure his smoke was lit. "We paid Pospisil a visit—deputy county attorney did the inquest. Lot of blood, he said. Soaked through the back of the clothes, big splotches on the chest. But when me and Jim came down here, wasn't hardly any. Where'd all that blood come from?"

"Oh hell, he doesn't know what he's talking about. That's

what you get, attorney playing coroner. Doesn't know his ass from his elbow."

Frank shut his eyes and rubbed his thumb between his brows. "Pete, there's three ways you could've answered the question. The first was how you did: he saw it wrong. The second was we saw it wrong—but you're bright—you know we didn't. The third way, one I'm after, was to say how not just Pospisil but a police surgeon and a whole goddamn coroner's jury saw all that blood." Jim and Frank hadn't talked to the police surgeon or anybody on the jury, but that seemed immaterial at the moment. "And something you said when Jim came by—you said you didn't know why the guy was so 'golldang popular.' Who was he popular with? Who was it said to make it look like homicide? And why the hell'd you go along with it?"

Pete waited, like he hoped Frank would offer a fourth option. When he didn't, Pete said, "O'Neill. That detective O'Neill said to do it. He said if I did, Elmer Kobb's about to get a commissioner's seat. Knows a way to get me back on as coroner."

Frank covered his face in his hands and let out a long grunt-huff of frustration.

Pete had been county coroner three times. He should've goddamned known, but since he didn't, Jim broke the news. "Pete. Coroner's office is a state deal. City commission's got nothing to do with it."

"Well, I know that." He sounded insulted. "But Kobb's got state backing. He's got the AG—all those people."

Before Jim could tease out whether Pete had a point or was being delusional, someone knocked on the steel door to the basement. Jim darted a look at Frank. Frank checked his watch, cursed it for stopping, and asked the time.

Before Jim could dig his out, Pete checked his watch. He whispered, "Five after nine."

"Who's that?" Frank said.

Pete said it was O'Neill. Dropping off Strba for the inquest tomorrow.

"He can't know we were here," Jim told him.

Pete's gangly arms waved them toward the stairwell. "Go on. Quick." He said they could sneak out the front.

They made their way upstairs and peeked through the drapes to see if anyone was posted outside or walking past. No one. They went out, heads down, eyes on the sidewalk. They took the long way around the block to the Ford.

Neither said anything until they were in the car. Once they were, Jim thought out loud, sifting through it. "Kobb and the AG—why the hell would a state official pull a city commissioner into some long game?"

"Christ," Frank said. "Even if Kobb don't get a seat, you know he'll get an appointment."

"Give me a cigarette." Jim remembered Yano going on about barstools and billiard balls. "How the hell's that not a ring—some kind of syndicate?"

Frank lit a cigarette and passed it to him. "Well, you know who we can ask about Kobb."

Jim sighed smoke and dread. "You know Maloney's mother's address?"

19

Mrs. Mary E. Maloney, Jack Maloney's widowed mother, owner of a Packard Six, license plate 1–1743, ran a decrepit rooming house that had no address. The city directory read, "Nineteenth and Capitol." It was five blocks northwest of the Henley-Barr, near the peak of the uniform mound that was downtown Omaha. Jim and Frank parked out front, on Nineteenth. A streetlight lit the whole mess. Before Jim's time, the rooming house was a tony mansion surrounded by other tony mansions, all built in the '60s. On the steep hillside behind the Ford was a high school where a pre-statehood territorial capitol had been—hence the name of the avenue— residue of a city's wishful thinking. The area was dubbed Capitol Hill District. It'd been Omaha's West Farnam before West Farnam, except its streets, which were now bricked up and paved, had allegedly been muddy enough to swallow horses. Jim guessed it was plausible. It was plausible that people who could afford to live on the hill back then could afford disposable horses. The people who couldn't lived on the river bottoms, where, it was said, mud-drowned horse corpses were dragged to decompose. It was a history the city clung to and repeated at every chance. Of course they did. If the story was true, it showed how far Omaha had come. So long as you forgot the squatters down by the dump.

Other homes that once stood near the rooming house were named: Henley Place, Pickard Home, McEvaney House. This one wasn't. It was commissioned by a dead banker who moved his family whenever a more fashionable neighborhood cropped up, so they weren't here long. They'd deserted Capitol Hill and named each house after it Sunnybrook. The first was just Sunnybrook, the second Sunnybrook Castle. The banker's kids still lived in Sunnybrook Farm, which had no farm. It was in a neighborhood. It had a goddamned yard. Maybe the banker thought adding "farm" implied the land had been in the family for generations, despite those generations being buried in someplace like goddamned Maryland. In any case, the rooming house never had a name or even an official address—only "Nineteenth and Capitol." Jim wondered if that was why it persisted—why the house still stood, the last vestige of Capitol Hill District, surrounded by auto garages and filling stations and the high school. Anonymity. No name, no number.

Jim was smoking again. He nursed the final pair of drags and dreaded the rooming house. The place dreaded him back. In a Hawthorne or Poe story, the mansion might've been a carriage house, but in Omaha it took up three-quarters of a city block and was less house than landlocked ship. The top floor, the third, was a dark-shingled roof with dormers that reminded him of portholes. The white clapboards below were clouded from coal dust and tear-streaked with snowmelt. Three brick chimneys resembled masts, and the place was set back high on the lot so when Jim stared without blinking, the thing seemed to be floating off. He wished it would. He wished it'd hurry the hell up. "You been in there?" he asked Frank.

Frank said he hadn't. He said it looked like a joint you'd get murdered in.

Tire tracks ran through the yard and around back. "If you never got called here, probably nobody got murdered here."

"Or: it's a joint where people get murdered real well."

That did seem more likely. Jim wondered if there was one city block without eight or ten corpses stashed under poured concrete basements. Frank popped open his door but didn't get out.

Jim dropped the stub of his cigarette. "Let's get it over with."

Despite all the tracks from tires and feet that crossed the yard, Jim and Frank followed the snaking steps and concrete walk to the stairs, which they mounted to reach the screen door. It was latched, but the inside door was open. Jim rapped on the wood frame and peeked into the chandelier-lit parlor. The room was exactly what Jim pictured when he heard the word *parlor*. Paintings strung on wires tilted out and hovered. Rugs from civilizations thousands of years old lay everywhere. Ferns in urns sat on pedestals built exclusively for fern urns to sit on. The furniture was wicker and cane, and a giant brass spittoon had green palm fronds fanning from it—where did somebody get fresh palm fronds in Nebraska in spring?

A woman appeared in an entryway at the parlor's edge. Jim felt faint at the sight. He felt like he'd drunk morphine again and was staring up at a Florsheim attached to a guy with burlap cat ears using a ridiculous phony voice, saying he wasn't who he was. Everything was off, like a fun house on a carnival midway. The house was Victorian, the woman Edwardian. She'd walked straight off a 1906 magazine cover. She either wore a corset under her dress or had worn one often enough to be permanently shaped like it, and her ass and hips must've been padded. They just—they must've been padded. She was tall and long and curved and her caramel hair was piled atop her head like a grand hat.

She glided—like she was on goddamned tracks—to the door and unlatched it. The streetlamp lit her face, which looked like something swiped off a cover of sheet music or a soap advertisement—white and poreless like a paper sketch, with rosy cheeks. If she had an age, if age applied to her, if she was not an apparition, she might've been thirty. A very youthful thirty-five, tops.

Jim managed to say he was looking for Jack Maloney. Did she know him? Why, yes, he's my son, she said. Jim registered the information while he quickly unfolded and folded the hand he'd used to knock. He was checking it for feeling. Between the time travel and the gliding, he wanted assurance he wasn't sleeping or dead.

She invited them in to sit on the davenport, which looked like it could've been an actual Davenport, and offered them tea. Jim wouldn't have thought Frank the type to go in for tea, but he said he would enjoy some very much, thank you.

"Is he home?" Jim asked. "Can I speak with him?" He felt like he was asking a medium at a séance.

Frank elbowed Jim's ribs. "Forgive my friend's manners. He keeps pretty coarse company."

Her head turned in a blush and she gave Frank a delicate smile before gliding away, disappearing behind the entryway. Somewhere in the rooming house was a noise. *Tack tack tack tack tack tack tack ding, tack tack tack tack tack tack tack vroot. Tack tack tack tack tack tack tack ding.*

"That thing I said about Maloney being a loser?" Frank said low. "I take it back. If that was my mother—"

Jim stopped him. "If that was your mother, she'd be your mother, you degenerate."

Tack tack tack tack tack tack tack ding. Tack tack tack tack tack tack tack. Somewhere behind the walls, she called, "Jack." The tacking stopped.

"Like an aria," Frank said. "Listen to that voice."

"You're a crackpot. Let's get out of here."

"You're the one went all moon-eyed when you seen her."

Jim couldn't explain to Frank that while, yes, the woman was picturesque, Jim hadn't gone all moon-eyed—he'd just felt like he'd drunk too much morphine and was hallucinating as the life left his body.

A floorboard creaked a flight or two above. It was followed by the lazy clip-clop of shoes familiar with a set of stairs. A "Yeah?" responded, and the woman said something melodic but unintelligible.

Maloney rounded the entryway in his Florsheims, fists shoved deep in his pockets. If he was the least bit surprised by Frank and Jim sitting in his alleged mother's parlor, he didn't look it. He smiled and greeted them. "Fellas." He sat in a plush blue velvet chair, a proper parlor chair with carved rosewood legs. Besides the Florsheims, he wore a pair of plaited sharkskin trousers, a white shirt that looked made to fit but billowed, and a garnet-colored cravat that matched his lip-rouge dashes of eyebrows. His hair was a coppery blond pomade curl. A mole on his right cheek was dabbed on with mascara.

"You looked better in a burlap sack." Jim studied Maloney as best he could without looking at him any more than necessary. That woman couldn't have been his mother. Maloney had to be thirty, even if he acted nineteen. Or just squirrely. Jim had been nineteen once—he hadn't acted like Maloney.

"No idea what you're talking about," Maloney said, then winked. He was chewing gum. "Ma," he called out. "Get me a malted milk."

Jim shook off the sense he was dreaming. "Pretend you got one rational thought in your head a minute. What's Elmer Kobb's long play?"

"Wouldn't you like to know."

Jim's patience was stretched thin enough to snap. "Yes. I would like to know. The only reason I'm sitting on this goddamned couch is I'd like to know."

"How's she your ma?" Frank asked.

Maloney ignored him. "What's it worth?"

Jim turned to Frank. "Forget it. I'd rather ask Kobb." Jim meant it, but Kobb wouldn't give up anything, at least not till after the election. Besides, Jim pictured that balloon-headed sad-beagle Kobb and couldn't take it. "What's it worth?" he asked Maloney. "Whatever they're doing, it's likely halfway done. If I knew what it was, what the hell could I even do about it?"

Maloney looked smug, and then Jim understood. All Maloney cared was that he knew something somebody else didn't. Well, Maloney could screw. Jim pushed himself upward, off the davenport, and nailed his head on an oil painting tilted out from the wall.

"Three bucks," Maloney said.

Jim studied his expression. Maloney was straight-faced. Not deadpan. He was serious.

"Give me three bucks, I'll tell you."

Jim turned to Frank again. Was he hearing this? "Three bucks?"

"All right, two," Maloney said.

Jim couldn't believe he was doing it, but he pulled three dollars from his pocket and put one back. He handed the two bucks to Maloney and sat again.

"Is she your stepmother?" Frank asked. "Like your real ma died, Dad found a gal half his age?"

Maloney shoved the money in a pocket. "First off," he said to Jim, "I'm not marrying Maymie Strunk. Period. I don't care how rich she is. I can get a rich broad that doesn't have gold fangs."

"Kobb," Jim said.

"Soon as he's on city commission, he puts me back on police. And when he makes mayor, I'm his special investigator. Me and a guy from the Secret Six. Not that I'll need income. I'll be flush by then. But status, you know."

"Secret Six are Chicago businessmen. You mean one of their investigators?"

"You know what I meant, bright boy."

"How's Kobb so sure he'll get a commissioner's seat?"

"It's a cinch. He's got the AG behind him, plus he's giving the DA a grand jury and trial that'll make Fatty Arbuckle's look like croquet on a lawn. And how wouldn't he get a seat? Gangland murders—"

"Better hope you don't get subpoenaed about those," Frank told him.

"Pshaw. I never murdered anybody."

"Neither did no gang." Frank turned to Jim, "He really just say, 'Pshaw'?"

"You didn't need to murder anybody," Jim told Maloney. "You're a lackey with lackeys."

Maloney was defensive. "I do plenty."

"Sure. Bean me, blow up my house—"

"Prove it. And you think I need to be 'subpoenaed'? I'll volunteer. I've got Harry Donnegan on retainer and twenty movie producers who'll pay top dollar for what I know." He swiped a hand through the air like he was gripping an invisible theater marquee as he read it. "*Star Witness*, they'll call it. I'll show up to court in double-breasted silk, cleansed by the holy water of immunity." He leaned back in the parlor chair, shut his eyes, and let his arms go limp, palms up, as if he were luxuriating in the water.

Jim and Frank exchanged a look. Maloney was out of his goddamned gourd.

Maloney opened his eyes again. "Hell, I even got a story about Haskell meeting Capone in Chicago last month. Top that."

"Capone was in Pennsylvania last month," Frank said. "In jail. Read a paper."

Maloney looked at Frank like he was some quaint dullard. "Who'll remember? Trial won't be till thirty-two."

That'd been Frank's math back at the office, between a grand jury and a trial—he'd said a year, two years out. Jim asked, "Why thirty-two?"

Maloney somehow raised one of the eyebrows that wasn't an eyebrow, like now Jim was the dimwit. "The AG's reelection. They got it all worked out. Him, Kobb, Wright, DA. It'll be the end of the road for old Bill Haskell, if he lives that long. When the underworld king's dethroned, the DA and AG look like they cleaned up Omaha. It'll convince the rest of the state the AG's worth keeping."

"Wouldn't put money on it," Frank said. "You think people out in sticks like drys? They got bootleggers in every nook and cranny."

"Like you know," Maloney said. "It's all apple pie and tent revivals out there. And if it isn't now, the stories I got about Haskell and gun molls and the Omaha rackets—it'll scare the Jesus into 'em."

The woman who couldn't have been Maloney's mother returned with a tray of tea and malted milk. Jim decided it was best he not look at her. He apologized for her going to so much trouble. He said they needed to be on their way. Frank gave Jim's ankle a sharp kick but got up.

Frank wished Maloney luck. Jim wished only to be out of there.

20

As Jim got his bearings from being inside the rooming house run by Maloney's alleged mother, he took Frank to his motorcycle, parked in front of City Hall.

Before Frank got out, Jim said, "Positioning."

"What?"

"After the permit renewal meeting. After I threw out Donnegan. You said maybe Kobb was 'positioning' him. Kobb made it look like Donnegan got backstabbed. If Donnegan's Maloney's defense in a mass indictment—"

"Okay, but Maloney's a kook."

"He's a kook, but if there's anything to it, if he really does end up star witness making all the accusations about a syndicate, it won't matter that Donnegan's a defense lawyer. He defends Maloney, he's on the prosecution right alongside the AG, the DA, and the brat. That aspirin-capsule-headed Clerk of the District Court Bob Wright's kid."

Frank gave a one-beat chuckle. "Aspirin capsule. A great big aspirin that gives you headaches instead of curing them."

Jim tried to take his mind off piecing things together. It was making him woozy like he'd been at the rooming house.

He wanted to lie down. He didn't know if he'd sleep, but he wanted to lie down and feel something solid beneath him. He told Frank to be safe and then waited, made sure the motorcycle started.

When Jim went back to the office, a phone message was slipped beneath his door. It was from Washington County Sheriff John Shumway, telling Jim to call tomorrow morning, Saturday. The number was in Blair, which meant if Shumway had come to Omaha to retrieve his father's body, he'd done it and gone home. Which could've been a good sign—lack of urgency. Then again, if he'd been hauling his dead dad in a truck bed, maybe Shumway hadn't been up for tooling around town.

And what wasn't a good sign was that Shumway called at all. Worse, he'd called on a Friday night. The time on the message was 10:30 p.m.

Jim tossed the message on his desk by the phone, unrolled the mattress, and lay there in his overcoat and holster and suit but with his eyes shut, hearing the *tack tack tack tack tack tack tack ding, tack tack tack tack tack tack tack vroot. Tack tack tack tack tack tack tack ding.*

It was a typewriter. Of course it was a goddamned typewriter. What else? Jim heard typewriters all day long. Maloney was probably drafting his screenplays or letters to Hollywood up there. Why hadn't Jim recognized the sound of a typewriter?

Because everything in that place had been off. The nameless, numberless house was dislodged from time. Context. So everything inside lacked context, too. Without context, a thing as familiar as a typewriter was unrecognizable. Like seeing your barber at Hinky Dinky buying canned milk. You knew who the hell he was but couldn't for the life of you place him.

The rooming house had worn him out. Between that joint and the message from Shumway, Jim felt weighted down and spent. He drifted off in his clothes without a sip of booze.

When the phone rang, he didn't answer. If it was Shumway, Jim needed to think through what he'd say. If the sheriff had been to Pete's and recognized Vern's tie, he might've asked Pete about it. If he did, what the hell would Pete have said?

It was still dark out. Jim checked the time. He'd slept two hours. Not long enough for today to count as tomorrow, and Jim didn't need any more today. Today had been more than enough. He got up, took off his overcoat and suit jacket and holster. The phone kept ringing as he loosened his tie and unbuttoned the shirt behind it. He sat down at his desk, pulled out the bottle of whiskey, and poured himself a few swallows. He took a cigarette from the silver case in his pen drawer, lit it, then left the case sitting open on his desktop. He was a smoker again. He might as well keep the cigarettes out.

When the phone didn't stop ringing, Jim gave in. If it was Shumway, he'd wing it. He answered.

It wasn't Shumway. It was Frank. "Pete's dead. Come to Pop's." He hung up.

21

Jim rebuttoned his shirt but scrapped the tie. He pulled on his holster and overcoat again and smoked. The news about Pete shook him awake, but he felt like he was dreaming as he mulled it over: Pete was dead. It felt crass, mulling that over. It felt crass polishing off a drink and smoking while Pete Gilson was dead.

As he headed down to the car, Jim remembered Pete a few hours before and sensing Pete was in for it. Jim had known there was a chance, as he'd stared down at the perforated drain, that Frank just might kill Pete. Jim had seen the tie with the hand-painted horseshoes and thought that tie was an omen, the sign of a terrible inevitability.

Maybe Jim didn't give old wives' tales enough credit. Maybe they did say what was coming. If so, they were still worthlessly unspecific. Jim and Frank had left, and Pete had been spared. He'd been spared so he could die sometime between then and when the phone rang. Because he'd still been in for it. Because everybody was. Because death was the only numbers game with sure odds.

Jim pulled up to park. Pop's should've been open for

people getting off second shift, but the storefront was dark, the blinds closed, the sign hung in the door saying Pop would be back at 9:08. Jim looked up and down the street. No one was lurking. No one Jim could see, anyway. He got out and checked the front door. It was locked. He listened for any sound there was to hear. Distant traffic. A train. Doomed cattle in the stockyards lowing, crying for lost calves. He thought to move the car. He drove around to the end of the block, made a left, and looked down the alley. No sign of anyone. He drove through the intersection and parked, shut off the Ford, and pulled the gun from his holster.

He jogged across the street. He searched for the back door made to blend seamlessly with the brick wall. The alley was lit by a lamppost, and Jim knew where to look, but finding where the wall opened still took a few nerve-wracking seconds. The latch was a quarter-inch piece of tin that stuck out and turned a plug of mortar. Jim remembered the wire he and Frank had run. He checked. It was still there. The wire snaked along the base of the building's bricks, partially hidden by dust and dirt. Jim and Frank hadn't wanted O'Neill to find the stairwell, so they'd run the wire to the cellar of the building next door.

Jim used a fingernail to turn the strip of tin clockwise, looked up the alley and down, and kept his pistol pointed groundward but took it in both hands. He nudged the wall open with his shoulder.

Light from the lamppost showed the stairwell empty. The stairs were concrete, so he didn't worry about boards groaning beneath his weight, only the sound of his shoes. He went in and slowly, silently pushed the wall shut, then felt for the lock on the other side of the mortar plug. He turned it, pulled to make sure it'd latched, and went down the stairs. A slim thread of light from the basement bled in at the bottom of the door. When Jim reached it, he listened for voices. They were hushed but familiar—Frank, Ward, Edith, and Pop. He listened long enough to be satisfied no one else was in the basement. He thought the sheered bricks might make a bullet ricochet, but he pressed his back against the stairwell wall, tried to make himself less of a target than he naturally was. He said in a loud whisper, "It's Jim," and kept himself flat as possible. Then he remembered to knock, two times, in quick succession. He did, and a chair leg scraped concrete. Half the thread of light bleeding in blotted out. "It's Jim," he said again. Two dull thuds came from the wall's other side. Jim unlocked and unlatched the door and went in.

Only the four of them were there. Edith said to put the gun away.

He slipped it back in the holster and joined them at the table. "What happened?"

Frank was wound tight and talked quick. "Before O'Neill showed at Pete's, remember my watch stopped? I asked Pete the time? He checked a wristwatch." He looked at Jim like the meaning was clear.

It wasn't.

"Pete don't wear no wristwatch. Carries one in his pocket. Always has. That watch was Dietz's. You were right—Pete pilfered it." Frank was smoking. He ashed on the concrete and took a quick drag. "Thought of it when you dropped me off, so I went back. Police ambulance was still out back. The one O'Neill used to bring Strba."

Frank had made a lap around the block and parked on Twenty-Fifth, where they'd left the Ford earlier. He'd snuck through the alley to the north side of Gilson's, where the embankment rose to a barred basement window. Strba was inside, bagged on a gurney, and Pete was on the floor, shot through the head. Frank saw his eyes. No more Pete. And the watch was gone. O'Neill had the wood door in the basement open, the one that hid the still. He was hauling everything out, piece by piece, plus bags of sugar, jars that were empty and full. He loaded it all in the ambulance. "Getting rid of the still—I don't know. Maybe he wanted it. But he was setting the scene, too. Ain't easy, though—making a scene read like you want. He'd want to look like he was the one found Pete, called it in. So he had to dump the still off somewhere, get Strba back in the ambulance."

Whatever O'Neill did with the still, Frank said he was quick about it. The ambulance took off east, down F. For twelve minutes Frank stared down at Pete. Gone Pete. O'Neill came back and wheeled the gurney out, pulled Strba into the ambulance again. Then O'Neill went inside and used Pete's phone. Frank suspected O'Neill was calling it in as a homicide, so Frank ran through the shadows to the motorcycle and sped down Twenty-Fourth to the south side station.

When he got there, Frank stopped by his boss's desk. Said he'd forgotten to drop off receipts, thought he'd check in. Cap told him Pete Gilson was murdered, told Frank and two detectives to go to the undertaking parlor. "So I went. I didn't know what O'Neill got out of Pete before he killed him, but I knew that little pissant bootlicker couldn't bluff me. If he knew I'd brought Dietz to Pete—he can't act that good."

"Think he knew?" Jim asked.

"Am I sitting here?" Frank took a long drag off his cigarette. Ward poured Frank some whiskey. Pop reached across the table and patted Frank's hand. "I would've thought he'd spill. Hell, he should've. Stupid old man." Frank's lower lids were pinkish and raw. "I don't know what he told O'Neill, but he didn't give me up." Frank brushed the underside of his nose with his shirtsleeve. Then he pulled Jim's notebook from his back pocket, the one with the wiretap list. He tossed it to Jim. "We gotta figure out what to do about the wires we ran. He seen them. Now it's a matter of when he figures out the gauge is different." Frank had ridden with O'Neill in the police ambulance. They'd still needed to drop Strba off somewhere. They took him to Al Kava's parlor, and O'Neill made detours on the way back, stopped and checked phone poles with his flashlight. Frank asked O'Neill what he was looking for. O'Neill said he and Dietz had been tracking down leads on the syndicate tapping phone lines. "I had that goddamned list on me the whole time."

"The syndicate tapping phone lines," Jim said. That was the truth of it. The real syndicate were the sons of bitches behind the wiretaps.

Frank took a drink. "I asked him—I even asked him. 'Where's Dietz?' I said."

Ward had been staring at the table. He rubbed at his hair. "Jesus."

"'Missouri,' he said. Didn't miss a goddamn beat. Said Dietz was in St. Joe."

"Suppose that's close to true." Jim flipped to the pages where he and Frank had run wires to buy time. He scanned up the list, to the crossed-out address where Dietz left off, the one before Pop's with a *D* beside it.

"So, we wait, then," Ward said with a lack of certainty, a guess bordering on a question. "Go about business as usual, hope he don't figure out it's the wrong wire, or if he does, he don't land on this being the last place Dietz was."

"It's the first place with a different gauge," Jim said. "He'll figure it out."

Pop's hands rested on the table, cupped like they hid invisible cards he'd been dealt. "He thinks someone killed his partner for tapping phones. When he sees the wrong wire, he'll assume the killer used it to buy time, like you did, and ran a line at their own place to fend off suspicion. But which place? He murdered a man for not saying who killed his partner. If anyone, from any of the places you two wired, could've done it, he'll make a mountain of dead bootleggers. Get a medal from Hoover himself."

"So, what do you think?" Jim had his own thoughts, but he would've preferred someone else, anyone else, say them.

"Tear down what you put up."

Ward offered, "You could take down all the wires."

Frank pulled the notebook back to himself and flipped through. "We could try."

"Too many," Jim said. "Five or six we might get away with. And this whole operation ain't just O'Neill. Him and Dietz were running taps, but they didn't come up with the idea. We know a few people in on it, but we don't know who else might be. If we went to everybody on the list, said, 'Rip down the wires'—for all we know, some taps could've been dummies. Ones people knew about. There could be a dummy wire down at Mickey O'Neill's, for show. And word travels too fast."

Frank nodded. He'd go to Pete Gilson's, make sure O'Neill was stuck there answering questions. "He should be, at least for a bit. Then you and me go take down the ones we ran." He looked to Pop. "You gotta shut down. Till things cool off. Lock the doors, don't answer no knocks. Hell, don't answer the phone."

Pop patted his hand again. He said to be careful.

Edith had been silent, brewing. "So, our bright idea is to make us sitting ducks? This is still the last place that dead cop was. If his partner shows here—when he shows here, even if we shut down a month—he kills us all, tosses a gun or two near our bodies. But one of us kills him, we get the chair."

"Well, one of us don't," Frank said.

"Christ, then—can't you just shoot him?"

"What in the world did your mother teach you?" Pop said. "You can't go around preemptively shooting everyone. That's a last resort, Edie."

Frank nodded, silent. He looked at his hands on the table. He slid one over the other, then drew them down in his lap. He nodded again.

22

Frank had left Pop's basement briefly. When he came back, he said O'Neill would be tied up at Pete's for hours while the police surgeon, Favano, worked. The county attorney had skipped the coroner's jury. That Pete had been murdered was apparent. Favano was dissecting Pete on one of the old man's own gurneys. "Three bullets went in, one came out," Frank said. "He's fishing for the other two."

Jim and Frank took off, leaving Ward, Edith, and Pop to get some shut-eye in Pop's back-room bachelor's quarters. Jim was relieved by that, the three of them sticking together for the time being.

In the darkness, he and Frank un-ran the fake taps they'd run. They started at Pop's then went to the other five places. When they were done, Jim stuffed the coiled wire in a barrel of garbage behind the Fontana. He and Frank passed a newsstand just as the twine popped from a bundle of morning *Tribune*s. They read in the light of a streetlamp.

The headline, PETE GILSON MURDERED, along with a photo that must've been twenty years old, ate up more space than the article. The details were scant, mostly Pete's biography, his professional history. About the killing, the article said only that O'Neill had brought Hal Strba's body to Gilson's to await a coroner's inquest. O'Neill found Pete shot three times in the back of the head. No sign of forced entry, no suspects, no known motive. Approximate time of death was between 8:00 and 9:00 p.m. It'd been more like five after, but close enough.

By the time the evening edition came out, Jim knew the reports wouldn't be any clearer. With each passing hour, each minute, whatever happened would be less and less clear, like a drop of ink in a pitcher of water. Strands of truth would stretch and pool and sink, and eventually the water would hardly bear a tint. People needed a reason, and to get one, they'd theorize, conjecture, ignore, and omit. All to reach consensus about why Pete was murdered and what his murder therefore meant or signified, as if a thing like that could have any sensible meaning. Sure, there was a why. The why was O'Neill saw a watch.

Jim remembered Shumway's message on his desk. Douglas and Washington counties shared a border. A headline about a murder in Omaha would be front-page news there, too. Jim didn't know if Shumway had been to Pete's. If Shumway had been and noticed the tie, Jim didn't know if Pete would've mentioned Jim. And Shumway couldn't know for certain Jim had seen the message, left shortly after Pete was killed. But if Shumway had picked up his father's body, if he'd seen and recognized the hand-painted tie, Pete getting murdered the same night Shumway left a message for Jim didn't look good. Shumway might think Jim killed Pete to ensure all Shumway had was the word of a dead guy.

On a practical level, if Pete had said anything to Shumway about getting the tie off a dead fella Jim brought in, it was true. All Shumway had was the word of a dead guy. That didn't mean Shumway couldn't make Jim's life hell, but he could get in goddamned line, so far as making Jim's life hell went.

Jim dropped the paper back on the pile. The fella who owned the newsstand groused, said he wasn't running a library. Jim took one step toward him and stared. The man turned away and busily rearranged boxes of gum.

Jim drove Frank to his motorcycle, which he'd parked two blocks from Pop's. Frank said he needed to clock out and sleep. Get his head on straight. Jim almost said to get it on straighter than usual, but the night had been too long for wisecracks. And something Frank said earlier nagged at him. "Back at Pop's, you said one of us wouldn't go to prison. For killing O'Neill."

"Just an observation."

"Yeah, well. Forget it." Jim told him to get some sleep. Jim needed sleep, too. He told Frank good night and left.

Of course, Jim didn't sleep. Back at the office, he left his phone on the hook, the line open in case Pop, Ward, or Edith needed to call. On top of worrying about them, he dreaded picking up and Shumway being on the line. Not one call rang through, but Jim jolted awake any time he drifted off.

He gave up on sleeping around noon, made coffee, and called Pop. All was fine there, Pop said, and it probably would be, so long as they stayed shuttered. But Frank had told them not to answer the phone, and Pop had, which didn't bode well.

When he hung up, Jim decided. He'd call Shumway. There was no precise calculation to make. He'd lob some dynamite and get it over with. Besides, if Jim was under suspicion, calling Shumway was the least suspicious thing he could do.

The sheriff picked up on the second ring. Jim said who he was, said he was returning Shumway's message.

"Omaha had quite the night, I hear."

"Hell in a handbasket," Jim said. "Senseless."

"You know, I went by Pete Gilson's parlor yesterday morning. Of all the places I could've been."

Of course. Of course he'd been by Pete's. Of course the sister who lived in Omaha hadn't taken care of transporting the body. "No kidding."

Shumway said what Jim already knew, that Shumway's father had passed away in Omaha. He was being buried tomorrow morning. Jim gave his condolences. Shumway thanked him, then shifted gears quick enough to strip them. "Say, I don't suppose you've seen Vern Meyer."

"Not lately. Heard he was in town, week or two ago. Lit out for the territories, I guess." Figuratively, it could've been true. "Saw he had a warrant out for him. Failure to appear?"

"Yeah, he's got statutory charges up here. Twelve-year-old girl."

Jim grunted. It was all he could muster or think to do, grunt disapprovingly. As far as reactions went, there wasn't an array of good options. Not without knowing what Shumway thought or what Pete might've said. And it was possible Shumway had called solely because Jim's house was Vern's last known residence outside Washington County.

"I noticed Pete wearing this tie," Shumway said, nullifying the possibility he'd called because Jim's place was Vern's last known residence. Jim wished he could pull a Lazarus on that son of a bitch just to kill him again. "I left the parlor and kept thinking, all the way back to Blair—where the heck else had I seen that tie? Wasn't till last night it hit me—that was the tie Vern Meyer wore to the preliminary hearing. I don't usually notice those things—don't believe me, ask my wife." He gave a light, good-natured laugh. Jim played parrot. He echoed a light, good-natured laugh. "But it struck me as odd, that tie."

"How's that?" Jim said.

"Well, it had these horseshoes on it. And from my understanding, Vern was a car mechanic? I don't suppose being a car mechanic means you can't be fond of horses. What's that—false equivocation?"

"Dichotomy, I want to say. False dichotomy."

"That's it," Shumway said. "Any rate, a man can like both, of course, but it's what made me notice the tie. And painted by hand! I guess Vern Meyer must've seen better days at some point, to have a tie like that. Painted by hand."

"Could've been a gift, I suppose." Jim's blood ran caustic and hot through the veins of his forearms. He didn't care for cat-and-mouse. Cat-and-mouse involved banter, and Jim did not like banter. Conversations, practically speaking, required four sentences. Ideally, two. One person said a thing, the other person agreed. If the other person disagreed, the first person said a different thing, and the other person agreed to that. If they didn't, the two people should've walked away from each other. Known they had no business talking.

"A gift," Shumway said. "That's true. That's true. And now you mention it, it's possible Vern Meyer turned around and gave that tie to Pete Gilson. As a gift."

"Well, if it was the same tie."

"Oh, I'm certain it was the same tie."

The volume of annoyance Jim was capable of bottling was less than he could hold in his bladder. That was not a lot and something he needed to see a doctor about. But if Shumway wanted to take the scenic route, Jim would feed him gas. "Guess Vern could've sold it, too. Stopped off, needed more money for the train, to get as far out of town as he could."

"Sold it," Shumway said, like that was some striking new possibility. Jim would've liked to strike Shumway with a goddamned office chair. "I guess that'd make sense, now, wouldn't it? You know what else would make sense?"

Jim didn't answer. He was done pumping gas.

"It'd make sense, to me, that the father of a girl who'd been—I don't know how to put it nicely—I apologize for that, Jim—but it'd make sense if the father of a girl Vern Meyer molested just turned around and killed the son of a gun. I don't have any daughters myself, only sons, but if I had a daughter, and if Vern Meyer—well, if he did what Vern Meyer's prone to doing—to my daughter? I can't say I wouldn't kill the son of a gun."

Jim knew the angle. He'd used it—tried to coerce a confession out of somebody by pretending anyone in that same person's shoes would've done the same thing. Jim never saw it work, but he knew the angle so well that an unexpected, mild smile crept onto his face. Because if Shumway was sitting in

Washington County, trying to coerce a confession out of Jim, over the phone, Shumway didn't have shit. Nothing material. And he couldn't have any. Because the only thing left of Vern was that tie. The rest was ash. And if Pete hadn't given up Frank over Dietz, hadn't given up a cop who gouged him on protection, hadn't given him up when doing it might've saved his own skin, there was no way in hell Pete gave up Jim over a goddamned tie.

Jim remembered the last time he saw Pete, waving those gangly arms, urging Jim and Frank to safety upstairs while O'Neill pounded at the door.

Jim realized then—he'd miss Pete.

"I could see that," Jim said.

"And if the father of that girl knew an undertaker, one who'd been known to cut some corners here and there, take a little under-the-table extra sometimes, why, what better way to get rid of a body than take it straight to that undertaker? A man could get a body gone in a jiffy."

"Sounds like quite a plan. But maybe since Pete's not even in the ground yet, it feels a little soon to be casting aspersions, John." They'd never met, but if Shumway felt he could take the liberty, Jim would, too. He pulled a cigarette from the case on the desk, lit it, and took a nice long drag. "Besides, does the father of that girl up in Kennard even know Pete Gilson?"

That shut him up a minute. "It sure is something, Gilson getting killed last night."

"I know it. Sounds like it happened about an hour, hour and a half before you left me a message." If Shumway thought Jim saw the message and snuffed Pete, Jim could do the professional courtesy of saying the timing didn't jibe. "It's a hell of a world."

"That it is. Tell you what. You hear any rumors or need to get anything off your chest, you've got my number."

"I sure do," Jim said. "I sure do."

23

When the evening editions hit the newsstand that afternoon, Jim bought copies. He huffed back up to the office steeling himself. Pete's death would suck up a lot of ink. Columns would collect shocked, outraged, lukewarm, and backbiting reactions from local politicians, clergy, and people whose wealth entitled them to opinions. Articles would dump out summaries of Pete's life, the crime, the investigation's progress. Quotations and editorials would postulate and speculate about why it'd happened. And once those last bits went from typewriter to editor to printing press, they might as well have been chiseled from stone by Moses.

Jim knew what he'd read would be ludicrous. He was accustomed to ludicrous. At this point in life's journey, he was intimately familiar with the bold and delicate hues of absurdity.

That said, when he sat and unfolded the paper, he saw absurdity had pulled a real goddamned number. Really outdid itself.

In words and letters and paragraphs, Pete had broken

free from a mortal cocoon that'd been less than perfect. A Pete made of words never could've been a politician so shady the state legislature dissolved his office. Print-Pete was not the kind of fella who almost definitely killed his first wife. No, Post-Life Pete was a Great Reformer who'd worked tirelessly against Vice and The Gang and The Political Machine. He'd striven for The Greater Good and paid with his Life.

It was a damn good thing O'Neill stole Pete's still.

The phone rang. Jim felt a skip in his chest, worried it could be bad news from Pop's, but it was Frank. "You read this horseshit?"

"Which pile? Looking at the front page of the *Tribune* right now."

"Page four, third column. Halfway down. Second paragraph."

Jim paged through, spotted it, and read. Pete was shot three times. One bullet: round-nose lead. Another: copper-jacket round-nose. The third: steel-jacket hollow-point. The same flea market that was in Dietz's gun. The inspector of detectives said while all the bullets were the same caliber, he thought it unlikely all were shot from the same weapon. Based on information received by the department, he suspected Gilson's murder was related to gangs in Kansas City and St. Joseph. The suspects were at large. Police Lieutenant Ted Wilford would leave tonight for Chicago, where the bullets would undergo more sophisticated analysis.

"Asinine," Jim said. "Three kinds of bullets means three suspects?"

"They know it's bunk. Don't say no more."

"I'm not worried about a transcript of this call getting used in a grand jury. It won't. It don't fit the story they're telling."

"Well, you want a brain aneurysm, turn back a page."

Jim turned back a page. It was a photo of Bob Wright, clerk of the district court, the old reformer who'd given Elmer Kobb the list of joints up for license renewal, minus Mickey O'Neill's. Wright's aspirin-capsule head glowed so pale from the printing press, Jim could barely make out a face—a line of a mouth, two little blowholes that should've been nostrils, eyes so light they were blank as Orphan Annie's. Wright was quoted for four half-columns straight, claiming he, Elmer Kobb, the DA, and the AG had received death threats that day—letters saying they'd better change their tune or they'd end up like Pete. Wright told the *Tribune* he was undaunted. He would not live in fear. And while friends and family had begged him to arm himself, he would not carry a weapon. Jim hoped a dozen murderous felons were reading the paper.

"I'm headed back over. To South O." Jim didn't mention Pop's on the off chance someone really was listening.

"Stay where you're at. I'll come by."

"Want to meet there?"

"No. What'd I just say? Stay where you're at." He hung up.

At the end of Bob Wright's hijacking of Pete Gilson's death, the paper read, "[photos, p. 6]." Jim flipped to 6. In the middle of a collage of portraits—Pete Gilson, Bob Wright, Elmer Kobb, and the AG—the paper printed a photo of the letter to Wright.

```
Bob Wright
Clerk of the District Court
Omaha, Nebr.

Mr. Wright,
In today's papers, you will read
of Pete Gilson's assassination.
Gilson was a reformer whose
interests went against the
Syndicate's. Despite our warnings,
Pete Gilson made clear he
supported crackdowns on Vice. In
his death, we also hope we make
ourselves clear.

Should you, the AG, the DA, or
Independent Federation candidate
Elmer Koll pursue any crackdowns,
be prepared to meet the same fate
as Pete Gilson.

"The Syndicate"
```

Maybe Jim had girded himself better than he thought. He wasn't surprised the same typewriter that'd turned the commissioners' meeting into a farce had churned out the death threat. If he was dumbfounded by anything, it was the level of brazenness, laziness, or idiocy that made the author feel confident in using a typewriter with problems that distinct.

He considered who the steno might've been. The AG

was unlikely. He was rarely in town. The DA gave speeches at lunches and meetings when he wasn't sending someone to the pen. Bob Wright was flagrant about transgressions, but he wasn't a dolt. And Elmer Kobb's pot might've been cracked, but the thing wasn't broken in two.

The profile that best fit the typist was that pompous, gawky, big-meloned, cravat-wearing loon with lip-rouged eyebrows doing all that *tack tack tack tack tack ding* in the rooming house from beyond.

Jim would show the paper to Frank. He'd decide what to do about Maloney and his typewriter when Frank got here.

In the meantime, Jim flipped back to the front page, to the quotes from businessmen and politicians and local religious figures. He knew better. Reading them was never any more productive than picking a fresh scab. But he justified it. It was in service of knowing the enemy.

He didn't need to look far to spot the son of a bitch. Elmer Kobb had top billing: "This unspeakable act, against a man who has been the city's bulwark, our rampart against a tide of criminality, must be punished swiftly and thoroughly. The criminal element has laid the final stitch in the flag it raises above our city. We must make a clean sweep. We must crush the vice syndicate through every legal channel available. If we fail in this, we are as culpable as Chicago's inept aldermen."

Jim could hear Kobb saying it. The sound made Jim's head pound, his eyes shimmer with stars. He had to hand it to Kobb—his words had an effect. Jim shut his eyes, but the ink was burned into them. One word: *Chicago.*

That was it. That was all any of this was. Chicago.

Jim went to the bathroom, to the pair of partitions hiding

a toilet and sink. He splashed cold water on his face. When Frank knocked, Jim answered, drying himself with a towel that needed washing. He was still in his undershirt from trying to sleep.

"You all right, Big Jim?"

"Sure. Don't I seem all right?"

Frank reached up and clapped his shoulder. "Wouldn't ask if you did. You look a little peaked."

"Chicago."

"Nah. San Diego. Better weather." He got on his tiptoes to check Jim's forehead with a wrist. "Don't got no fever. You sleep any?"

Jim slipped into his shirt and buttoned it. "Remember what you said about the Saint Valentine's murders? What happened was probably what it looked like? Two uniforms, two plainclothes walk into a warehouse, everybody lines up for the bust and gets mowed down?"

"Sounds like me."

"Maybe what happened in Chicago was what it looked like, and here, nothing happens like it looks. Not how it looks in the police report or the papers." He slipped into his holster. "Gus passes out drunk, gets ruled a murder victim. I get beaned by Maloney and told to watch out for 'the gang,' whole thing's a setup for a headline—and then the bombs go off during the fundraiser—during it—so they can announce it from a goddamned podium. Pete's bootlegging, gets killed and turned into a martyr." He knew the way things were coming out was disjointed, but he was tugging the pieces together. "Other day in the *Tribune*, Kobb says if Omaha has a liquor syndicate, the city winds up as rough as Chicago.

He said it again today. That's it. That's their whole angle. They're making Omaha—a wide-open town where laws are for show—out to be Chicago—a city in the alleged thrall of organized gangsters. It's why they're insisting there's a syndicate. Making Pete out like a reformer, some white knight against crime—he gets gunned down, nobody's safe."

Frank mulled it over. "Get people scared out of their wits, vote for the guys who promise to make it all hunky-dory. Sure. First Kobb gets elected, later—if Maloney ain't just a crank—the AG gets re-upped for looking like he reformed the town." He used Jim's desktop lighter to spark a cigarette and kept talking through the half of his mouth that was available. "Makes sense, but Omaha—" He took a drag and exhaled. "The ninety-nine out of a hundred that don't go to the Fontana—they won't buy it. Even if they did, AG runs during general election, not local. Anybody with half a brain and a ballot's gonna blame Volstead for the killings and rackets. Thirty-two election's a landslide for the first guy promises to repeal Prohibition." He'd taken another drag and exhaled. "Know who I like? That one down in Louisiana. That Huey Long fella."

"Sure, but what till then? If making the city out to be Chicago's their only play, they'll out-Chicago Chicago. Even if it don't work, it'll be goddamned bedlam."

Frank smiled. "Say, is Bill Haskell gonna play O'Banion or Capone?" Jim didn't laugh but got the joke; O'Banion was dead. "Ask me, Capone probably ain't even Capone. Just another goat."

They were standing by the desk. Jim pulled the newspaper close and tapped the photo of the letter. "So maybe we jerk a knot in their tails. Use this." Jim pointed out the *P*'s and *b*'s missing half their bubbles. "The same machine that typed that letter changed the list at the permit renewal meeting." He explained his reasoning, why he figured Maloney was the typist.

Frank took a minute, running it through his head, getting worked up. Then he wound right back down. "Nah, ain't enough. Not for a warrant. And it's a thin case against Maloney anyhow. Donnegan'll argue it's a rooming house. Anybody could've gone in a room and used a typewriter. Plus, use your noggin, Big Jim. You think the DA would prosecute?"

The DA. Christ. Even if the DA could bring the case without implicating himself, he wouldn't. He'd been at the Fontana fundraiser, he'd gotten one of the supposed death threats, and he'd set Bob Wright's kid up as his assistant. They were all in bed together. "So we go to the papers. Or if we get the typewriter—"

"We'd have a guilty goddamn typewriter. That's it. *Post* might take the bait and print it for scandal and sales, but we gotta have something besides our word. Otherwise we got a machine we're claiming Maloney typed on and a libel suit. Even if we got prints off it, matched the prints to Maloney, Donnegan's gonna say all it proves is Maloney used the machine. Don't prove he typed that letter."

"The letters. What about prints on the letters?"

"Big Jim," he said. "Buddy. You need sleep. Who's got the letters?"

Christ. Everything behind Jim's ribs sank. "If we got the list—"

"Kobb turns around, says he got it that way from Donnegan."

"And Donnegan points the finger back at me."

"Like he did at the meeting, yeah."

Jim was a goddamned rube. Sleep-deprived or not, he should've figured it out. Even if Maloney signed a goddamned confession, the DA wouldn't do shit about it.

"I know," Frank said. "I know it." He tapped the back of a hand to Jim's chest. "But that little observation I made at Pop's. About how one of us wouldn't get the chair. You know. If something happened to Maloney."

Jim didn't like the sound of it. "Forget it."

"Listen. Pop can't stay closed for good. Him, Ward, Edith—they can't hide out forever. They're not safe as is. A cop wants revenge over a dead partner." He told Jim to sit down, have a smoke, a drink.

Jim sat down. He didn't drink. He lit a cigarette and listened.

"There'll be a raid."

"Nope. No there won't."

"Just listen." Frank said Pop would step out beforehand, go to Carl Ziske's. Frank would go in, get Ward to serve him a whiskey at the upstairs bar so nobody'd find out about the basement. After Ward served him, O'Neill would come in with a pair of feds. The feds would take Ward to jail, pawn off evidence collection on Frank and O'Neill. Frank knew a couple feds who always pawned off grunt-work. "They leave, I shoot O'Neill. Unfortunate but unavoidable incident. Guy lost his head—been acting strange since Pete got killed. I asked him about it. Lack of sleep, jitters from finding Pete.

Then he said all this paranoid garbage—about the feds, about Pete and a watch—pulled his weapon, shot at me. Thought I was in on some plot."

Afterward, two south side detectives would show up—Frank would call them. They'd check out O'Neill's gun, find all the different bullets, connect O'Neill with Pete's murder. On top of it, once people realized Dietz was missing, everybody'd guess O'Neill killed him, too.

"Are you done?" Jim said.

"That's it."

"Good. No. There's too many goddamned variables."

"It won't go wrong, Big Jim."

Maybe it wouldn't go wrong, but the possibility of how it could was like a lead medicine ball sitting on Jim's chest. It was a weight he wouldn't have expected three or four days ago. "I can't let you do it. If O'Neill got the jump on you—" Jim shook his head.

Frank's face turned partly away. He smiled like he had in the Ford outside Gilson's, after they'd seen Gus's body. When he'd said they made good buddies. The Kewpie smile.

"Oh, go screw." Jim pictured the feds marching into Pop's and arresting Ward, dragging him around the far end of the bar, passing the door to the basement. "Listen. If we went through with this half-boiled plot, which we won't—you don't think the feds would search the whole place?"

"Nah, these guys—laziest feds you ever seen. They'll come in, cuff Ward, take him in. Look like a couple G-man heroes."

"G-men. Christ. What's a fed bond run these days?"

"In Ward's case? Not cheap. Going rate's upwards of a

thousand, and Ward's got priors. Joint itself's got priors. The U.S. commissioner—she don't like priors. Three grand? I know you don't got it. Me, neither. But we'll figure it out. And he'll be safe while we do. Jailers they got downtown ain't like they used to be."

Three grand. Jim had a little over two left from what Donnegan paid him. Pop didn't have another thousand. Edith and Ward and Pop all together didn't have it. Jim thought of Maymie. She was likely more cutthroat on interest than Haskell used to be. And Jim wouldn't go to a bondsman. Jim wished some anarchists would do to bondsmen what they should've been doing to streetcars with no unions.

But like Frank said, Pop's couldn't stay closed indefinitely. Pop, Ward, and Edith couldn't hide out forever. And right now, this was a figment. An idiotic, hypothetical figment. "You don't think they'd check the basement."

"Nah—not these morons."

"Then you plant me behind the door. On the top stair. What else would I do—sit here? I couldn't sit here knowing all that was going on."

"Basement door got a lock?"

"You just said they won't check the basement."

"They won't. But, you know. In case they do."

Jim smoked and walked himself through it, put himself there on the top step, listening as everything went right, then as everything went wrong. "Forget it. You got Jennie and the kids. You got reasons to keep breathing."

"Nothing happens to me. And look, I don't got a death wish. I'm just the only one can pull it off. I got reasons to keep breathing, sure. So's everybody."

"If somebody's got to kill O'Neill, nobody's counting on me." Jim knew it when Frank had brought up skipping town for San Diego. With Molly and Addie around, Jim had reasons. Reasons to work, not smoke and drink all day. Reasons to stay late at the office, not go home. Reasons for all kinds of things. But not now. "Besides, I'm the one who got us jammed up in this mess."

"Ah, that's horseshit. Knowing you, you would've got yourself mixed up in some other garbage, but I was the one pulled you into Donnegan's thing."

"Well, you couldn't have if I hadn't—" He cut himself off. "Forget it."

"Listen, I count on you. And I like you hanging around. You can't think of no other reason to stay out of the electric chair, do it for me." He stubbed out his cigarette. "I know the plan ain't ideal. But Edith's right. It comes down to them or O'Neill. And Pop's right, too. Last resort. But I'm the only one who can get away with it, make things right."

Make things right. Jim was fairly sure there was no making anything right. There was only reaction to reaction to reaction to reaction.

24

Before Frank went through with his harebrained plan to kill O'Neill, Jim had one more idea. It was far-flung and last-ditch, likely to work about as well as rubbing a foot chopped off a dead rabbit, but he'd try it. He'd go see Bill Haskell.

If Haskell had any pull at all, he might know a cop or official who'd throw O'Neill in jail. Not for killing Pete—no matter what side cops and officials were on, admitting a cop murdered Pete would plunge the department into chaos. Too much public scrutiny. They wouldn't risk it. But there was still the wiretaps. The phone company hadn't let the cops listen in, so the feds hadn't signed off, which meant the taps were illegal. If O'Neill was locked up a minute, a judge would order the taps torn down. And by the time O'Neill was out, he couldn't use the missing wires to figure out where Dietz was snuffed. They'd all be gone.

It wasn't late, but it was dark, and Jim didn't have time to get his bell rung by Maloney or anyone else, so he drove the two blocks to Fifteenth. He parked between Farnam and Harney and checked the time. It was nine-fifteen, not banking hours, but Bill Haskell hadn't kept banking hours even when he was a loan shark.

Haskell's office was above Walt Feffer's Golden Spike, the basement cigar shop that took bets on elections and ran a sports wire. Before he got out of the car, Jim smoked and looked at the entrance. A thought struck him. Why the hell did Bill Haskell have an office?

The guy had been a farmhand, a miner, and a faro dealer, then come to Omaha and run gambling joints, dabbled in whatnot that likely did require an office. Loan sharking. Real estate. But nowadays, his line was breeding little show dogs. Why pay rent on an office when all you needed was some kennels and a couple humping dogs?

Sure, there was the politics. Besides playing middleman between corporate money and candidates, Haskell managed campaigns in his ward. He registered voters regardless of age or whether or not their addresses were vacant lots. Organized canvassers. Beforehand, he no doubt met with railroad and bank presidents, newspaper editors—but wouldn't he have gone to those guys' offices? Ones that weren't crammed in the back of the old Elks building? Being a glorified poll worker was part-time, seasonal work. It didn't justify paying rent on an office. So what did?

Maybe Jim hadn't given Haskell enough credit. Maybe coming here was a good deal more reliable than a severed rabbit foot.

The entrance was in the alley, which was well lit. No armed guards or bouncers were staked there, and when Jim stepped inside the corridor, no one was seated outside

Haskell's door. Jim knocked, and a voice called out, said it was open.

The voice was Ted Wilford's. He was eating at a small dining table in his street clothes. Wilford was the lieutenant tasked with taking the bullets that'd killed Pete to Chicago. So far as Jim knew, Wilford was the only officer who was colored who'd been promoted past detective. Since he was Haskell's closest friend, a lot of people thought that explained the promotion—Haskell must've pulled some strings. The *Tribune* egged on the speculation, used every opportunity to insinuate Wilford was a police lieutenant because he was Haskell's underworld lieutenant. Maybe there was something to it, but the commendations Wilford had gotten for tracking down fugitives weren't mentioned much. His getting shot during a prisoner transport and dropping off the felons before going to a hospital didn't come up, either.

Jim apologized for interrupting Wilford's dinner. Wilford said it was fine, he was getting a quick bite before he ran Haskell home. Haskell was downstairs in the Golden Spike.

"Think he'd mind if I popped in?" Jim said.

Wilford checked his watch. "This late, he's just jawing with Walt down there. Never wagers, anyway. Bill's picks are theoretical." Wilford told Jim to remind the old man they needed to get going.

Jim headed down to the basement, a smart setup that lent itself to a high-stakes operation. Small-ante card and dice rooms were tucked in the back rooms of grocery stores, hidden above restaurants and jewelers. But basements were tough to raid—gamblers could leave through tunnels under the downtown streets. So Feffer didn't bother messing with dice or cards or making the place clandestine. He ran a full-on bookmaking joint that looked like a low-rent bank. A counter ran the width of the room. Above it, iron bars stretched to the ceiling. The cashier cages' barred doors swung open during business hours, when gamblers played the ponies or wagered on ball games, prizefights, elections, you name it.

Not that the Golden Spike was unique. There were enough joints like it, you could be a stickler about the company you kept. The Tattler, the Harlem Room, Izzie's, and B&G's catered to particular genders, races, classes, and creeds, while at Nick's, Ballpark Central, and Old Mo's, you threw your lot in with the spectrum of humanity. Golden Spike was one of the latter. If it specialized in any kind of people, they were ones classified as career or compulsive, depending on how much and how often they won or lost.

The only people there when Jim walked in were Walt Feffer, a kid in a flat cap pushing a broom, and Bill Haskell, who sat on a bench like a church pew lining the wall. The kid swept his way toward the back, behind the cages, and Feffer nodded at Jim on his way out a side exit. Feffer told Haskell he'd be back. He needed to drop off the night deposit.

Haskell was getting old, all right. His bowler was on the bench beside him, and his bare pink scalp was freckled in liver spots. When Jim approached to shake hands, Haskell seemed to have a tough time making him out. He squinted and drew his thin lips tight. As always, he was dressed for court, suit jacket draped across his lap. He was getting a paunch, so the bottom of his vest was unbuttoned.

Jim shook his hand.

"Jim Beely. Sneaking tomorrow's tickets in early?"

Jim said he wasn't much for gambling. Haskell moved the bowler to his lap and invited Jim to have a seat. "Hear about Pete Gilson?" Jim asked.

"I did. Never liked him. Grifter. Worst kind—took advantage of people in mourning. Still. Didn't wish a bullet through his head."

Jim made sure the kid was out of earshot. "Wanted to pass along a tip, ask your advice."

"Hope the tip's about a horse called Low Gear down at Hialeah. Hope somebody shot the son of a bitch."

"No, but I hear you don't usually lose much."

"Bragging rights. Face. Not like this mug's some great loss. Never gamble for money. For money, I'll take a sure thing. But you don't need to wager to care who wins."

A sure thing. Only a person who couldn't remember relying on a bet in his life would talk about a single sure thing besides death. Whether or not you could afford rent or should buy tools, whether you bought four cans of evaporated milk this week or two—all of it was wagering. That was why Jim never had a taste for dice. He rolled them all day long. It was goddamned tedious.

"A cop's tapping phone lines," Jim said. "Phone company didn't let him do it, he's climbing poles. Which means the feds ain't signed off, and it's illegal under state law. I was wondering if you knew anybody—lawyer, cops, both—somebody who could shut him down."

"Know what it's about?"

"State's working up a mass indictment. Criminal conspiracy. Could be a hundred defendants." He watched Haskell's expression. It was dutifully but insincerely concerned. "You don't seem too worried."

"I'm not."

"Well, they'll need a ringleader, and you're the obvious pick. They'll likely claim you're head of a syndicate—liquor, prostitution, and gambling. Omaha's Capone. Sounds inconvenient, at least."

Haskell gave a middling laugh. Unsurprised. "Oh, it'll be a circus. But no need to worry about me. Never dealt in women. My place sold liquor when it was legal, but they shut me down before they even outlawed booze. Nowadays, it's just me and the dogs. You like dogs?"

Jim said sure. Sure, he liked dogs. He wanted to get Haskell back on topic. Maybe he'd care if he knew the whole thing was political. "They're timing the trial to line up with the thirty-two election. Make it look like they took down you and your machine to keep the AG in office."

"If I'm still breathing in thirty-two, it's an angle. Not real original, but it's an angle." He ran a pair of pinched fingers down the crease of his trousers, sharpening it. "Won't save the AG, though. That pari-mutuel ban stuck in a lot of big craws. And the first fella who promises to repeal the Volstead Act'll sweep the whole party out." Haskell leaned back to look at Jim like he was fine print. "I can tell you're genuinely worried, not here for a payout. Don't mean to sound ungrateful, but what's it to you, son?"

How he'd spoken wasn't warm, but Jim found the word *son* oddly comforting. Maybe the reminder that somebody was older and more tired than Jim was reassuring.

"This have to do with Kobb blowing up your house? Or the murdered fella? One who worked for you?"

Jim shouldn't have been surprised Haskell knew about front-page news, but Haskell was usually the headline. It was odd to think the headline was a guy who picked up the paper, read about the other people in it. "He wasn't murdered," Jim said. "Somebody went out of their way to make it—" Jim was tired of explaining. "No. I got family, friends getting framed up in this syndicate garbage, and the cop tapping phones has it in for them. They're in trouble. I'm trying to figure a way—"

"You can't." The words weren't curt, but they were plain. Absolute.

Jim studied him. Haskell's face softened a little. Jim's hands were braced on his knees.

Haskell patted the one closest to him. "Cops, lawyers, politicians—they won't do a damn thing about it. That don't mean nothing can be done, only I can't help. I wish to hell I could." He peeked around, made sure the kid with the broom was nowhere near. Then he rested his arm along the top of the bench like it was his couch. "I'll tell you something. I think you got a fair idea anyway. And listen, I'm no gangster, but enough people think I am, you tell another soul, you'll bleed out in a gutter. Sure as we're sitting here. Understand?"

If what Haskell said was a bluff, Jim wasn't about to call him on it. Jim stayed put on the bench. Haskell looked him in one eye, then the other, till he gave a slight nod, like a pitcher waiting for the sign he wanted.

"People—not politicians, I mean people with souls—they

think I run the city. I know you never did. You always struck me as somebody who knows what's Shinola and how to use it. But it's part true. I got as much power as they think I do, which goes a good distance. Don't cross the finish line—I'm not rich—but it goes a good ways."

Haskell turned a gold ring with a big icy rock around his finger. He caught Jim looking at it. Jim didn't mind being caught. He gave Haskell a look that said, respectfully, he didn't buy it. Haskell not being rich.

"Oh, money's passed through these hands, sure. And I can get it when I need it. Not for free, but I can get it. When I'm dead, though, they'll be digging holes in my yard, hunting for gold bars I never had. Never been rich. Even when I was messing with those loans. You remember those." He chuckled. Jim didn't. "Still a sore spot. Any rate, money's water and I'm a damn sieve. So I've made myself useful. I've been useful, and the trade-off's I never wanted for much. That and I kept my brothers in good jobs."

Haskell's brothers worked for the city. People said their jobs were more proof he ran the town. Never mind that anybody with a steady job, especially one with the city, got it by being somebody's in-law or blood relative.

"To the point," Haskell said. "I've never been dishonest about it; nobody thinks to ask. But between you, me, and the fence post, I'm a patsy, Jim. A professional goat."

Jim searched Haskell's expression for confirmation of what he'd said. Haskell nodded.

He was a patsy. A willing patsy?

"Always?" Jim said.

"As long as making me city bogeyman's been useful. Making me bogeyman keeps people from wondering who the real string-pullers are."

Jim took it in. While he took it in, he said the only thing he could think of. "Why have an office? Why pay the rent?"

"You think I pay it?" Haskell chuckled again. "For show. Any respectable bogeyman's got an office. At least mine's upstairs from this joint. Convenient."

Haskell was a willing patsy. Of course he was. That was how he'd stayed out of prison. That was why Haskell wasn't surprised by the mass indictment. He knew all about it. His was the one phone line there'd been no need to tap. Jim felt that odd sensation he'd had at the rooming house and the night Maloney beaned him. It didn't make him smile, but he felt it, the physical sensation of absurdity. "A professional goat."

"Yeah, but I'm an old goat. About used up. People need to believe somebody's all-powerful. God, invisible governments, conspiracies—they need to think somebody's hands are moving the pieces. Otherwise, there's no sense to it."

There wasn't. "I suspect there isn't."

"I suspect you're right." Haskell took a long draw of breath that said he was tired. His words came out on a sigh. "A man gets old enough, he outlives what people are willing to believe about him. You break a hip, get dotty, go the way of Jake Berman." He still turned the ring and Jim saw it was less out of habit than from loose fit. "No use being bitter. Change of the guard. I can't stop it, you can't stop it."

Jim pictured Pete, then Pete's old hearse. The old black carriage. Soon it'd be tinder, horses sent to auction, then turned into dog food. Glue or gelatin. "I suppose we can't."

"Maybe it's no comfort right now, cop tapping phone lines, friends in trouble, but get them through that, I'll say this: The charges in thirty-two won't stick. Oh, it'll be a hassle. Syphon money to a bunch of lawyers nobody can afford. But in the end, whole thing's a play. Make-believe end to a make-believe racket. All so a couple fellas claiming they're square dealers can cash in. Get their turn for a while."

Jim pictured that balloon-headed sad beagle. The walking Anti-Saloon League pamphlet with a soul of wet cardboard. "Goddamned Elmer Kobb."

Haskell laughed then—a real, spontaneous laugh. "Goddamned Bob Wright, you mean. Clerk of the district court, my ass. More like the damn Emperor of Omaha. Kobb's clinging to coattails. That son of a bitch Wright knows more law than any lawyer in town. Sends anybody who looks at him sideways to the funny farm, signs off on election boards, pockets all those filing fees. What that son of a bitch can do with a pen—something else. And now his kid. Assistant DA. If that's the new guard in thirty-two, I'll head back out West."

Haskell's legs were crossed and the one on top must've been asleep. He gripped the ironed crease he'd been straightening to move it.

"So long as I got your ear," Jim said, "you're right—I'm not down here for a payout. And you sure as hell know I don't want a loan. But maybe you can point me toward somebody. It's my brother, Ward. Looks like he might get pinched by the feds for serving liquor."

"Damn federal bonds. Highway robbery."

"I know it. I've got about two-thirds—"

"Tell you what. He gets in trouble, I got a lawyer I've paid so much by now, he owes me. He can haggle it down. Still got a few friends at the courthouse, too. I'll have one call me if he shows up. You know when?"

"Tomorrow night."

"Ward Beely, is it?"

Jim said that was him.

"What kind of name is that, anyway? Beely."

Jim thought about saying Irish. Testing out Frank's theory of convenience. Maybe it was even true, but it would've felt like lying. "Not a real one. Don't know where the old man came up with it."

"Suppose they're all made up at some point."

Jim thanked Haskell, then reminded him Wilford said they needed to get going.

Haskell wished Jim luck and reassured him. "Remember what I said—syndicate charges won't stick. Don't let anybody go broke on lawyers. Lawyers always figure out how to cost exactly what you got."

Jim went back upstairs and out to the Ford. He drove to the Henley-Barr and took his time trudging up the stairs. When he was inside the office, he slipped off his overcoat and out of his holster. He called and left a message for Frank at the station. Then Jim lit a smoke, poured two drinks, and waited.

When Frank showed up, Jim slid him a drink. "Saw Haskell. Asked about the syndicate thing. Says none of the charges'll stick."

"You believe him?"

"I do."

"That don't solve the O'Neill problem."

"It don't."

"So what do we do?"

Jim took a drink to brace himself. "Last resort."

Frank was more somber than Jim recalled ever seeing him. Frank said he'd go to Pop's. Pop would take some convincing, but he'd come around. Frank would tell them all what to do and where to be. Then he'd go find O'Neill, ask if Dietz was back from St. Joe yet, say he needed a partner tomorrow night. A couple feds were raiding a south side joint, wanted Frank to do the buy.

"Listen," Frank said. "You got to trust me. I know how it sounds. I tell my own kids, don't never trust nobody who says you got to. But you got to right now, Big Jim."

Jim studied Frank's eyes. They were hazel. A little green, a little brown. Jim studied them for anything he might not want to see. Betrayal, a tell, some sign Frank saw an easy mark. But there was none of those things. Only gravity.

"I do." Jim could hardly believe it, but he did.

25

The next night, Frank called and said he was headed to the station, which meant he'd talked to the feds and convinced O'Neill to go with him to Pop's. Frank was being careful about what he said, no doubt in case somebody was listening in, but Jim wondered if Jennie and the kids were nearby. The thought made him want to call it off. Frank must've sensed it. He kept Jim talking. He asked what Jim was up to tonight. Jim said he planned to get dinner around nine or ten. Frank said he heard Monte C's was least busy at ten-thirty. The lasagna was pretty good. Jim said he'd give it a try.

Shortly before ten, Jim parked on Twenty-Third and M. Then he tried to leisurely, or at least halfway naturally, stroll the two blocks to Pop's. When he got there, all of them were upstairs—Pop, Edith, and Ward. They'd brought three bottles of whiskey and an empty barrel up from the basement and put them behind the bar. Pop was nervous, distracted. Jim tried to reassure him. Jim would be right behind the basement door. There was no way he'd let anybody get to Edith, and he'd be ready if Frank needed help. Frank or

Jim would call Pop at Carl Ziske's soft drink parlor when it was done, ring once, and hang up.

Ward had drunk more than usual, numbing his nerves. Jim tried to reassure him, too. Jim said he had two-thirds of the bond and a line on how to take care of the rest. Jim didn't say the line was Bill Haskell's lawyer, because if Ward heard Haskell's name, he'd think Jim was in too deep. And if Jim explained why he wasn't, told Ward that Haskell was a professional goat, Jim really would be in too deep.

Edith was Edith. She wasn't thrilled, but Jim didn't know what a thrilled Edith looked like. She must've been worried for Pop and Ward, but she was steadier than the four of them combined. She asked Pop for his shotgun. She'd take it in the stairwell with her, along with the downstairs dolly of barrels and bottles. She'd be fine in the stairwell, one way or another. After Frank shot O'Neill, Jim would go down there, knock twice, and he and Edith would take off. They'd hunker down at her and Ward's row house. Frank would call them when the detectives were done.

Pop hugged each of them before he left. He whispered in Jim's ear. "Keep Frank safe. The children, Jennie—they need him."

As soon as the old man left, Jim inspected the basement door so Edith and Ward could have a moment. The inspection paid off. He avoided watching the two of them get sentimental while noticing the building had settled. A crack ran between the doorjamb and wall, slim but wide enough to peer through.

After Edith went downstairs, Jim listened for the dolly,

but they kept the wheels oiled. All he caught was the sound of the wall being latched.

Jim and Ward were finally alone. Jim said, "Listen, I know it don't begin to cut it, but I'm sorry. I'm sorry I dragged everybody into this."

"I know you are." He shrugged and lit a cigarette. "Hell, I heard that owl hoot—night down on the river. Should've known something would go wrong. Should've grabbed Vern, let him have a heart attack on the train instead."

Jim thought of Pete wearing Vern's tie, the sense of it being an omen. Jim thought to say there might be something to old wives' tales, after all.

Ward said, "Anything happens—"

"It won't." It could, but Jim couldn't think about how.

Ward checked his watch, told Jim to hustle.

Jim positioned himself behind the basement door and tested the stair for groans. It creaked only in the middle, so he straddled the weakness and shifted the lock shut. The crack between the wall and the doorjamb gave him a decent sliver of vision. He could see the front door and a fair portion of the room. The view cut off anything behind the bar, but seeing anything was better than nothing.

He waited and wished his pulse were quieter so he could hear better. Then he made a point to quit wishing. When he let himself wish for one thing, he'd wind up down a hole of it. Before he knew, he'd have wished himself back to the last century. And he'd been there, last century. There was nothing fruitful back there. What was done was done. Right now he was here, Vern was dead, and Molly and Addie were in Spokane. He would've liked to think the two of them started over, better, without him. But a change of city didn't change what'd happened. Molly might've left behind as much as she could, Victrola and quilts and photos, but the stuff that took up more space, the stuff that fogged up half of what you saw when you looked at the world, she and Addie took all that with them. And maybe that gave Molly a right to loom over him, a disembodied harpy that could send telegrams. After all, plenty loomed over her and Addie.

At least they'd left him behind. He hoped it helped. He did.

When the front door drew open, the bell above it tinkled and Frank came in, said hello to Ward. There was a tightness in Frank's shoulders. That was his tell, apparently. Jim was relieved Frank had one. He bobbed to the bar and leaned his elbows, asked about Ward's day, made small talk. Then he ordered a drink. Ward's hand set a glass on the counter. That was all Jim could see of Ward, a hand on a glass. A cork pulled from a bottle with a low thud. Liquid lapped into the glass. Frank took a drink and set some change down, Ward's hand swiped it up. The cash register drawer clanked open and shut. Frank looked down into the glass when he waved at the front door.

The tinkle of the bell was muted by a rush of footfalls, though only three people entered. The feds were a pair of gray suits brandishing badges and automatic pistols they likely called "rods." One guy was squatty, the other a string bean, and both apparently read too many cheap detective-story magazines. They reminded Jim of Maloney, the way they made their voices loud and low and tried to look stern. Maybe Frank was right about them being lazy, but even lazy feds turned out to be squirrelly clowns, high on adrenaline. They stumbled over each other's lines as they announced themselves, said this was a raid, said Ward was under arrest. Both said everything four times because they kept cutting each other off.

Ward said, "Yeah, I got it," to help them out. Behind them, O'Neill had his kitchen-greased hair, chin sunk in like he'd made progress swallowing it, but he was hopped up on the thrill, too. Or nervous. He looked like he'd done a sniff. His eyes were wired. Jim pictured him looking like that right before he shot Pete three times in the head.

String Bean sprinted to the open end of the bar, which was only a few feet from the basement door and out of Jim's sight. He repeated himself, said Ward was under arrest, and Ward told him, again, he got it. Fabric rustled. Glasses thudded and shattered. Ward surely wasn't making a fuss, but that wouldn't stop these morons from making a scene of it.

The squatty one darted toward the basement door. Jim pulled his face clear of the wall's crack and loosened his fingers carefully, easily, so the knob wouldn't move on the other side.

The knob shifted quick, back and forth. Squatty's voice was aimed away, back over his shoulder. "What's this?"

"Storage," Frank said. "Owner rents it out separate." Then he said, "Well, look what we got here."

"How much?" Squatty asked.

Jim peered through the crack again. Frank was gone. He must've been behind the bar. He said there were three pints and an empty barrel. "You want the barrel?"

"If there's traces, can't hurt."

String Bean had Ward cuffed at the front door. "Let's run him in. Frank, you mind?"

"Sure. O'Neill, you want to give me a hand?"

Squatty caught up with his pal and the bell gave its tinny refrain. The feds led Ward out to the sidewalk and turned left. The door's window blinds were open, but the rest of the storefront's were closed. Jim couldn't see a car, but he heard doors shut. An engine started, revved, idled, then faded off. Jim put his thumb and forefinger on the lock, careful not to rattle it.

"Thought there'd be more than this," Frank said from behind the bar.

"More than what?" O'Neill's hands perched on his waist, his right closer to his gun than Jim liked. Jim slowly, quietly shifted the lock open.

"Than what's here, genius." The bottles clanked and the barrel thudded into view at the far end of the counter.

"I'll tell you where there was more."

"What's that?" Frank sounded distracted, which meant he was trying to sound distracted.

"Pete Gilson's."

"What about him?"

"He was running a still. Right there in the basement, behind a door."

"No kidding."

The hammer of a revolver clicked. O'Neill hadn't moved. Jim checked the bar. Frank's hands held his revolver steady above the polished wood. Jim grabbed his own from his holster. He watched O'Neill for any slight twitch.

"Hey. Frank. What's—what's this about?"

"Put your gun on the floor, kick it toward me."

"What?"

"We're gonna talk." Frank waited. "I said—" O'Neill pulled the gun from the holster. Jim trained his barrel on him.

O'Neill held his free hand up in surrender. He bent to set his gun down, then rose, slowly. He used the sole of his shoe to push the gun toward Frank. It skidded across a floor-board and stopped. The wood was uneven. O'Neill looked at the gun like it was pointed at him. When he swallowed, Jim could've sworn O'Neill's chin sank in and didn't come back out as far. "It didn't go," he said. "I tried to kick it—it didn't go."

"You scooted it. You didn't kick it, you scooted it. Kick it."

O'Neill had both hands raised, palms facing Frank. He took a step toward the gun, set his sole on it again, and pushed. It skidded a few more floorboards.

"That's a *scoot*," Frank said. "Ain't you never kicked a thing in your goddamn life? Forget it. Step back. Take two big steps back and stay there."

O'Neill did. Frank came out from behind the bar and plucked up O'Neill's gun. He set it on the counter, then leaned his elbows back on the rail. He held his gun in his left hand and chewed a matchstick, likely because he wanted a smoke but didn't have enough hands to light one. "Why'd you kill him? Pete Gilson."

"Frank—"

"Don't say you didn't. I know you did. Just say why."

"But I—"

Frank let a shot off. It hit the wall between O'Neill and the basement door and echoed like a flicked sheet of metal.

Till the echo died off, nobody spoke. Or if they did, Jim couldn't hear it over the ringing and the pulse in his head.

Then O'Neill talked, fast and panicked. "Maloney. Maloney said to. He's mixed up with politicians—said they needed a civilian. Somebody who wasn't a bootlegger. He said do Pete Gilson. He told me about the still, said get rid of it."

Jim studied O'Neill. He was barely older than a kid. Twenty-one, twenty-two.

"Why Pete?"

"I don't know."

"Sure you do."

"He did a favor, they said. They were scared he'd talk."

They were right about that, Kobb and the rest. Pete had talked. He'd talked to Jim and Frank, said O'Neill told him to make Gus look like a homicide. O'Neill knew good and goddamned well what the favor was.

Frank was scrutinizing O'Neill. Chewing the match. "Where's the watch Gilson had on?"

"What?"

"You trying to use up my bullets? Don't. I got a lot. Where the hell's the watch?"

O'Neill was stuttering, stuck between an "I didn't" and "I don't." He shook his head, quick. "I didn't see any—I don't know anything about a watch." He was scared, holding his hands like this was a stickup, eyes wide.

Christ.

Pete knew Dietz was O'Neill's partner. They delivered bodies to him. When O'Neill showed up, Pete would've taken off Dietz's watch, put it in his pocket or thrown it somewhere—in a drawer, in the crematory, behind some formaldehyde bottles.

This was why Jim didn't play chess. He got too far ahead of himself. Predicted wrong. Assumed.

Worse, Jim and Frank had done the same thing everybody waiting for the evening edition of the paper did. They'd rooted around for a why, a specific reason O'Neill killed Pete. They hadn't dug up anything profound, but they'd come up with an answer. And the answer was wrong.

Frank went quiet. Jim couldn't tell what Frank was thinking. "Where's Dietz?"

"I don't know. I swear to you, Frank—I know what I said—I told you and Cap both he's in St. Joe. It's all I could think of. He's got family down there. I was covering for him."

"Yeah?" Frank took a moment, still thinking. "What all's he got you covering?"

"What? I mean so he don't get fired." O'Neill went quiet then, like a thought struck him. "Wait. If he did something—I mean outside us, outside work or Maloney's thing—I don't know about it, Frank, I don't. Anything he's done—I don't know."

O'Neill didn't just look like a weasel, then. One shot at a wall, a couple questions from Frank, and O'Neill gave up his partner. But O'Neill did look like a sincere weasel. He really didn't seem to know where Dietz was.

Frank was mulling something over.

"Frank, I—"

"Shut up. So you don't know nothing. About Dietz skipping town." Jim eyed him. Frank had a plan. Jim didn't know what it was, but Frank had one.

"Shit." O'Neill looked to the floor, thinking. "I don't. I don't know anything. But now you say it, it makes sense. Kid on the way, wife's family hates him."

"That ain't what I mean and you know it. You think he'd go to St. Joe?"

"Frank, I don't know what he did. I swear."

Frank repeated the question louder and enunciated it: "Do you think he'd go to St. Joe?"

"Not if he don't want to be found." Then a spark lit in O'Neill's eyes. "He mentioned someplace. Redwoods? Is there a Redwoods? In California?"

Frank used the hand that wasn't holding a gun to pinch the bridge of his nose. Jim suspected Frank wanted to shoot O'Neill for asking if there were redwoods in California. "You mean Redlands?"

"That's it—Redlands—he talked about it—couple times—you think he went there?"

"He could've," Frank said, like it was possible, on some metaphysical plane. Frank's shoulders loosened then, and the air in the room shifted. The electricity left it. When Frank spoke, all the sharpness, the interrogation, was gone. "Shit. Look, I'm sorry. Maloney and Kobb got you wrapped up in their thing, with the wiretaps, frame-ups—"

"You know about all that? The wiretaps?"

Frank said Dietz told him about it. Didn't know all the details, but they'd talked a little. "Then Dietz goes and pulls—" Frank took a heavy breath, like everything was too much. "Look, it all got crisscrossed, and I'm sorry. I'm sorry I put you on the spot, kid. I thought the thing with Pete Gilson was fallout from what Dietz got himself into. I figured he had you in on it, just because you're partners." Frank had been gesturing with his gun. Now he holstered it.

O'Neill let his arms down but he stayed put. "Shit—what'd he do?"

"Nah, now—this? What just happened here? It was too close. I ain't getting you mixed up in Dietz's mess. Not when Maloney's got you neck-deep in all that other garbage—by the way, no hard feelings. About the wiretap."

"Wait—what? No," O'Neill said. "We wired your—*FT*," he said, like the letters were a revelation. "You over on Twenty-Second?"

"Yeah, it's all right. If I ain't doing nothing wrong, don't gotta be scared of no wiretap, right?"

"Sure, but—Frank, that ain't right. I'll go take it down. Maloney won't know the difference."

"Nah, it's fine. Oh, hey," he said, offhanded, like an afterthought. "But I took down some wires you guys ran—six. Don't get sore—not like I'm trying to help Maloney, but it was the wrong gauge. Didn't know if it could short out somebody's phone line. Why'd you switch gauges?"

"What? I didn't switch gauges." O'Neill was relaxed enough to have half his chin back. "So that's why they looked wrong. The wires. After you and me ran Strba to Kava's, you know how I was checking—wait. You knew I was feeding you a line about the syndicate? Tapping phones?"

"Don't worry about it. I know I ain't supposed to know details."

"Yeah, but still. I'm sorry. I was seeing where Dietz did his, how many was left. How many I'd have to do if he didn't show back up. I knew something didn't look right. He switched gauges?"

"Must've. Maybe ran out. I don't know. Fella had a lot on his plate." Frank reached upward, stretched his back, and yawned.

Frank had resurrected Dietz, put him on the lam, and now even the missing wiretaps were explained away. Jim could've popped from the basement door right now and slapped the doll-headed squirt on the back.

Frank grabbed two of the three bottles from the bar, then must've seen O'Neill's revolver there. Frank handed it over. Jim kept his barrel trained, but O'Neill slid the gun in his holster.

"Say, one thing I didn't ask Dietz," Frank said. "You know that dead Fritz? Rounder down by the coal pile? Nobody said what he was up to, where to find him?" He handed O'Neill the empty whiskey barrel and slid the third bottle between his forearm and chest.

"Nah—thought he was passed out. Was gonna take him in as a vagrant, but he was dead."

"No blood, though—how'd it even get an inquest?"

Frank said he hadn't asked Dietz about it. He wasn't supposed to know. About Pete's favor—drenching Gus's clothes in somebody else's blood.

"They were all backed up." O'Neill hadn't caught on. Maybe he wouldn't. Maybe he was so dense or confused he'd never get it. "Maloney says make anything we find look like gangland. I shot him a few times—" He stopped, gave an embarrassed laugh. "Didn't think—dead guy won't bleed. But I told Cap it looked like a gunshot victim, and only me, Dietz, and Gilson—" O'Neill stopped. "Wait, why do you—how did you—"

Jim's shoulders drew tight. O'Neill was far enough left the bullet wouldn't hit Frank. Jim held his breath and pulled the hammer back. O'Neill's grip on the empty whiskey barrel loosened. Time slowed enough that the empty barrel floated free. Jim pulled the trigger. Dust puffed from a brick by the front door. Jim pulled the hammer back again as the barrel hit the floor. O'Neill's hand was on his pistol grip. Frank looked back at Jim, confused. Confusion didn't look right on Frank. Jim pulled the trigger again. The pop clogged his ears so everything past his heartbeat was muffled.

O'Neill swatted his neck, like a deerfly had landed and bit. It was his gun hand. He looked at his fingers like he might've seen the dirt-brown bug. He must've seen blood, but he swatted again. Then again. He kept swatting, steady, like he was locked in the moment he first felt the urge to. Frank stared at him, still holding the bottles. Jim cocked his hammer once more. He reached and felt for the doorknob. He turned it and the door yawned open. Frank stared at O'Neill's swatting. Frank's head flinched back with each slap. As Jim neared, he saw Frank flinched because O'Neill was swatting blood on him.

Jim was close enough to reach Frank's shoulder. He pulled Frank away. There was a hole in the back of O'Neill's head. Right above the neck. Jim bent around to get a look at O'Neill's face. One of his eyes was crossed.

"See a bullet come out?" Jim asked Frank.

"What?"

It was bouncing around. Or it had, enough that O'Neill's brain had been whipped like an egg beater got inside. He needed put down. The blinds on the door were still open. Jim shut them and locked the door. Then he reached, slow, like O'Neill's revolver was a snake's neck, and pulled the pistol free. He hadn't needed to be cautious. O'Neill didn't notice. O'Neill couldn't notice anything anymore. Jim stepped back. So the shot would come from a bit of distance. He pulled the trigger. The swatting hand dropped. Then O'Neill did.

"You all right?" Jim asked Frank.

"Nah."

Jim appreciated his honesty. Jim wasn't all right, either. He was hollowed out, ears ringing.

"The fuck happened?"

Jim's voice came hollow, too. "You said you didn't ask Dietz about Gus. Weren't supposed to know Pete made it look like homicide. He went for his gun, I got a shot off. Went in, made a mess, didn't come out."

"Holy Christ."

Jim couldn't feel his hands but saw them open the cylinder of O'Neill's gun. He checked the bullets. Flea market of ammo. Jim fired a round into the far end of the bar. He moved Frank aside and fired another, low, into the wall. He thought to use his handkerchief to wipe his prints, then squatted down. He didn't understand why he couldn't feel his own hands, only O'Neill's—his palm, warm and damp. Jim wrapped the hand around the gun, then let go. Let the pistol fall to the floor.

Jim told Frank the story for the detectives. O'Neill was out of his head. When he neared the door, he fired a shot back at Frank rounding the bar. Frank shot and missed, hit the brick. Frank shot again, same distance, then rushed him. They struggled, Frank forced O'Neill's arm down, and O'Neill got a shot off, hit the wall. Frank leapt back, fired the last bullet.

Frank's voice and eyes were flat. Maybe he was hollowed out, too. "There's another one. Slug I shot in the wall. To get him talking."

Jim said he'd wipe up the dust, mix it with spackle. The detectives wouldn't see it if they weren't looking. He'd check the crack he shot through, clean that up, too. "Let me see your gun." Frank handed it over. It was the same caliber as Jim's. "What if you got a Colt? Instead of Smith and Wesson."

Frank sounded less hollow than hypnotized. Half asleep. "Been shifted around so many departments—gun wasn't issued anyway. It's mine." His voice changed. Sharpened. "Christ. Christ. Why'd I keep talking?"

Jim wanted to stay hollowed out. "You'd resurrected a dead guy and saved Pop's skin. You were on a roll." Jim slid Frank's revolver in his own holster and handed his over. Jim said he'd clean up the shot in the wall and turned away. Frank reached up, gripped Jim's shoulder. Jim looked at him. Frank's eyes were welling.

Jim quit looking at him. "You didn't do it, I did. You tried harder to avoid it than anybody would've."

Jim didn't say trying didn't count for a goddamned thing. Not when a guy barely older than a kid was dead and didn't have to be. Jim needed Frank to get his head on straight. Then Jim needed to go to the office. Get his own head as crooked as whiskey and morphine could make it.

Before he could walk toward the basement door, Frank

grabbed him with both arms. He latched on like a wrestling hold—Jim's arms were pinned to his sides. Jim didn't know what the hell Frank was doing. Frank was too small to wrestle Jim.

Then Jim knew what was happening. After a delay. Like the time he'd gotten shocked rewiring Ma's place, like the time Maloney beaned him.

Frank was holding him. Jim let him. He let Frank hold on to him and tremble.

On the floor, the kid's crossed eye was empty.

26

Jim knocked twice on the stairwell panel in Pop's basement, and he and Edith left for Carl Ziske's. Edith went in. When Pop was in the Ford, he was panicked—he'd expected the single ring of the phone. Where was Frank? Was Frank okay?

Jim told him Frank was fine. Frank wasn't fine, but he wasn't dead.

Jim said the detectives would be a while. He pulled up to the row house and went in with them. He washed in the bathroom, saw blood on the soles of his shoes, on his overcoat and shirt. He washed his shoes in the sink. He took off the overcoat and shirt. He'd throw them in a garbage bin on the street between here and the office. His pants were dark. He dabbed the few spots he could see and called for Edith, asked to borrow one of Ward's undershirts. She slipped it through the cracked bathroom door.

When he was done, he asked if the two of them needed anything. They said they didn't. "What do we do about Ward's bond?" Edith asked.

"I'll take care of it. He'll be all right." Jim was more spent with every word that came out of him. He said he needed to go to the office. He said to call if they needed anything.

He took Twenty-Fourth to pass Pop's on his way downtown. A squad car and a police ambulance were parked at the curb.

Before he got to the Henley-Barr, he pulled over on a deserted block of Seventeenth and shoved the overcoat and shirt in a garbage bin. Then he drove on, parked outside the office, and took the back stairs. He went up slow, to preserve his breath. Before he entered the hallway, he listened. The corridor was quiet. When he rounded the corner, he saw he'd left his light on. At the door, he fumbled with the key, but the knob turned. It was unlocked.

The door drew open. Shumway was inside, sitting in Frank's chair. Jim knew it was Shumway by the sheriff's getup. Standing behind him was an Omaha cop. Downtown station. Jim recognized the face but didn't know him. Jim walked to his desk and pulled back his chair.

"Don't get comfortable," Shumway said. "You're under arrest."

It was appropriate, but Jim asked anyway. "What for?"

"Murder of Pete Gilson."

Jim hadn't pulled the trigger, but maybe there was something to it. If he hadn't killed Vern, Jim wouldn't have taken Vern to Gilson. Jim wouldn't have been hired by Donnegan, and Jim wouldn't have hired Gus, who wouldn't have died at the coal pile the night O'Neill found him. Pete wouldn't have been picked to be Kobb's civilian because he wouldn't have been a loose end. So, sure enough. Jim hadn't pulled the trigger, but he was responsible for Pete's murder.

Shumway looked like his voice sounded on the phone. Old farm boy, probably German parents, face wrinkled from squinting at the sun. His jaw sprouted a three- or four-o'clock shadow. Under his department-issued Stetson, his hair was likely gray, the kind of gray that used to be blond, the kind that took a long time to turn. "During our phone call, I noticed you're a little ill-tempered." Shumway must not have liked it when Jim had agreed with him, said that he had Shumway's number. Maybe Shumway didn't enjoy wordplay. "And you had motive—circumstantial evidence of a necktie suggests you killed Vern, took him to Gilson. After I saw Gilson and left you a phone message, you killed him to cover your tracks. Thin, but it's motive. And you've got means. Speaking of which, leave your gun on the desk." Shumway didn't pull his own weapon. He likely saw Jim was too tired—too out of sorts—to fight him.

Jim took Frank's revolver from his holster and set it on the desk. "The timing don't line up." He wasn't arguing. He was reminding Shumway as a professional courtesy.

"It don't. But you got to start somewhere."

Start somewhere. If Shumway thought he could jump into somewhere and find the start, Jim wished him luck. Good luck finding the start of the series of reactions that led to them looking at each other right here, right now. But Jim didn't have the energy to wish Shumway luck. It took all the energy Jim had to wish Pete was still Pete. To wish O'Neill wasn't lying cross-eyed on a floor across town.

Besides, Jim got the gist. "Starting somewhere" meant Shumway planned to make Jim a hobby. Send him to jail two nights here, three nights there, until he decided Jim had served an equivalent to whatever sentence he might've gotten for killing Vern Meyer. It was fair enough.

The downtown cop was the one who cuffed him, but if he thought he was bringing in the murderer of Pete Gilson, he lacked the pomp of pinching a suspect in a high-profile killing.

Jim noticed the cop and Shumway had the same eyes, same jaw. Jim asked if they were related.

Shumway said the cop was his nephew.

Jim nodded. "Resemblance."

They didn't have far to travel, only across the street and the courthouse lawn. Jim had been in the courthouse more times than he'd been inside Council Chambers, but it was always during daylight hours. Now, at night, the place was practically empty. He passed the gold cashier cages and crossed the marble and mosaics. The place was like Greek ruins before they'd been ruined. The wreckage of monuments must've been a product of time. Of sitting back, waiting, doing nothing. Jim was more accustomed to hastier varieties.

Shumway and his nephew chatted as they made their way to the top floor, where the cells were. They made small talk. They exchanged news about shared acquaintances, shirt-tail relations. While Jim was being printed, photographed, frisked, and assigned to a bunk, he hoped to get a glimpse of Ward, make sure he was all right. That the G-men hadn't roughed him up. But the jailer led Jim to the first cell in the corridor, which was narrow, and all the cells were on the left, a concrete wall on the right. Shumway told Jim to get a good night's sleep. He said he was headed over to the Hotel Fontana for the night. That seemed fitting, too. Jim had once made the Fontana patrons a hobby; now one of their guests was making Jim one.

After the jailer locked the cell and walked out of sight, Jim called, "Ward?"

The jailer was close by, apparently. He barked, "Quiet."

Ward didn't answer, but Jim recognized his brother's snore. It was lower-pitched than it'd been years ago, when they lived with Ma out past the beltway. Jim let him sleep. Ward deserved a rest. Jim lay down on the thin tick mattress of the bottom bunk. It wasn't much different from the one in the office across the street.

With his eyes shut, he tried not to see anything—no Molly, no sandbars, no deerflies.

Minutes passed. They might've added up to hours. Jim couldn't say.

"Ward Beely," the jailer called. He sounded like he was reading off a roster, making sure everyone was accounted-for. Jim waited to hear his own name, but it didn't come. No other names came, either. Somewhere in the concrete corridor, Ward snorted and cleared his throat. Metal creaked, and boot soles brushed the concrete. The jailer passed Jim's cell studying a clipboard. Then keys jangled, and a lock shifted with a thunk. A cell door rattled and slid.

Jim sat up as much as he could without hitting the empty bunk above him. He rested back on his elbows. Ward followed the jailer, no cuffs or shackles. He looked over. "Jim."

"Quiet."

Jim asked where the jailer was taking Ward.

"Bonded out. Quiet."

27

Jim lay on the cot after Ward was bonded out but didn't sleep. Each time he closed his eyes, he pictured O'Neill's hand, swatting. Eyes open, he pictured Ward walking by, looking confused. Jim couldn't be glad his brother was out—he didn't know what it meant. He didn't know who had the money for a federal bond, besides Maymie, who had no reason to help Ward, and Elmer Kobb, who'd made a point to say he knew Jim's family. Maybe framing up Pop, Ward, and Edith with a wiretap wasn't enough for someone who'd had Jim's house bombed.

Jim needed to call the row house. Find out if Ward had gotten there safe, make sure he hadn't been sprung so Kobb could have him gunned down in the street.

Jim yelled, said he needed to make a phone call.

No one answered. The minutes passed. Hours, maybe.

A door opened and shut. A pair of voices echoed against the concrete and brick. One was the jailer, the other Shumway.

Shumway stopped in front of the cell and leaned back against the blank wall that faced it. "Get some shut-eye?"

Jim almost said a jail bunk wasn't the Fontana, but it'd work in a pinch. Then he remembered Shumway didn't care for wordplay. "Know where my brother is? Ward Beely? Heard anything?"

"I don't know anything about your brother."

That offered a little relief. If Ward had been gunned down and Shumway saw the name "Beely" in the paper, he likely wouldn't hold back about it.

"I got to thinking last night I didn't explain myself well. Just expected you to know why I'd put you here. And that's not right. If a man doesn't know why he's locked up, he can't learn from it."

Since the scene at Pop's, Jim hadn't felt much. Hollow. Dread. Some panic over Ward. But Shumway talking like Jim was a kid who'd broken a window with a slingshot, been beaten with a switch over it, and now needed a sermon made Jim feel his pulse beat in his head again.

"On the phone I said if I had a daughter and Vern Meyer did to her—well, what he does—I might turn around and kill him." Shumway drew a breath and looked toward the ceiling. "Well, in truth, I'd like to think I wouldn't."

Jim didn't know what was worse: Shumway's tack when he tried to coerce a confession, pretending he could put himself in Jim's shoes, or this, the sheriff thinking he really knew how he'd act if he was somebody else. "Maybe I'd like to think I wouldn't, either."

Shumway stared into Jim's right eye, then his left. "You might think whatever you did to Vern Meyer was a favor. To your daughter. To the girl up in Kennard. Her parents. Favor to the whole world."

Shumway was giving Jim too much credit. Sure, Jim had thought it. That the world was better off. But that was hindsight. The kind that let you live with a thing. When he'd killed Vern, Jim hadn't been doing anybody a favor. Down on the river that night, Jim wanted to stop feeling what he felt. That was all. That was the whole of it. And to some extent, it worked. Like a tourniquet. It stopped the hemorrhaging, but it didn't cauterize, didn't stitch. A tourniquet didn't stop a thing that'd happened, a thing that couldn't be undone.

"I'm here to tell you it wasn't a favor." Shumway stayed leaned back against the wall but shifted his weight. Made himself more comfortable. He planned on taking his time, apparently. "That girl's parents up in Kennard deserved something. And you took it. You stole it. They deserved to make that man—if you can call him that—they deserved to make him look them in the eye, knowing what he did. They deserved him to know they saw him. For what he was."

"What he was." Jim rolled to his side and pushed himself up to sit. All his life, people asked Jim what he was. What kind of a name was Beely. As if a name said anything about what a person was. But people didn't like it, when they couldn't peg you easy. And Jim was guilty of doing the same goddamned thing.

There was a time Jim thought Vern was a mad dog. An animal so far gone he only knew to attack. Even if it'd been true, a mad dog alone in the world was a sad thing. "You think Vern boils down to something he did. But that's not all somebody is. A thing they did."

"So you've got a soft spot for Meyer, is that it? Hold no malice against him for molesting your daughter?"

"I'm saying all I know about Vern is he helped me once when nobody would've, then turned around and—" He didn't need to say it. "Whatever else he was, I don't know. I don't know what somebody walks around hoping or remembering. But I'd guess it's more than a thing they've done."

When Jim killed Vern, he hadn't undone what Vern did to Addie. He'd killed everything else Vern was and could've been. And now Jim had killed a man who was little more than a kid. A kid who'd murdered Pete, sure, but killing that kid didn't unkill Pete. It just ended him. Stopped him from being everything else he was. Stopped him from ever feeling the weight of what he'd done, or of trying, for the rest of his days, to do no more harm. Or do less, anyway. To be better.

Granted, maybe O'Neill never would've felt the weight. Maybe he was a good man by Pop's definition. Maybe he had no brains. Was a budding tyrant. But that was just pegging somebody, too, Pop's definition. Slicing somebody down to one sliver, one pin, that could be poked into a cushion. Put in its place, tidied away.

Shumway wasn't interested in conversation, apparently. Shumway had a point to make. "That girl's parents deserved to hear a judge sentence him. They deserved to know he'd pay for what he did."

Jim wondered if Shumway, honest to God, believed that. If he honest to God believed people could look at each other and see what they were. If he believed wrongs could be righted through math. Some hours. Jim wanted to say wrongs couldn't be righted by eradicating someone from the earth, much less locking them in a room for a specific number of hours. Maybe Shumway had campaigned for sheriff so many times he'd started believing the slogans. "Pay," Jim said. "Like a gas bill? A man does a thing, pays for it like a can of beans at the Hinky Dinky?"

"Yeah, well, it's what we've got. And it's all we got."

"Then we're in some rough goddamned shape."

A door opened again. A pair of voices bit back and forth, heated. One was the jailer. The other was Frank, and he was loud. Jim's heart beat hard in his chest and his head but it couldn't decide why. The heart didn't know whether to beat with hope, with relief that Frank was here and had some heat back in his voice, or to beat with dread. If Frank was heated because something went wrong, if he'd been pinched for killing O'Neill, Jim didn't know if the heart in his chest could take it. He breathed shallow, tried to quiet the pounding.

"You think I give a shit?" Frank said. "Get your goddamn keys out. Get them out." Keys. Maybe Frank was cuffed, but the demand sounded more like he had a gun on the jailer. Jim needed to see what the hell was going on. But the corridor was too narrow. The line of sight was too slim.

The jailer said, "Frank, you got no—"

Frank's voice cut low and menacing. "I got no what? You gonna tell me I got no paperwork? Some form needs filled out? I got no what, you hayseed prick?"

Shumway had turned to watch the melee, right hand resting on his sidearm.

"I wouldn't," Jim said.

Shumway didn't. He watched, brows knit.

Frank told the jailer to go fuck himself. The jailer said he was calling Frank's captain. "Good," Frank said. "Call him. Go fuck yourself while you call him."

Frank stepped into view. He was in uniform, Jim's pistol in his holster. He glanced over, a short look that didn't tell Jim anything other than Frank was riled. Frank looked up and studied Shumway's face, then checked his badge. He reached a forefinger to flip the bottom of it. "What's that, Washington County? You ain't got enough farmers to pinch for fucking cows up there?"

Shumway was stone-faced. Maybe the livestock thing was a sore spot. He looked to Jim. "Who's this charmer?"

Frank snapped his fingers. "Over here." Shumway tilted his head back to say his patience was worn thin. Frank wasn't quite a foot shorter than Shumway, but he was close. He straightened and strained to get as high as he could. His voice went low again. "You know good and well who the fuck I am. You seen me in the papers. 'Who's this charmer?' This charmer's Frank Tvrdik. Jim Beely's alibi for the night Pete Gilson got murdered. He was helping me with a case. South Omaha. That's all you need to know about it."

"You know each other pretty well, then," Shumway said. "Good pals? Don't suppose you know anything about Vern Meyer."

Frank's whole body shifted then. Relaxed. "Vern Meyer? Sure." Now Frank sounded like Shumway was his next-door neighbor and they'd run into each other here, as if here was a hardware store. "Heard he ducked into town last night, bonded out Ward Beely, took off again." His volume lowered like he was broaching a delicate topic. "Word around town's he put Jim's family through all kinds of hell." Hands on his waist, he shrugged. "Maybe he figured bonding out Ward was something. Ticket-seller down at the Burlington says he showed up, then left again about an hour later. You got time and want to check, I can run you down there," he offered. "Eddie Tvrdik's the fella sells tickets. You want to verify Meyer posted bond, we can check the ledger downstairs."

The two of them stood in silence, Frank casual, Shumway's jaw clenched. Shumway was first to blink. He puckered his mouth a bit, looked to the floor with a nod. "Omaha's finest."

The door down the hall opened again. Keys jangled against keys. No one said anything as the jailer approached the cell. He didn't look at Frank or Shumway or Jim. The lock shifted open with a thunk.

Jim and Frank left Shumway upstairs, arguing with the jailer. On their way out of the courthouse, Frank gave an inconspicuous, low wave for Jim to follow. Frank led him to a gold cashier's cage. The woman behind the counter slid Frank a ledger, turned her back, and walked away, toward some filing cabinets. Frank pulled the book through the opening and pointed. It was the register of bond receipts. Across the page from Ward's name and "$3,000.00" was a signature: Vurn Mier.

"Don't suppose you're cozy with Bill Haskell," Frank said.

Maybe Haskell decided Jim had overpaid on that loan years back. Or maybe bonding out Ward was encouragement for Jim to keep a lid on Haskell's secret—that he was a willing patsy, a professional goat. Haskell likely suspected Jim didn't lose much sleep over the prospect of bleeding out in a gutter. "I don't have the cash or clout to be cozy to Haskell," Jim finally managed.

"Ward's home with Edith," Frank said.

28

Jim and Frank walked out of the courthouse. It was morning. They crossed the lawn then Farnam Street. Frank stopped at a car outside the Henley-Barr. It was his own car. Jim recognized it from the garage where they'd dug through buckets and bins for spools of wire. Frank pulled out some clothes piled on the front seat. He shut the door and he and Jim went upstairs to the office.

While Frank changed behind the bathroom partitions, he said the south side detectives found the array of bullets in O'Neill's gun. Once the ballistics came back from Chicago, they'd link the gun to Pete's murder. "And then I quit," Frank said.

"You didn't."

"I did." The captain hadn't wanted him to; he'd wanted Frank to take some time off and think about it. Frank said he didn't need to think about it. He was through. He said he'd finish his shift and be done.

He'd called the row house to see how Pop and Edith were holding up. Ward answered and said the jailer told him Shumway locked Jim up for murdering Pete. Frank stayed a cop long enough to go to the courthouse, check the ledger to see who'd bonded Ward out, and clear Jim of the charges. "Jennie's wanted me to quit for years. She'll smack the hell out of me over money, then kiss me for quitting." He said he was fair with carpentry. He liked carpentry.

He came out dressed in his street clothes and sat in his chair. He wasn't riled up anymore. Once Frank sat down, Jim saw Frank's eyes were dimmer. If they'd been flashlights, their batteries would've been running low. Jim poured him a drink, gave him a cigarette.

Frank took a swallow. "Remember that thing you said— no use hating a squirrel for being what it is? About how Vern and Gus didn't pick what they were?"

Jim remembered. He remembered he'd said it to change the subject.

"Some things you can pick. Last night, I picked. When I quit, that was me picking." He'd lit a cigarette and took a long drag. "You know that's what *heresy* means? It's Greek. 'To pick.'"

"It's a wonder you don't fall over, that big head so crammed."

"The part I don't know's how you live with what you been."

Jim didn't know either. "We'll figure it out."

"Doubt it." He exhaled smoke. "That kid." He shook his head once, quick.

Jim would've said "that kid" killed Pete Gilson, but it didn't make a single thing different.

"I sat there with him, after you left," Frank said. "Waited

on a barstool. Thought, *Who the fuck am I, sitting on a barstool?*"

"You didn't pull the trigger."

Frank gave him a look. Closed-lipped and unconvinced. "You hadn't, he would've. Or I would've. No matter which, somebody's sitting on a barstool, waiting with a dead guy. Watching a clock."

"Yeah, well, you wouldn't've been there—" Jim stopped. But he'd say it. O'Neill wasn't Frank's fault. Frank should know it. "None of us would've been there—Pete and Gus wouldn't be dead. Not if I hadn't killed Vern."

Frank had already smoked the cigarette down to his fingers. He stubbed it out and lit another. Jim couldn't tell if Frank had registered what Jim said.

"I killed him, Frank."

Frank looked at him with mild confusion, as if Jim had said a common name and Frank was figuring out which person Jim meant. "Did you think I thought he fell in a cistern?" Frank blinked. His eyes narrowed, not in menace. Disbelief. Then his nostrils gave a slight flare. His eyes lit a little. "You did. You thought I bought it." A quick, flat chuckle bubbled out of him. An uncontrollable thud of surprise.

"I didn't know. I just never said it. Out loud."

"Well, you probably shouldn't. 'Cistern.' 'Freak accident.' Big Jim, I ain't stupid. Not saying a thing don't make it less apparent."

"Listen, Ward don't know. What I did. You and me, that's it."

"Think Shumway's got a pretty good idea, but he can't

prove it." Frank took another drink, another drag. "Anyway, you and me got other problems. Killed people and kept breathing. Breathing ain't living. How you live after that?"

Jim didn't know. He didn't have the first idea. "Say, 'There but by the grace of God'?"

"Grace?"

"It was something to say."

"Yeah, but maybe it's grace. Maybe grace ain't something somebody doles out like a pardon."

"Then I suspect it ain't grace."

Frank sifted ideas in his head. The lights in his eyes brightened a touch more. "What's the word, then? The one that lets you live with who you been but keeps your head on straight. Knowing you ain't above or below. Ain't in the position to accept or forgive or condemn nobody."

"I don't know that one."

"Well, I say we call it grace till we find out. Because whatever it is, we need it. You and me both. Otherwise, I don't know where the hell we are."

Jim had a fair idea. "A pit."

"That's it. That's where we're at, all right. Bottom of a goddamn pit."

They weren't down on a sandbar at night, staring out at the river and bluffs, but the skin at the back of Jim's neck prickled. Maybe two sets of eyes could see the same. Not all the time, not necessarily simultaneously. Maybe only in rare glimpses. But rare glimpses were something.

"Guess we might as well try climbing up," Frank said.

Jim supposed they might as well. As long as they were still here, they might as well try.

29

One early Friday evening in May 1933, Jim finished the week's books while Frank read the *Tribune* at his desk across the room. Roughly three years had passed since the building superintendent of the Henley-Barr whittled the gold-stenciled BEELY NAT'L INVESTIGATIONS off the mottled glass. Jim and Frank dropped the "national" angle and opted for BEELY & TVRDIK INVESTIGATORS. It cost only one more letter than Jim shelled out for originally.

"What a prick." Frank lit a cigarette.

"Who now?"

"Eh, Wright's brat." Wright's kid might've been the DA's assistant, but he'd done more lawyering in the mass indictment and trial than the actual DA. And he hadn't shut up about it since the circus ended, nearly six months ago. "Says the judge didn't call Maloney abnormal."

"Don't think he did. Think it was 'abnormally deceitful.'"

"Say—Maloney could still pitch that picture." Frank held up his hand like he was gripping an invisible theater marquee as he read it. *"Abnormally Deceitful Star Witness."*

A movie called *Star Witness* had come out before Maloney

even took the stand. Stole his thunder. Jim and Frank watched it at the Palisade around the time Maloney was suspended from the police again. Kobb had won the police commissioner's seat in '30 and reinstated Maloney as sergeant, but Maloney got tangled up with the wife of a rich gambler, impersonated the guy at an auto garage, and stole his car. Donnegan got Maloney off the hook, scored him immunity for his testimony in the liquor syndicate trial. The trial ended in a hung jury shortly after the AG lost reelection. The prosecution opted not to retry the case, since prosecuting hadn't been the point. It'd all been more election-year antics. And now Wright's kid seemed to think if he kept saying he'd been successful, taken down Bill Haskell and his machine, people would eventually believe it.

At any rate, Haskell was right, none of the charges stuck. Now Kobb was mayor and Maloney was his "special investigator," along with a grifter who claimed he'd worked for Chicago's Secret Six.

"First the brat says the jury's rigged. Then the system's wrong—should be ten votes out of twelve."

"Said feds signed off on the wiretaps, too." The feds hadn't. And the cops who did the listening wrote conversations in longhand, then swore they knew the difference between fifty different voices. "He says a lot of things. Sore loser."

"I wish that loser was sore. Mistrial. Gets to say he didn't lose, leave out he didn't win."

"Let him talk. All anybody's got to do is read the trial transcripts, see it was a farce." Jim pulled a cork from the bottle of whiskey in his desk drawer. "You want some?"

Frank checked his watch. "Nah, wait till you get home for that."

Jim put the cork back.

He hadn't asked Frank to be his partner; Frank just said he would be. He said he was tired of not solving cases when suspects were too important or victims weren't important enough. Plus, he'd been sore when O'Neill's gun went missing from an evidence locker and Pete wound up a "homicide: no suspects." Jim warned Frank half the work was finding stolen cars and the occasional undergarment, but Frank didn't care. He wanted to work with Jim. He had only one condition. Jim had to get an apartment. Stop sleeping in the goddamn office and keeping his dirty washcloths and towels there. It was depressing.

"*Abnormally Deceitful Star Witness,*" Frank repeated with a chuckle.

"It's a good title. I'd watch it if I hadn't already." Jim capped his fountain pen and closed the ledger. "Say, I'm heading out."

"See you in the funny papers. Hey, don't forget—Jennie wants to feed you Sunday."

Jim stood and put on his hat. "What are we eating? Ox ass?"

"Nah. You got an ox ass already. It'd be cannibalism."

Jim swatted a good night at him and headed down the stairs of the Henley-Barr, but he didn't round the corner to the Ford. He didn't drive to work anymore. He'd moved into the place Pospisil had vacated on Nineteenth, five blocks from the office. Jim had to pass the Quivira's courtyard and its iron gate twice a day, but he crossed the street and didn't look at it.

The night air was hot for May. He was sweating when he climbed the sidewalk of Nineteenth. He wondered what the climb would've been like before all the road grading. He went up the concrete stairs and flipped open the mailbox. Every night he checked it, and every night he held his breath a little less tight in his chest. There was no postcard, no letter, nothing from Molly or Addie. He was glad. Each time the mailbox was empty, he was a little surer they'd moved on. Not wholly. He knew they carried around everything that'd happened. So did he. But day by day, new things piled on old and somehow lessened the weight.

He unlocked the door, which opened to a steep staircase. The apartment wasn't laid out like a row house or anything else Jim had seen. He trudged up to the top landing, then made a U-turn where the hall ran back the opposite way. He walked down it and made a right into the living room. He put on "East St. Louis Toodle-Oo," poured himself a drink, lit a smoke, and walked back out to the landing, which led to a sunporch.

He was glad the night was unseasonably hot. On hot nights, he'd sleep out here, the windows open so he could feel the breeze. Some nights he fell asleep thinking he didn't deserve to be here, above the streets and sidewalks and gutters, still breathing. Other nights he was grateful.

All of the nights, he thought about grace.

ACKNOWLEDGMENTS

I'd like to acknowledge everyone who's tolerated me during the writing of this book. Special thanks to Will, as always and in particular.

Thanks to my agent, Emily Forland; my editor, Daphne Durham; and Daphne's assistant, Brianna Fairman.

Thanks and apologies to patient friends who waded through the first-draft muck: Orenda Fink, Jason Allison, John Woods, Richard Stock, and BFF Mike Walker. An extra helping of gratitude goes to Jonathan Tvrdik, who is of no relation to Frank.

For aid with resources, I'm grateful to Amy Schindler, Director of Archives and Special Collections held by the University of Nebraska at Omaha, as well as the Nebraska State Historical Society, the Douglas County Historical Society, the Omaha Public Library, Nebraska Health and Human Services' Office of Vital Records, and Dr. Orville D. Menard's collection of recorded interviews and his book *River City Empire: Tom Dennison's Omaha.*

Chris Harding Thornton, a seventh-generation Nebraskan, is the author of *Pickard County Atlas*. In addition to holding an MFA and a PhD, Harding Thornton has worked as an overseer of quality assurance at a condom company, a jar-lid screwer at a plastics plant, a closer at Burger King, a clerk at a record store, a manager of an all-ages club, a PR writer, and a teacher of writing and literature.